DOUGLA

MW00899345

THE
CHAMPIONS
OF ANNA'S MILL

The Champions of Anna's Mill
All Rights Reserved.
Copyright © 2020 Douglas Toal
v7.0

This is a work of fiction. Names, characters, businesses, places, events, locales, and incidents are either the products of the author's imagination or used in a fictitious manner. Any resemblance to actual persons, living or dead, or actual events is purely coincidental.

The opinions expressed in this manuscript are solely the opinions of the author and do not represent the opinions or thoughts of the publisher. The author has represented and warranted full ownership and/or legal right to publish all the materials in this book.

This book may not be reproduced, transmitted, or stored in whole or in part by any means, including graphic, electronic, or mechanical without the express written consent of the publisher except in the case of brief quotations embodied in critical articles and reviews.

Outskirts Press, Inc.
http://www.outskirtspress.com

ISBN: 978-1-9772-2369-2

Cover Photo © 2020 www.gettyimages.com.. All rights reserved - used with permission.

Outskirts Press and the "OP" logo are trademarks belonging to Outskirts Press, Inc.

PRINTED IN THE UNITED STATES OF AMERICA

To Rob, D.J. and Scott and the times we had at raceway infields, where this story began. To June and my children for all your loving support.

Chapter 1

Richard Hobbs extended his arm from the window and felt a warm breeze flow past. Old County Road 19 stretched before him and on both sides the Georgia plains flushed white with snowy cotton puffs as far as the eye could see. Cotton drifted past his windshield and swirled behind his Ford pick-up truck as it sped along. The hazy morning sky portended thick and oppressive humidity.

Hobbs welcomed the heat. *It'll be a fine day,* he thought to himself. If he and his two companions found work, it'll be finer still.

To his right sat J.R. Rentz, a close friend since the age of ten and travel companion since the age of sixteen. For the last eleven years, Hobbs and J.R. traveled the country, sharing food and space and sojourning from one speedway track to the next as they followed the professional stockcar races on its yearly circuit. Living day to day on bare rations, the friends accepted the hardships and welcomed each race day with a sense of relief and joy.

Hobbs stood six feet, five inches tall with a solid build. He greased his dark brown, curly hair for management and parted it just above the left ear. His facial expression fell naturally into a frown and he possessed a slight cast in the left eye. Most people avoided him on looks alone, but the few friends he had looked past the outward appearance and saw a kind and considerate man, rarely disagreeable and extremely loyal.

After a full night's trek from the Miami raceway to central Georgia, Hobbs cherished simple moments such as this; trucking through the Georgia countryside, he relaxed, enjoyed the scenery, and tried to banish all frets over where and when the next meal would come and how to drum up enough cash to buy infield tickets to the last race of the season in Atlanta.

Hobbs' second traveling companion, Dippy Jordan, sat opposite J.R. in the passenger-side seat. Even Dippy's jabber mouth couldn't distract from Hobbs' peaceful hiatus. Now he barely registered Dippy's complaints about their lack of cash. During the fourteen-hour long road trip, Dippy talked of mathematics and racing physics and commiserated about the unlucky set of events that was his life. Of course, Dippy took no responsibility for the events and happily credited others, notably Hobbs and J.R. All through the long night, Hobbs and J.R. sat in silence while Dippy ranted. He eventually relented but Hobbs knew it was temporary.

Hobbs remembered a time two years previous when he and J.R. traveled the stockcar circuit alone, without Dippy. Then one day as they traveled to Charlotte, they picked up a hitch hiker and things got more complicated. "Where are you headed?" Hobbs had asked. "Wherever you're going," Dippy responded. Dippy refused to leave when they got to the Charlotte Motor Speedway and decided to stay on as Hobbs and J.R. traveled to Pennsylvania and Texas. Now, two years later and Dippy still had not left. It was probably the longest hitched ride in history, Hobbs guessed.

Hobbs knew that Dippy's attraction to racing had nothing to do with a love of the sport and everything to do with his fascination with racing physics and mathematics. He was a genius with mathematical formulations and for Dippy, stockcar racing provided a treasure trove of numbers to be crunched, manipulated, and coerced. He was particularly interested in collecting lap times from various cars during a race to make predictions on the eventual race outcome. At each raceway they visited, Dippy found a way to hack into the local computer system that cataloged lap times. From a lap top computer, Dippy collected lap times and fed them into a complicated set of formulations.

Hobbs marveled at his friend's expertise and did not understand his work nor did he comprehend why an educated man like Dippy hung out with two degenerate rednecks like he and J.R. To be clear, Dippy was no blue-blooded scholar; he was raised on a poor farm in North Carolina and when not talking about mathematics, Dippy easily reverted to redneck slang. He possessed a passion for his work and believed that he had made important discoveries that would impact racing for years to come.

To Hobbs, his friend was slightly delusional. He considered Dippy's preoccupation with lap times and formulations as just one oddity in an extremely odd and discontented man.

Hobbs breathed in the fresh country air and ignored the peculiar hitch hiker in the passenger's seat of his truck.

Chapter 2

Dippy Jordan resembled a twenty-five-year old Barney Fife with a large nose and thin lips. He stood a foot shorter than his two traveling companions and one hundred pounds lighter. After two years of unfulfilling work in the Graduate Program of Mathematics at a North Carolina University, Dippy skipped graduation and hitched a ride to nowhere in particular. He had become disillusioned with academic life and hated the thought that most mathematicians with graduate degrees ended up as teachers; he wanted to apply his knowledge to solving everyday dilemmas. More than anything else, he wanted an escape from his scripted and predetermined course. By happenstance he hitched a ride with Richard Hobbs and discovered a lifestyle that few experienced. By traveling the stockcar circuit he enjoyed freedom from the status quo. He also found a venue to apply his knowledge and expertise in a way that few could've considered.

Now, after two years of data gathering, he believed he was on the brink of discovery. Perhaps one last race remained before his work would be complete. Unfortunately, due to a lack of cash, the Atlanta Motor Speedway looked further away than ever, and a real chance existed that he would not complete the work he had started two years previous.

"Richard, I think our next stop should be at Two Pines Cotton Gin," Dippy said with a sense of urgency. With the Want Ads section of the local paper spread across his lap, he consulted a map of Bibb County.

"I don't know why you decided to drag us down this old road," Dippy complained. "It's bad strategy Richard, we should be heading north toward Atlanta. The next race is in Atlanta anyway." He glanced past J.R. Rentz in the middle seat and looked at Hobbs. "Did you hear me? I said it's bad strategy. There're more jobs up north of here." A small bulb of cotton blew into the truck and settled on Dippy's head. He grabbed it and studied it for a moment. "Ain't nothing down here but cotton," he said and glanced once more at his friend. Hobbs smiled pleasantly and appeared oblivious to Dippy's complaints. Dippy sighed and slumped deep into his seat. "Unless people start listening to reason around here, we ain't ever gonna find work."

"We'll find a job, Dippy," J.R. Rentz said. "Shoot, we came awful close to getting hired at that diner a couple miles back."

Dippy turned and looked up at his long, skinny mate. From Dippy's vantage it appeared that J.R.'s head might bounce off his shoulders at any moment. Every slight bump in the road made J.R.'s head wobble as if it and his long neck engaged in a constant balancing act to maintain contact.

"We'd probably be working right now if you hadn't told the cook that you could fry a burger in fifteen seconds," Dippy said, his eyes bobbing up and down, following J.R.'s bouncing head.

"I've seen it done before," J.R. responded in defense.

"You've seen it done at fast food restaurants where the burgers are paper thin and arrive frozen and cooked. At Mel's Diner back there, those burgers are blood red and bigger than your softball-sized brain."

J.R.'s head bounced a couple more times and he looked down at Dippy. "I've seen it done before, that's all I'm saying."

"Remind me to avoid your burgers J.R. I don't fancy getting poison from your blood red burgers. People die from poison in under-cooked meat. Didn't you know that?"

J.R. gave no response. Dippy looked out the front windshield for a moment and then turned back to J.R. He wasn't finished with this conversation just yet; a mathematical analysis seemed in order.

"Do you realize that if you cooked one burger every fifteen seconds, you'd have cooked one thousand, nine-hundred and twenty burgers in an eight-hour shift?" Dippy paused to do the math once more in his head. "That's a lot of greasy dinners. What's Mel gonna do with that many burgers? He's probably lucky if he cooks one thousand in a year. Did you ever think about that when you opened your mouth and spoiled any chance of getting jobs?"

"Hush up Dippy," Hobbs said in a husky voice. "We had no chance back there to begin with, they were looking for full time workers, not drifters like us. There's no reason to badger J.R."

"Well, welcome back, Richard," Dippy said. "J.R. and I gave you up for dead."

Hobbs ignored the comment and jammed on the brakes. A small man stood in the road directly ahead and held a stop sign.

"Beware of fearless strangers with stop signs," Dippy yelled as he braced himself against the seat and prepared for impact.

Chapter 3

The truck skidded to a stop in a thick cloud of tire smoke and managed to miss the stranger by mere feet. Camping supplies in the bed of the truck crashed against the rear window and a tent peg escaped, bouncing off the paved road and into a ditch.

When the smoke from the burnt rubber cleared, Dippy breathed a sigh of relief that the small man holding the stop sign looked unharmed. He stood in the exact spot, oblivious to the fact that he had almost lost his life. For several long moments Dippy stared at the man, unsure of his intentions. He looked past the man down the long narrow road and then turned to look behind. No other cars were in sight. In fact, for the last ten minutes he had failed to see a single vehicle on the lonely and deserted road.

"This is an unusual occurrence," Dippy concluded as he studied the strange looking man standing before them.

The man was a leather-skinned, old Mexican with a tattered Atlanta Braves baseball cap and a face that hadn't seen a razor for several days. Twine secured his heavily worn britches. The old man fidgeted and looked behind him at the empty road. He turned to face the truck and pulled a crude wristwatch from his pocket. After studying the watch for a long moment, he returned it to his pocket and held on to the stop sign with both hands. The long post on the sign looked as if it had been removed from the ground at some traffic intersection. He planted the post on the pavement and stared at the grill of the truck, careful to avoid eye contact with its passengers.

"What does he want, Richard?" J.R. asked.

"Not sure," Hobbs answered. "But when a man stands in the middle of a road with a stop sign it's likely that he knows what he's doing. I expect he'll reveal his intentions soon enough."

They sat in silence and watched the sign toting old man as he fidgeted once again and glanced at the fields and road behind. "Go around him, Richard," Dippy said. "There's nothing wrong with this road."

"He's got a reason," Hobbs responded. "We'll wait him out. After all, he risked his life to get us to stop."

Dippy let out an exasperated sigh. "I don't have your patience, Richard." He opened the door and slid from the truck. "I don't feel like sitting here all day. I'm gonna find out what this is all about."

J.R. scooted from the truck and followed Dippy.

The approach of J.R. and Dippy seemed to excite the old man further. He scratched the back of his neck, removed his cap, and wiped sweat from his brow. After glancing at the empty road again, he lowered his head and stared at his feet.

"What's all this about hombre?" Dippy demanded with hands on hips. He liked the fact that he could look down at the old man. "What gives you the right to stand in the middle of the road with a stop sign?"

The old man gave Dippy an uncomfortable and frustrated look. It was obvious he didn't want to talk but Dippy was relentless.

"You've got to have a reason for stopping traffic," Dippy

complained. "There ain't no reason for you to keep us from heading down this road. Look," he said pointing down the long, straight road, "it's completely empty."

Feeling the pressure of Dippy's questions, the man finally spoke. "I hungry," he said. "Mi Familia hungry. I get food, I work now," he said pointing to the ground.

"Well join the party bud. I'm hungry too."

"I've got some old crackers you can have," J.R. said helpfully.

"Keep quiet J.R." Dippy exclaimed. "I'll handle this."

Dippy appraised the man for a few moments. He crossed his arms and studied him from head to foot as the man resumed his submissive posture. The base of the sign-post looked as if it had been hacked off with a saw. The more Dippy thought about the situation, the angrier he got. "You've got a lot of nerve, mister," he said finally. "It may be customary to hold up traffic and demand food where you come from, but around here it's against the law. People around here earn money and buy their food at the market."

The old man grumbled a few words under his breath.

"This guy's some piece of work, huh J.R.?" Dippy asked his companion. "He's standing here with a stop sign pulled from the earth, robbing innocent travelers of their food. That's two **laws** you're breaking mister," he said loudly, pointing to the old man. "Number one you can't go around destroying public property and number two you can't stop traffic on a public road and steal food. You need to find another way to feed your family amigo because this won't do."

"I don't know about that Dippy," Hobbs said as he leaned against the hood of the truck and held the tent **peg** in one hand. "Seems like this old guy's taking an original approach," he said with a smile.

"Oh yeah, Richard, you think this is funny," Dippy responded. "I wonder how funny you'll think this is when the old coot ends up in the slammer. I'm just trying to help this poor guy by educating him to our ways and all you want to do is make fun."

"Don't get so worked up," Hobbs said, looking toward the cotton fields to his left. "I'm sure he's got a perfectly good reason for stopping us. He just can't communicate it to you."

"His reason for stopping us is to rob us, that's all. It's highway robbery."

Dippy turned his attention back to the old man. "Listen, hombre," he said in a conciliatory tone as he stepped closer to the man. "Why don't you just stroll on over to the side of the road and let us pass and we'll forget this ever happened." Dippy grabbed the man's elbow and tried to escort him from the road.

"No," the man yelled and slapped Dippy's hand. He picked up the signpost and planted it in the road between his feet. "I work aqui. I make money aqui." His face flushed and he looked at Dippy with a mix of determination and spite.

"Oh, so now you want our money too," Dippy exclaimed in disbelief. "Let's get out of here, Richard." He marched toward the truck. "Come on, J.R."

"No gringo. You no go," the old man exclaimed looking squarely at Dippy. He uttered a few loud words that sounded like curses. "Monstruo maquina, monstruo maquina," he yelled and adamantly pointed to the road.

"What's he fuming about?" Dippy asked, looking back at the animated old man.

"I'm not sure, I ain't Mexican and I don't know his language," Hobbs answered. "But while you've been yapping at this poor old guy, I've been watching those big harvest tractors yonder." He motioned toward a thin line of pines one-hundred yards up the road. Between the pines they watched several large cotton pickers move rapidly through the fields and emerge onto the road ahead in a thick cloud of dust and cotton. The big green machines came to a stop on the road, turned, and charged back.

"Monstruo maquina!" the old man screamed at Dippy and pointed toward the cotton pickers. "I hungry, I make money now, I work now, and no gringos die."

"Oh," Dippy said. He hastily walked toward the passenger side door as the man continued with the curses. "Well, ah, keep up the good work," he said quickly, motioning as if granting permission for the old man to carry on. His face turned red as he scrambled into the truck while the Mexican waved a fist.

It's a cotton-picking embarrassment, Dippy mused.

Chapter 4

Hobbs said a few words to the old man by way of an apology and entered the truck behind J.R. "Well Dippy I'm sure glad you were here to handle the situation. I don't know what we'd have done without your help."

Dippy made no response as they watched the man walk to the side of the road and wave the truck through. He threw in a few extra hand gestures and verbal curses to send them on their way.

Hobbs glanced over at Dippy sitting low in the passenger side seat. "What do you have to say for yourself, Dippy?"

"I ain't saying nothing," he responded sourly. He crossed his arms and buried his chin into his chest.

"J.R.," Hobbs said to his lanky friend. "If there ever was a time that you wanted to make a harassing comment at Dippy, now's the time. He's a humbled man and likely to be quiet for some time now."

J.R. sat with a puzzled look on his face, trying to piece together the encounter with the strange little man. He looked down at Dippy with a look of concern. "Dippy," he said, "I guess that old boy didn't want our food, he was just doing his job, huh?"

"Yeah, J.R.," Hobbs interjected. "He was doing his job

and saving lives. I'd say he's an outstanding member of society and our good buddy over there ridiculed him to the point of tears."

Dippy glanced past J.R. and gave Hobbs a hateful look. "You knew what was going on all along," he said quietly.

"What's that?" Hobbs said with his eyes on the road. "I didn't hear you."

"I said you knew what was going on," Dippy said louder. "You knew them tractors were crossing that road and you just let me carry on and make a fool out of myself."

"When you work up an anger, which is often, you're a natural born fool," Hobbs replied. "You don't need my help in that department."

"So, I guess you're just trying to teach me a lesson, is that it?"

"Well now that you mention it," Hobbs said thoughtfully. "I guess there is lesson to be learned. What do you think, J.R.?"

J.R. thought for a moment and then turned in his seat to face Dippy. "I'm not very good at giving lessons, but..."

"No, you're not," Dippy agreed with a sullen look. He buried his head once again.

J.R. continued, "...the way I see it, you can look at a person and either have good thoughts or bad thoughts. Me? I like to have good thoughts. Maybe you should try that every so often."

"There you go Dippy, there's your lesson," Hobbs said with finality, hoping the conversation was ended.

Dippy may have been humbled but he wasn't lowered to the point of receiving lectures from the likes of J.R. "If I took that advice to heart," Dippy said, looking at his two companions, "then the three of us would make a mighty boring trio. This little adventure we're on would be 'bout exciting as watching an egg boil. Look at you two," he said as he sat up and pointed with a grin. "You'd have to be the age of a kindergartner to find J.R.'s conversation useful. Other than watching his head bounce up and down he provides no entertainment whatsoever. And as for you Richard, you're about as talkative as a medical school cadaver. I derive more excitement from watching road kill pass than I do from conversing with the two of you."

"What's a cadaver?" J.R. asked.

"Admit it boys," Dippy continued, ignoring J.R.'s question. "I provide spice to our little group. You can lecture me all you want but I ain't changing and thank God for that. The next time I see a sign-toting Mexican blocking our way, I intend to express myself."

Hobbs shook his head in disgust. "What's our next stop?" he asked while Dippy bemoaned the immigration of illegal aliens. It wouldn't be such a nuisance if they could communicate properly, he was saying.

Dippy stopped in mid-sentence as if taken off guard. He retrieved the map and consulted it for a moment. "Two Pines Cotton Gin is ten more miles up the road."

He looked out the side window and studied the broad white fields of cotton. "Have you ever worked in a cotton gin before?" he asked Hobbs

"Once or twice," Hobbs answered.

"I hope they don't speak Spanish."

The trio rode in silence for several miles as Dippy debated the merits of learning to speak Spanish. The experience with the old man could have been avoided if he had known a smattering of the poor man's language. As he watched a group of migrant workers erecting a roadside gate, he decided that once he got the opportunity, he would buy some language tapes and learn something new.

"What's a cadaver?" J.R. asked again.

Dippy shook his head as if clearing his thoughts and looked up at J.R. "You've been racking your brain about that word for the last five minutes, haven't you?"

J.R. nodded.

"You're a constant source of entertainment, J.R.," Dippy said with a look of disbelief. "I take back what I said about you being a bore. Every thought you have is a struggle and adventure. It's an amazing thing to watch."

J.R. smiled. "Thanks," he said enthusiastically. "I think that was a compliment, don't you think so Richard?"

"Coming from Dippy, it's as close as you're gonna get," Hobbs responded dryly.

Chapter 5

The truck bounced down a neglected, pothole-filled road. Cracks filled and divided the pavement like checkered board and pine trees crowded in on both sides. Flimsy branches merged overhead, blocking out what little sunlight remained in the long day. Hobbs reached down and flicked on the headlights. A sudden wind rocked the truck and the high, thin pines swayed back and forth as pine needles rained down.

"We'll be walking before long," Hobbs said to his friend, J.R. He eyed the fuel gauge. They had used the last bit of money on fuel and now that was nearly spent.

J.R. looked out at the pines from the middle seat, smiling. His long, thick eyelashes framed large and hopeful eyes. His wavy brown hair fell below his ears and dimples formed at his cheeks. Dippy dozed fitfully, his short legs stretching to the floor.

"I just know we'll find some work in this next town," J.R. said.

"We've been looking all day," Hobbs responded. "I hate to say it, but Dippy was right. We ain't gonna find work. Not today; not around here."

"Don't give up hope yet. I've got a good feeling about this next stop."

Hobbs looked at J.R. with amazement. Despite the incredibly bleak and fruitless day, J.R.'s optimism never failed. They'd been to Zebulon, Aldora, Concord, Meansville, and many more places searching for jobs. Rejected at every stop, and yet J.R. remained hopeful.

Hobbs struggled to understand the source of J.R.'s cheerfulness. Like Hobbs, J.R. grew up underprivileged; but worse, he was challenged with a learning disability. At the age of 16, J.R. ran from an abusive home and partnered with Hobbs. J.R.'s optimism contrasted with Hobbs' pessimism and it confounded Hobbs that his friend shirked off life's hard blows with such ease.

The wind outside the truck ceased and a surreal calm filled the pine forest. Twilight settled in and the shadows of the forest merged so that nothing remained but darkness. The dim headlights revealed low, skinny, and pale branches that reached out at them from all directions like some creature from a horror movie.

Their last hope for the day rested on a small town by the name of Anna's Mill and an auto shop by the name of Voyals. The difficult part was locating the scratch town in a sea of Georgia pines and the barren road provided no comfort. Hobbs half expected the drive to end at a dilapidated shack with a couple of shot gun toting degenerates on the front porch.

Hobbs pulled his truck to a stop in front of a road sign, mostly hidden by overgrowth. The headlights from the truck reflected off the signs dull surface. It read, *"Welcome the Anna's Mill, Population 1,258."* A neglected placard dangled precariously by a single chain. Hobbs tilted his head to match the angle of the placard. It read, *"HOME OF THE GREEN UGLY."*

With foreboding thoughts, Hobbs looked out the front window of the truck at the small town of Anna's Mill. The pines receded and, in the distance, he could see a few lights in the center of town. No people were in sight as the first raindrops began to fall.

Hobbs placed the truck into drive and inched slowly toward Anna's Mill, population 1,258; home of The Green Ugly.

The truck eased passed a full-service gasoline station called "Joe's Gas Stop." A gray-haired attendant, *probably Joe himself*, sat on a wooden stool and eyed the truck suspiciously. When J.R. waved, the man's expression turned sour. *With old Joe as the welcoming committee, it's no wonder the town has so few occupants,* Hobbs thought. *Joe's evil eye scares away any would be visitor.*

He stopped the truck at a four-way stop and surveyed the small town. In the distance, he saw another stop sign, and beyond that, a dirt road. He counted eighteen buildings in all, ten on one side of Main Street and eight on the other. Three-foot high sidewalks elevated the buildings. The sidewalks reminded Hobbs of an old western town where a wooden catwalk is elevated above the street on both sides. Skinny poles containing a single power line connected the structures.

The four-way stop intersected a single lane dirt road that curved around the buildings on both sides. A row of neatly packed houses lined the dirt roads and extended behind the main buildings. Hobbs guessed that both roads intersected again at the stop sign on the other side of town and from his position at the stop sign, Hobbs looked upon the entire town of Anna's Mill, both residential and business districts. The whole community; packed together and surrounded by tall pines.

The quaint town gave off a neat appearance and the lighted homes provided a warm and friendly glow; a welcomed sight after traversing ten miles of pine forest in an old truck, dodging potholes and fallen trees. Hobbs' stomach growled and he thought about the dinner.

He was not averse to knocking on doors for food in

exchange for hard labor and had half a mind to walk up to the nearest home to test the town's hospitality. But then he remembered old Joe at the gas station. He glanced in the rearview mirror to see the old attendant glaring at him. The old crow stood in the distance next to the road with his hands on his hips as if he was the local crime watcher. *He must think it's his civil duty to stare off any troublemakers,* Hobbs thought to himself with a frown. *Maybe this town ain't as friendly as it appears.* He decided his hunger could wait; they had a job to look for, and then maybe some food and a place to sleep.

"What's the name of that auto shop, J.R.?" Hobbs asked as he drove slowly through the town. On his right he spotted The Old Country Store. A large pane glass window displayed various items including dresses and ten-pound sacks of sugar. *The store probably served as both a grocer and clothier,* Hobbs thought.

"It's called Voyals Auto Parts and Repair," J.R. said as he scanned the town for anything resembling an auto mechanic shop.

On his left, Hobbs found the local barbershop. He stretched his neck to look up into the shop and saw the barber hard at work, shaving a fully lathered face with a long shiny blade. The barber looked out onto the street as the truck passed and Hobbs thought he saw something resembling a smile and a nod.

Further down the road he noticed a dark and empty building with a sign that read "Women's Clothing." The store had an "Out of Business" sign; *no doubt the women were buying clothing from The Old Country Store.*

The Mid Town Theater stood next to the abandoned store. The largest structure in town, it could easily have been three stories high. The theater featured *Smoky and the Bandit* as its feature presentation and Hobbs envisioned large crowds on Saturday nights. Next Saturday's film featured Robert Redford and Clint Eastwood in *Butch Cassidy and the Sundance Kid*.

"I got a bad feeling that Voyals Auto Shop ain't even in this town," Hobbs said. They drove nearly the length of the paved road and all potential sites for an auto shop had rapidly diminished.

The post office was the last building on the left. The thin structure barely allowed enough room to fit a door and window. Aunt Mae's Cafe and Boarding House sat directly across from the post office. The Cafe was a solid looking two-story structure made of dark stained wood. The warm glow of soft, yellow interior lighting gave Aunt Mae's a cozy feel and Hobbs saw several people sitting at tables enjoying supper. A young waitress scurried about with plates of food and drink.

Hobbs pulled the truck to a stop at the second and final crossroad. The truck headlights shone down a dark and empty dirt road that bordered a small gated pasture. A group of fat cows huddled together by the gated enclosure, looking miserable in the rain.

They saw no sign of Voyals Auto Shop. *All this way for nothing,* Hobbs thought bitterly. The long drive down the abandoned road proved fruitless. He rubbed his tired eyes and began formulating a plan to turn around and get back to civilization. With any luck they'd find a job tomorrow.

Hobbs swore under his breath. He turned around, looked past the dimly lit town and studied the deserted road. Tall pines dwarfed the thin path and he frowned at the thought of driving back down it. The winds pick up again and heavy droplets of rain began to fall. The pines swayed back and forth.

Hobbs shook his head in disgust as he thought about their predicament; starving with no place to sleep and stranded in a small, dead end town, and worst of all, unemployed. The Atlanta Motor Speedway seemed farther away than ever before.

"Richard, we can't give up yet," J.R. said, sensing frustration. "It's only seven o' clock and there's still hope that Voyals is open late tonight. Maybe if we hurry-up we can find it and get some work."

"There's no shop here, J.R. We've done traveled through this dinky town and we ain't seen nothing. Do you understand that?" Hobbs said, frustrated and tired. "We got to head back before the storm hits full force. We'll be lucky to get back down that road without running into a fallen tree."

J.R. sighed and scanned the surroundings. He saw a young boy sprinting along the dirt road on an old rusty bicycle. J.R. reached across Dippy and rolled down the window as the boy approached.

"Hey, boy," J.R. yelled.

The boy applied the brakes and small pebbles of clay splattered the truck as the bicycle fishtailed to a stop. The child shielded his eyes from the falling rain and looked at J.R. as if he had just seen a ghost.

"Can you tell us where Voyals Auto Shop is?" J.R. asked loudly. Without a word, the boy gestured toward the dirt road ahead.

Before J.R. could thank him, the boy crossed in front of the truck and was soon at a full sprint.

J.R. rolled up the window and slapped a hand over his knee. "I knew we'd find it," he exclaimed. "Let's go Richard before it's too late."

Chapter 6

Hobbs found Voyals Auto Parts and Repair a half mile past Anna's Mill at the end of an old muddy road. The dirty cinder blocked building sat juxtaposed to a junkyard filled with old cars on one side, and the city dump on the other; the perfect setting for an auto repair shop that held little regard for neatness and order. A chain-linked fence surrounded both the shop and junkyard and as Hobbs pulled his truck into the graveled parking lot, he saw a mass of cars, tractors and various other vehicles scattered about the front and side yards of the building. He maneuvered the truck between rusty engines, stacks of old tires and shattered windshields. It was difficult to determine where the junkyard ended, and the auto shop began. The place looked as if a tornado had just passed through and Hobbs was startled by the contrast between the clean little town of Anna's Mill and its auto shop. It would seem Anna's Mill banished Voyals, along with all other eyesores, to the far reaches of town.

Rain fell heavily as Hobbs parked the truck at the front door and next to a broken-down tractor. He surveyed the surroundings. A sign in the murky pane glass window welcomed all visitors, *We Do It Right the First Time,* it declared in big black letters.

With the nearest auto repair shop twenty miles distant, the people of Anna's Mill used Voyals whether they did it right the first time or not, they had little choice, Hobbs thought.

To the rear of the truck he noticed a thick metal pole and platform. At one time a car had sat on top of the platform as a tacky form of advertisement, but someone had taken it down long ago.

"If the EPA ever caught wind of this place, they'd condemn it," Dippy said, looking out the side window at a large diesel engine. The engine sat in the middle of a thick puddle of used oil. Rolls of soggy paper towels were scattered about in a vain attempt to absorb the waste.

Hobbs saw light in the shop. *Perhaps someone was at work inside and the shop was still open,* he thought. "Let's go see about a job," he said wearily.

When the three men exited the truck, the stench of trash from the town dump assaulted their senses. The rain did little to quench the strong aroma of decaying waste, grease, and motor oil. They ran to the front door shielding their heads from the heavy rain. Relieved to find the entrance unlocked, they rushed in, seeking refuge from the downpour.

They entered a dark and dusty reception area where dim light shone from an open door leading to the garage. Hobbs brushed water from his thick curly hair and walked to the reception counter. He looked past the door and into the garage where a jack elevated a 1985 Chevy Impala and underneath the car, a man grunted and strained to remove some part. The man's legs extended from under the car and fought for leverage. Hobbs heard a wrench clatter to the cement floor followed by a loud curse.

Dippy stood behind Hobbs and watched the man scramble for the fallen tool. Before long the man was grunting and straining once more. "Looks like they're too busy to notice visitors," he said to Hobbs in a whisper.

Hobbs ignored Dippy's comment and surveyed the reception area. A wooden chair and well-used recliner sat in one corner and served as the only furniture. In the other corner, several stacks of newspapers and magazines reached almost to the ceiling. Next to the stacks of paper, he saw J.R. studying framed photographs. *You'd think he'd show some enthusiasm,* Hobbs thought. They had driven through hell and high water to get to this godforsaken place and J.R. acted as if he didn't have a care in the world, as if he was on some museum tour. Hobbs shook his head and wondered, for the millionth time, what was going on inside his buddy's head.

Hobbs returned his attention to the garage. The man still labored under the Chevy and country music played on a scratchy radio broadcast in the background. He rang a small bell on the counter and the man under the car stopped moving.

Hobbs rang the bell again.

"Shhhh, shhhh, shush it up," the man said. "Be quiet."

Hobbs and Dippy looked at each other quizzically. Someone turned off the music and heavy raindrops pattered the front window. Hobbs felt he'd just entered someone's home unannounced.

"Who's there," the man barked.

"It's just us," Dippy responded.

Hobbs looked at Dippy, perturbed. "Just us?" he whispered. "He doesn't know us from Adam." Dippy shrugged his shoulders.

The man cursed and heaved himself from under the car. He looked at Hobbs.

"We're from out of town and looking for work," Hobbs clarified.

The short and stocky man had a thick and unkempt beard. He sat on the floor and glared at Hobbs. "You've come to the wrong place, stranger. Get on out."

"We'd like to talk with you if you don't mind," Dippy said in a squeaky voice.

The man stared at Dippy for several moments and then stood up. He made a motion with his hand to some unseen person and instantly the music began again. He walked toward the lobby, reached into his back pocket and pulled out a black and greasy rag. He wiped his face on the rag and placed it back into his pocket.

"I said you've come to the wrong place if you're looking for work. We ain't got any." He leaned against the doorframe and pointed toward the door. "Get out," he said casually as if he'd done it many times before.

"That's no way to treat visitors," Dippy shot back, offended by the ill manners. "All we've done is to come in here and ask for a job. If you don't want visitors, you ought to lock your front door."

The man offered no response and nonchalantly walked up to the counter. He pulled out a can of beer from a hidden ice chest, opened it and took a long swig. He let out a loud belch and wiped his mouth with a thick hairy forearm. "This is my place and you ain't welcome." The man gulped down the rest of the beer in a few seconds and followed it by another long belch. He threw the can in the corner and turned toward Hobbs and Dippy. "Get out of my shop," he said again, more forcibly. He loosened his belt strap to make room for the extra 12 ounces of liquid.

"Is there someplace we can bed down for the night?" Hobbs asked. "It's getting late and I don't fancy driving back down that road in this storm."

"Yeah," the man said, and he walked toward the exit. "I know of a place." He opened the door and glared at Hobbs. Outside the downpour continued.

Hobbs and Dippy waited for the man to finish his sentence. After a few tense moments Dippy blurted out in a high-pitch squeal, "Well, where is the place you ingrate?"

The mechanic responded with another belch.

Not amused by the antics of the rude mechanic, Hobbs began to walk toward the exit. As Hobbs approached the open door, the man noticed J.R. lurking in a dark corner studying the photographs on the wall. "Hey," the man yelled pointing toward J.R. "What are you doing over there?"

"Let's go J.R., we ain't welcome," Hobbs said.

"Is this your car?" J.R. asked calmly. He faced the wall, looking at several framed pictures of stock cars.

"Yes, it is, young man" said a friendly voice from the garage. Hobbs turned and saw a grandfatherly figure standing in the doorway behind the corner. The man smiled at Hobbs and winked.

"That there, is the Green Ugly," the old man said with a proud smile.

Chapter 7

"Wait a minute Bill," the stocky mechanic said, his face red with anger. "These boys were just leaving. This ain't a time to get friendly." He turned back toward J.R. "Get away from those pictures boy and get out of my shop."

Old Bill entered the lobby and turned the lights on. He faced the rude mechanic standing at the door. "I know your Daddy taught you better manners, Clarence. Close the door, you're letting the rain in."

Bill shuffled slowly across the lobby toward J.R. and smiled at Hobbs and Dippy as he passed. He wore house slippers and a navy-blue, full body mechanic suit with "Bill" stitched on the breast. His friendly blue eyes peered over low fitted bifocals.

"Wow," J.R. said. He wiped dust from a picture with his shirtsleeve. "Come check these Road Stock Cars out Richard. This one is a 1992 Thunderbird and that one over there is an 84 Monte Carlo." J.R. acted like a kid in a candy store as he moved from one picture to the next.

Hobbs cast a wary eye toward Clarence who slammed the door shut and glared at J.R. with disdain.

Old Bill stood behind J.R. and rested his hands on his frail hips. He smiled; apparently pleased that J.R. took a liking to his collection of photographs.

"Look here, Richard, wasn't that picture taken at the Valdosta track?" J.R. asked excitedly and pointed at a picture high on the wall. Hobbs joined J.R.

"That's the Speedway in Valdosta," J.R. said again looking at his friend.

Hobbs looked at the pictures. Thirty or forty framed photographs of different puke green stock cars with the number "00" painted on the sides hung on the wall. The photographs had been taken over a period of many years. The oldest looked more than forty years old, taken some time in the 1960's. Looking closely at a more recent photograph, he saw a man in his sixties standing next to a 1988 Thunderbird with his helmet in one hand and a checkered flag in the other. Another photograph, this one taken many years previous, showed the same man, much younger now, sitting on the roof of the car. The man had the same stocky features as Clarence, but the resemblance wasn't identical. *A father or uncle*, Hobbs guessed. He noticed immediately that all the cars were "Road Stock," meaning they were factory manufactured cars with customized modifications; the type of car raced in entry-level, grassroots competitions on local tracks by amateur drivers. He and J.R. had grown up around such cars in their hometown of Valdosta, Georgia.

Hobbs scanned the photographs and smiled. The sight of the Road Stock cars brought back happy memories from his youth. He studied the photograph that J.R. pointed at. It was a close-up of the number "00" car streaking down a straightaway. The photograph centered on the car and provided little detail of the track, but Hobbs noticed the distinctive low white and blue cement, steel bar barricade wall of the Valdosta track.

"Have you boys been to the Valdosta track before?" Old Bill asked.

"Yes sir," J.R. exclaimed. He looked at Bill for the first

time and smiled. "Richard and I were born in Valdosta. We've been to that track hundreds of times. Shoot we were practically raised at that track. Ain't that right Richard?"

"Yep," Hobbs said. At the age of ten, and for years afterward, he and J.R. attended every race. Initially they watched the races from the outside, behind a chain link fence. Eventually they found a hole in the fence and watched the action from the stands. But that wasn't good enough, they wanted to be closer still and soon the boys found access to the infield pits. There, for once in their life, Richard and J.R. found a place they belonged.

Young Richard and J.R., enthralled by the sights and sound of the busy pit area during race nights, spent hours studying the habits and actions of the volunteer mechanics as they twisted, turned, and molded common streetcars into powerful racing machines.

Whenever a mechanic asked for assistance to retrieve some part or tool, the boys helped eagerly. Before long they accomplished chores normally reserved for mechanics and soon built engines as full-fledged mechanics.

"I ain't ever seen this car before," Hobbs admitted. He looked closely at the car in the photograph.

"Well Richard you can't be expected to know every single racecar that's ever been driven," Dippy said sarcastically, joining the three men close to the wall. Hobbs knew that Dippy rarely tolerated being left out of a conversation.

"Richard's determined to know more about racing than any man that ever lived," he explained to Bill. "He's a little put out that he don't recognize your car."

"Well," Bill said to Dippy with a friendly smile, "I'm not surprised that he ain't ever seen The Green Ugly before. It's been many years since we raced down in Valdosta."

"Green Ugly is an odd name Mister," Dippy said. The comment was more of an accusation than a statement.

Bill chuckled. "It ain't so odd. I'd call that a very ugly

green car," he said, nodding at the photographs.

"He's got a point, Dippy," Hobbs said. He studied more of the pictures. The paint on the car looked fluorescent and dull at the same time. "You've got to work hard to concoct a color as ugly as that."

"Well there you go Bill," Clarence barked from behind the wood counter and opened another can of beer. "Are you gonna stand around and let these no-good drifters criticize Daddy's car? Or are you gonna throw 'em out in the rain where they belong?"

"Never mind Clarence," Bill said quietly to Hobbs. "Ever since his Daddy left us three years ago, he's forgotten his manners."

Hobbs stole a glance at Clarence as he guzzled down another beer.

"If you can't mind your manners then go make yourself useful and finish replacing the muffler on Widow Baker's car," Bill declared to Clarence. "She's been expecting that car for a week now."

"You don't boss me," Clarence said. "Besides I don't trust your new friends here. I believe I'll just stand guard to prevent them from causing trouble." He smiled arrogantly and belched.

Bill made a quick and erratic swatting motion toward Clarence. "Don't mind him, he's as harmless as a dried-up worm on a hot summer's day."

"Mister," Dippy said to Bill quietly, "you ought to connect that man to a pipe. He's likely to provide enough natural gas to keep this town humming for weeks."

Bill laughed.

"What did you say, shorty?" Clarence bellowed at Dippy.

"Nothing," Bill snapped back with another quick swatting gesture. "Mind your own bees wax." A pulsating vein poked out on Bill's forehead and to Hobbs it appeared that Clarence was apt to provoke a stroke from the old geezer.

"Excuse me, sir," J.R. said to Bill. "Did you build the Green Ugly?"

The vein disappeared and Bill's face brightened into a smile. "I did," he responded with pride. "But I have to say," the old man continued, "I got a lot of help from Clearance and his daddy."

"Is the Green Ugly still around?" J.R. asked excitedly. "Richard and I might want to take a good look at it. It's been a while since we last seen a Road Stock."

"Well hold on J.R.," Hobbs said with raised hand. "I believe we've outlasted our welcome. It's time we leave."

"Amen to that brother," Clarence said. He eyed the ice chest as if trying to decide if he should go for another beer.

"Nonsense," old Bill said. "You ain't spent your welcome." He looked at the door leading to the garage and contemplated for moment. He turned towards his visitors and with a twinkle in his eyes he whispered, "I don't normally show off the Green Ugly to common strangers, but I can tell you boys are true enthusiasts. Come on," he said with excitement and a wave of his hand. "I got something to show you."

Clarence positioned himself at the entrance to the garage as the trio followed Bill. "You ain't showing that dammed car to these boys," he said with determination.

Clarence's stocky frame barred the garage and he watched Bill approach. "You know I don't like you showing off that car."

"Your Daddy may have left this garage to you Clarence," Bill said with clenched teeth. The purple vein reemerged on his forehead again. "But I'm still your uncle and I'm guessing that by the time I make it to that door you'll be far removed."

Clarence glared at Hobbs for a moment and quickly disappeared into the garage with a look of disgust.

Chapter 8

The garage appeared in as much disarray as the front yard. Large sections of chassis and engine blocks covered the floor and tools of various sizes littered the workbenches. Other than the 1985 Chevy Impala it was difficult to determine what, if any, work was in progress.

"I'm afraid that you'll also have to forgive Clarence for his lack of orderliness," Bill said. "When that boy's Daddy owned this place, we kept it spotless. I'm too old to clean up after his mess so I just keep to my own bench." The old man motioned toward a corner at the far end of the garage. "At my age I can at least keep a corner of this place clean."

Hobbs looked at Bill's corner workbench and noticed that it was indeed very clean and orderly. Shiny hand tools hung from the wall and parts from an old carburetor soaked in a beaker of detergent.

"I'm nearly useless now," Bill said with resignation in his voice. He passed his bench and continued toward the back of the garage. "All I do now is break down parts and put 'em back together." He stopped and turned to address J.R. "When I pull stuff apart and put it back together it forces me to think. It's good therapy for an old coot like me. Don't you think?"

"Yes Sir," J.R. said with a broad smile.

Bill regarded J.R. for a moment. "I like you, boy. You've got an agreeable disposition." He padded J.R. on the arm and walked to a door on the back wall. "I've got too many disagreeable people in my life," he mumbled to himself.

"Do you build race cars in this garage?" J.R. asked. He scanned the garage for anything resembling a modified speedster.

"We did at one time," Bill said. "My brother and I started this auto shop in 1959." He looked around the shop, reminiscing. "There was a time when Anna's Mill was a lot more prosperous and we did a fine piece of business."

Bill fumbled through his pockets and produced a key. He unlocked the latch and turned to address his visitors.

"One day," Bill continued, "my brother had the idea of building a stock car." He pointed to an area of the garage stacked high with cardboard boxes. "We built her over there," he said with a dreamy, far-away look. "We labored three whole years on that car with nothing but blood, sweat, and tears to show for it."

"It was my brother's idea to name the car Green Ugly. They say that nothing worthwhile comes easy," he said. "All that hard work eventually paid back dividends because we built one dandy of a car."

Bill turned to look at Dippy. "Have you ever created something that you were proud of? Something that would make people sit up and take notice?"

"I do my best," Dippy said in all seriousness. "But then again I'm not exactly surrounded by greatness."

Hobbs elbowed Dippy and scowled.

Old Bill glared at Clarence who stood next to the Chevy Impala and watched the group from the far end of the garage. "But we don't build race cars no more," he said loudly so that his nephew could hear. "Clarence lacks a certain level of ambition and I've long ago lost the strength. It's a real disappointment."

"Follow me," Bill said. He turned toward the door and pulled the latch. "You said you wanted to see the Green Ugly; well, here's your chance. She's the fastest road stock car in all of Georgia."

When Bill opened the door and entered the room, Hobbs looked once again at Clarence. The casual and rude behavior Clarence displayed earlier disappeared and now he glared at Hobbs with bitter hatred. Earlier, Clarence had not welcomed Hobbs but now the message was different. Now, Hobbs trespassed on sacred ground and Clarence would make him pay.

With a keen eye on Clarence, Hobbs turned and followed Bill into the room.

Chapter 9

When Hobbs entered the sparsely lit back room, he detected a serene and tranquil atmosphere that, strangely enough, reminded him of a church sanctuary. He had the strong urge to speak in hushed tones and to step lightly.

The two back walls of the room contained hundreds of newly polished trophies sitting upon rows of oak shelving. Checkered flags, driver apparel, and other memorabilia, designed to evoke a sense of time and tradition, accented the display and soft lighting provided highlights to specific areas. A museum curator could not have designed a more fitting tribute to racing. Hobbs looked at the display with awe.

After a quick glance at the neatly packed rows of trophies, he scanned the rest of the room. The dim lighting made it difficult to see far away details but close by he detected oil and fluid stains on the cement floor. *Mechanics had worked in this room in the past,* he thought to himself, but now it was some sort of shrine.

"Well, I'll be," Dippy said quietly, looking at the gold trophies. "I guess Fort Knox ain't got nothing on you."

"Ain't none of its gold." Bill responded. "They look like gold because I polish 'em often. Gold or not, don't matter, it's the memories that's valuable. When you get to be my age, memories are more valuable than gold anyhow."

"Did you do all this?" Dippy asked.

"I created the display but as far as winning all these trophies, I share that distinction with my brother, Jack. And Clarence too, believe it or not. When Jack was still around Clarence played an equal part in our race team. He did all the bodywork, I was the mechanic, and Jack was the driver."

As Bill talked, Hobbs noticed a nondescript form in the center of the room. With all the light directed toward the walls, Hobbs thought the center of the room empty. He peered into the darkness and noticed the unmistakable silhouette of J.R standing next to the form. He watched J.R. walk beside the form, feeling its contours.

"Looks like you've discovered the real treasure in this room," Bill said to J.R. "Let's lighten things up in here."

Bill flipped the light switch and the room filled with industrial strength lighting from rows of florescent tubes imbedded within the ceiling. Resisting the urge to shield his eyes from the intense light, Hobbs focused on the form. There, surrounded by the beautiful collection of trophies and checkered flags, sat a stock car sporting the ugliest green color Hobbs had ever seen. He gawked as gold and silver clashed and gave way to a horrendous green color that assaulted his senses. The harsh transition forced Hobbs to momentarily shut his eyes.

"Boys," Bill exclaimed with pride, "I present to you the Green Ugly."

Once the initial shock abated, Hobbs took a closer look at the celebrated car; a 1992 Ford Thunderbird with minimum modifications including a full, welded-in roll cage, welded doors and window mesh. Like most road stock cars, the stripped interior provided no conveniences except for a driver's seat and five-point safety harness. The car had double zeros etched onto the passenger-side door and the backside panels carried the words *Pride of Anna's Mill*. Hobbs guessed that at one time it had been a family car before being transformed into its present condition. Unlike most amateur racecars constructed with limited budgets and held together with duct tape, this car was in pristine condition. Other than a slightly twisted back bumper, the car looked as if it had never seen a racetrack.

Hobbs knew however, that the car had seen its share of races and then some. Novice bystanders might look at the car and see nothing out of the ordinary except for an obvious God-awful green finish. But Hobbs looked past the obvious and appraised the craftsmanship with an expert eye. What he saw was a masterpiece, each panel on the car, meticulously and expertly molded. There were no overlapping or jagged sheets common on amateur cars and the welding was hidden so that each part rested against the other, the entire car, from front to back, looked as if it had been constructed from the same continuous sheet. Few professional stock cars possessed this type of workmanship. *If Clarence created this piece of work,* Hobbs thought to himself, *then the rude, beer-drinking mechanic missed his calling in life. He should be molding body frames in a professional race shop.*

Hobbs watched as J.R. crouched low and ran an index finger along the contours of the body frame. After a moment of concentration, J.R. exhaled and raised his eyebrows in amazement. He stood and took a step back to appraise the car from a greater distance. He sensed Hobbs' gaze and looked past the car to where his friend stood. The two shared a knowing glance. The body design on the Green Ugly was unlike any road stock car they had ever seen. Hobbs wanted to get a look at the engine. If the craftsmanship of the engine matched that of the body, then they had truly discovered a rare find.

"Boys," Bill said as he shuffled toward the car, "you're looking at the fastest amateur stock car to ever race in central Georgia. This car ain't ever been beat in this state and she holds track records as far west as Columbus and as far east as Statesboro." The old mechanic placed a tender hand upon the hood of the car and turned to look into Hobbs' eyes. The gaze was direct and penetrating. "You say you boys have been around amateur racecars most of your life," he said in a serious and confident voice, "believe me when I tell you. This one's a lick faster than any road stock you've ever seen."

Bill's words might be the empty boasting of an old sentimental fool, but Hobbs sensed truth to the comment. The victories on the wall and the master craftsmanship displayed within the body all attested to the fact that the car was a cut above the rest.

"It's kind of dull ain't it, Bill?" Dippy observed.

Hobbs winced at the comment. *Only Dippy could concoct a comment so rude and untimely,* Hobbs thought. *The old guy had obviously made this car his life's work.*

"Can't you wax it or something? It's an ugly apparition compared to the fine gold trophy's you've got in here."

"There's more to a car than its color, Dippy," Hobbs retorted harshly.

"No, no," Bill said with a wave at Hobbs. "Dippy's right. I've tried just about everything to bring a shine to this old car, but it won't take. God himself would find it difficult. It's a lifelong vexation to me that my brother chose this color. He never provided an adequate explanation and when I see him in the by and by, I intend to ask him again first thing."

"She's beautiful," J.R. said.

"Are you blind, J.R.?" Dippy blurted out.

Bill chuckled and watched as J.R. felt along the front grill. "He ain't blind." He walked to the front of the car to release the hood. "In fact, I can tell that J.R.'s got a keen eye when it comes to fast cars."

Hobbs and J.R. helped Bill lift the hood to reveal a sparkling V-8, 351 horse powered engine. Hobbs eyes lit up as he and J.R. surveyed the engine.

"The crankshaft's got 4340 alloy steel forgings," Hobbs observed.

"Check out the bolts on the shaft, they're splayed," J.R. responded with excitement.

"Do you like that?" Bill asked. "That was my idea. The splayed bolts increase the strength of the cap."

"Dog gone it, Richard," J.R. exclaimed. He edged further into the engine. "The piston crowns have domes and they're fly-cut."

"Let me see," Richard responded. He heaved himself further into the compartment.

The engine was like a treasure trove to Hobbs; each new discovery needed to be thoroughly analyzed. He wanted to pull apart the components, but he knew the engine was no plaything. It was a finely tuned instrument with parts that fit exactly as they should. He poked and prodded carefully.

After several minutes of exploration, Hobbs noticed that Bill and Dippy had walked over to the trophy case. He nudged J.R. "Hey," he whispered.

J.R. had managed to work his head between the frame and engine block. It was comical to watch J.R. work on engines. No component was hidden from view as J.R. twisted and strained his lanky frame.

"Hey," Hobbs said again and poked his friend. J.R. responded and bumped his head several times before finally emerging.

"I've been looking at the drive train," J.R. said.

"I can see that," Hobbs whispered and looked over at Bill. "Do you notice anything familiar about this car?"

"No, do you?" J.R. said. He rubbed the bumps on his head.

"Ever since I saw those pictures in the lobby, I've been racking my brain to come up with an explanation as to why I haven't heard about the Green Ugly. If this car is so famous in Georgia, how come we haven't heard about it?"

"Yeah but we're from South Georgia. Maybe the Green Ugly never raced down there."

"It did race in Valdosta. Remember the picture in the lobby?"

"Well that picture looked twenty years old, Richard. Maybe it raced before we were old enough to know better."

Hobbs rested his elbows on the engine and racked his brain, certain he had never seen the car in action but somewhere and at some time, he had heard about this car.

"Maybe one of the old timers down in Valdosta could help you remember," J.R. said, tinkering with a worn belt. "Those boys knew everything and weren't shy about telling stories."

Hobbs thought about that for a moment. Johnny Watts and Bugger Vance were old men that frequented the track infield in Valdosta. Each Friday night a van from the nursing home dropped them off and Hobbs never saw one without the other. Johnny possessed an encyclopedic knowledge of amateur racing and Hobbs cherished the stories he told. Many of the stories were exaggerated accounts of wrecks and daring feats of bravery exhibited by drivers long forgotten. Some stories were obvious fabrications, but others were true; stories of fantastic wrecks at the finish line, of men who raced with broken limbs and shattered vertebrate, of cars that finished races engulfed in flames. Johnny and Bugger told hundreds of stories. If anyone in Valdosta remembered the Green Ugly, it would have been them.

"The old timers never talked about the Green Ugly," Hobbs said, visibly frustrated. "I would have remembered that name. You don't forget a car by the name of Green Ugly."

"Maybe they didn't know the car by that name. Maybe they used the driver's name."

"No," Hobbs responded. "I never heard them talk about Jack Voyals either. Bill says that the Green Ugly has never been beat in Georgia and I know for a fact that if this car raced in Valdosta, and won, then Johnny and Bugger would know about it. They would have talked about it too."

In his mind, Hobbs reviewed details of the photograph he had seen in the lobby. Perhaps the image of the car would shake loose some distant memory. He recalled that the car had oil and debris splattered across the side panels and shadows under the front wheel created the false impression that the car was flying. On the bottom part of the driver side door, just under the double zero, Hobbs had detected a small streak of rubber where a competitor's tire had gotten too close. The rubber streak provided a dark underlining mark to the number. The "double zero" is not an unusual number in amateur racing but for some reason the "double zero" on the photograph struck Hobbs as unique. He could not shake the image of the Green Ugly flying down the backstretch with the double zero emblazoned on its side panel. The number clung on to his mind and called out for attention.

"That's it," Hobbs exclaimed. He slapped the engine block with an open palm.

"What?" J.R. responded.

"Johnny and Bugger used to talk about a car from up north," Hobbs exclaimed in muted tones to contain his excitement.

"I wonder if they're still alive. Johnny used to make me laugh," J.R. said.

"Do you remember when Troy Dalley won those three straight championships and started bragging about how he had the fastest car that ever race in Lowdes County?"

"Yeah."

"Well I was there when Johnny and Bugger laughed at Troy and told him to shut up. They said that the "Double Zero" held that distinction and unless Troy could top the track record, he was just second best."

"I don't get it," J.R. said. "What's the Double Zero?"

"The Double Zero was the car that owned the track record down there. Troy didn't believe them, so Johnny and Bugger pulled out the record books and right there on top of the list was a double zero. It got the record sometime in the early 70's and I remember there was no name next to the entry. Troy said that since there was no name then it wasn't legitimate. He said that some jealous old men placed it there."

J.R. looked at Hobbs with astonishment. "You think this car is the double zero that owns the track record in Valdosta?"

"Not this car but some earlier version. I think there's a strong possibility." Hobbs looked over at Bill. "Let's go find out."

Chapter 10

Bill Voyals talked with Dippy beside the trophy display and Hobbs approached tentatively, wondering if he had accidentally discovered the mysterious stock car of his youth. Ever since he'd learned of the legendary Double Zero car from Johnny Watts, he'd dreamed of someday finding the famed car and its driver. *It might be too late to find the driver,* he thought, *but the car might be right under my nose.*

"Excuse me, Mr. Voyals," he said.

Bill turned and looked up at Hobbs, his soft blue eyes peering over low fitted bifocals.

"Excuse me sir," Hobbs said again respectfully. "But I was wondering if I could ask you something about your car."

"You can call me Bill," the old man said. "And by all means ask whatever you like."

"Did you say that the Green Ugly raced in Valdosta?" Hobbs asked.

"I don't remember saying that Richard, but I'm sure we did. At one time we raced her ever chance we got."

"Do you think you would have raced down there sometime in the early 1970's?"

"That seems about right," Bill said stroking his chin. He folded his bifocals and placed them neatly within a shirt pocket. "Back then Jack was ambitious and anxious to prove his mettle against all the top amateurs. When he heard of some hotshot driver in some far away locale, Jack loaded up the car and headed off to whip him. He looked for challenges all the time. We'd go to west Georgia and he'd hear about some guy in Montgomery and off we'd go. In Montgomery he'd hear about so and so racing in Mississippi and the next week we'd find ourselves on a backwoods dirt track outside of Tupelo. We've raced and won on every major amateur track in Georgia, including, I'm sure, Valdosta. Sometimes we'd race two or three times a night at different tracks. We'd blow into some places and hardly have time to register the car. After the race we'd cut out and speed to the next track down the road." Bill smiled as he recalled memories. "We were foot loose and fancy free back then, and careless too I think."

Hobbs and J.R stole a glance at each other. "You won't believe it," Hobbs said with an uncharacteristic touch of giddiness, "but I think your car still holds the track record down in Valdosta."

"Really? How nice," Bill said.

"They still talk about your car. People have no idea about the driver and the only identity the records give is that the car had a double zero. After the race, the car and driver were nowhere to be seen."

"We did that a lot back then," Bill said. "Since there was no money to be won in most amateur races, we packed up and scooted. We probably had a second race that night."

"I wish I could've seen her race," J.R. said. He looked at the car as if imagining her thundering past competition, leaving nothing but dust in her wake. He turned and looked at Bill. "Why did you stop racing so long ago?"

"We didn't stop racing, we just stopped traveling so far away for the races. We pushed our cars and ourselves for twenty years, racing in places as far away as Fort Smith, Arkansas and Durham in North Carolina. We'd come home and everybody wanted to know all about it. They'd badger us with questions until we plum ran out of breath. They'd ask questions like 'Why'd we have to race so far away?' and 'How come you can't race closer to home?' We had no good answers and the plain truth was that after twenty years of whipping every top amateur in the South, Jack and I just ran out of challenges. We realized that the only fun races left were the ones in Bibb County because our families and friends could come out and watch. So, for the last twenty years, and up until Jack's untimely demise, we raced the Green Ugly strictly in this area."

After a moment of reflection, Bill turned towards Hobbs. "Young man," Bill said, "I'm honored that the people in your hometown think so highly of the Green Ugly. But you should understand that my brother and I raced this car for nearly forty years. During that time, we built and raced more than fifteen different versions of the Green Ugly. We raced thousands of times and I can count on one hand the number of times we didn't win. We set more track records than I care to number. In fact, we didn't care much about the track records then and I don't really give a hoot now. No disrespect but I don't care if people in Valdosta or Bainbridge or Jacksonville or any other far-away place knows who we are or what we did."

"In fact," he continued, "the only recognition I seek is from family and friends and the people in this dirt-poor town."

Hobbs nodded his head, "The people around here are lucky to have this car to cheer on," he said.

"Everyone in this town knows what it's like to be an underdog," Bill said. "That's why the Green Ugly is so important to Anna's Mill." He looked over at the car parked in the center of the room.

"Most towns around here have high school football teams to cheer on or peanut growing festivals to fuss about, but Anna's Mill lacks all those things. We've got nothing but poor peanut farmers and a few desolate families who scrape out a living by collecting pinesap for turpentine. The entire state of Georgia has forgotten about this place and in twenty years, by the time our young people are old enough to leave, Anna's Mill won't be nothing but a bald spot amongst pine trees."

Hobbs studied the back panel of the car. The words 'Pride of Anna's Mill' had a new meaning as Bill continued talking.

"The people here are my family and friends. I'd do anything to help my family out, to help them feel better about their unlucky situation. So, your right, Anna's Mill is grateful to have the Green Ugly to cheer for. But she and I are just as lucky to have Anna's Mill. I guess you might call it a mutually dependent relationship, if that makes any sense."

An uncomfortable silence fell on the room. Hobbs wanted to veer the discussion towards a more sterile and technical topic. He wanted to talk about the 4340-alloy steel forging on the crankshaft and the Holly 4150 carburetor under the hood.

"Sir, have you raced this car lately?" J.R. asked

"The Green Ugly hasn't left this room in three years. It was three years ago that Jack left us."

"Well," J.R. said, looking at Hobbs and then the car, "other than a few worn out belts and a carburetor that needs a good working over, the car is in excellent racing condition. It wouldn't take very long to get her ready."

"I appreciate your enthusiasm, J.R, I really do." Bill walked to the car and placed a hand on the frame where his brother's name was painted in bright yellow letters. "Jack ain't around to race her no more and his son has no interest."

"You know," Bill continued with a smile, "this Friday night is the annual Central Georgia Amateur Stock Car

THE CHAMPIONS OF ANNA'S MILL

Championships at Bibb County Raceway. When Jack was around and we were still racing the Green Ugly, the entire town of Anna's Mill would throw a huge party. You'd think the circus had come to town with the way folks carried on. We called it the Green Ugly Day," he said with a chuckle. "It was a regular festival with pie tasting contests and horse shoe throwing, the whole bit. We even elected a Queen of the festivities. What a hoot." He slapped the top of the car and laughed loudly. "Most young ladies would be ashamed to be crowned Ms. Green Ugly. But not here in Anna's Mill. It was a real honor to wear that crown."

The old man paused for a moment, caught up in a flood of fond memories from a happier time. He turned and placed a hand on his beloved car. "The celebration would culminate when the town folk lined both sides of the Main Street and rooted their encouragement as they sent the Green Ugly off to the races. Then the entire town loaded up in vans and pickup trucks and headed to Macon for the race."

"The entire town?" Dippy asked in disbelief

"Every last soul, from the oldest to the youngest. Of course, there wasn't much suspense to the outcome of the race since Jack and the Green Ugly has been winning that championship for four decades. But still, they all came; everyone. It was a sight to see. A whole section of the grandstands would be filled with Anna's Mill people all dressed in green, waving flags and pom-poms. When we rode into town the next morning, we'd receive a hero's welcome."

Bill frowned. "Since the Green Ugly don't race in the championship anymore there's nothing to celebrate. There was a lot of joy back then but now the whole town's depressed when Green Ugly Day comes around. It's hard to get out of bed on that day."

"Is there any money to be won at this championship race?" J.R. asked. He looked at Hobbs as if to say *this could be our*

♦ 47 ♦

ticket into the Atlanta Speedway.

"Well," Bill responded, "last I heard they offer $5,000 for first, $2,500 for second and $1,250 for third. There's not much money in amateur racing. You've got to have passion for it because you'll never recoup the investment it takes to build and race these cars."

Hobbs watched J.R. with a sidelong glance. He knew J.R. wanted to race the Green Ugly and even though the money sounded good, there was no guarantee of victory. Their trip to Voyals Auto Shop had turned out to be an enjoyable detour but with only a few days left before the Atlanta race, they dared not waste even one day getting the Green Ugly ready to race.

For a long moment Hobbs and J.R. looked at each other, J.R. pleading his case silently.

"Bill," J.R. said and he turned slowly from Hobbs to the old man. "What would you say if we built the car up to race this Friday night?"

"What?" Dippy exclaimed. "You're off your rocker if you think we're going to hang around here till Friday. We ain't ever gonna make Atlanta with you fiddling around here for three more days. Forget it."

"There's money to be won, Dippy," J.R. exclaimed excitedly. His face turned beet red. "We'll win it for sure." He turned to Hobbs. "You know this car will win. Five thousand dollars will be more than enough. Can we do it Richard? Come on."

Hobbs watched Bill as J.R. pleaded his case. He wondered what type of response the old man would give to J.R.'s proposition. Bill's blue eyes grew wide with excitement and he looked like a man who had just won at bingo and merely waited for the judges to confirm his winning card.

"We could get the car ready to race, J.R.," Hobbs said in an even manner. He slowly took his eyes off Bill and looked at his excited friend. "But we ain't got a driver. Besides, what makes you think that Bill wants us to race the Green Ugly?"

"Any money you win is yours to keep," Bill responded quickly, playing it cool.

Hobbs frowned at Bill. If it were any other time, he would've jumped at the opportunity. But with the Atlanta race only a few days off, he felt he couldn't wait around. It was too risky. Even with a fast car like the Green Ugly there was always the chance of a cut tire or wreck. *Surely there's a more dependable way to earn the money,* Hobbs thought

"We ain't got a driver," Hobbs said with finality. "And since even the Green Ugly can't drive itself, then that settles it. There's no sense in getting the car ready to race without a driver."

"I'll drive it," J.R. exclaimed with a confidence and conviction that surprised Hobbs. J.R. stood taller than normal, his chin held high.

"Oh man, now I know you're crazy," Dippy exclaimed loudly.

"You have my permission to drive her, young man," Bill said in a manner that reminded Hobbs of a father looking to marry off his old maid daughter.

"Excuse us, Bill," Hobbs said.

Hobbs pulled J.R. to the side with Dippy close by. "You ain't even got a driver's license, J.R. What makes you think you can handle a stock car with forty experienced drivers looking to gun you down? If you crawl into that car, with its legend status, you'll be a marked man." Hobbs spoke rapidly, trying to contain his anger.

"I've seen teenagers without licenses driving stock cars," J.R. responded forcefully. "If a teenager can drive in a stock car race, so can I."

"Well since you've got the brain of a six-year old, that's not a very fair comparison," Dippy said.

Hobbs turned to J.R. and regarded him for several moments. J.R. had never shown this level of determination and was normally very pliable. He rarely voiced opinion and certainly never stood his ground under pressure.

"Why are you so determined to do this?" he asked.

"Ever since we rode into this town, I've had this deep-down feeling. We don't need to look for money anywhere else because we can get it right here. We can do this, I just know it."

"It's a big risk, J.R.," Hobbs said, shaking his head. "Too big," Dippy chimed in.

"You've seen the car, Richard," J.R. countered. "There's none like it anywhere and I just know she'll help us win some money."

J.R.'s determination and conviction unnerved Hobbs. His friend expected and received very little in life and if Hobbs denied him this small request, it would break J.R.'s heart.

"J.R., it's dangerous, you could be injured or killed," Hobbs said, pleading his case.

"I really want to do this, Richard. Let me do this. It's important."

Hobbs studied his friend for a long moment, mystified at his confidence. Despite better judgment, Hobbs consented. He took a deep breath, exhaled, and nodded.

J.R. beamed with joy.

Dippy moaned. "You can't be serious, Richard," he exclaimed

"We've run out of options Dippy," Hobbs said, looking at J.R. "We've looked for work all day without success. This is our best chance."

"If you think I'm gonna wait around here watching y'all work on that old car then you're crazy," Dippy fumed. He no longer cared to speak quietly, and Bill listened from afar. "Number one," he said waving a finger at J.R. and Hobbs,

"I'm not sitting in this podunk town another day while you boys get your kicks out of tinkering in this garage for free." Waving two fingers, he continued, "and number two, since you won't be going to the Atlanta race this weekend then there's no sense for me to wait around here. First thing tomorrow I'm hitching my way up to Atlanta and I'm gonna find my way onto the infield. One way or another I'm gonna make it to this race. I have to make it to this race."

"We've missed races before for lack of money," J.R. said. "Why are you so determined to be at this next race?"

Dippy stole a quick glance at Bill and leaned toward Hobbs and J.R. "I've got my reasons," he whispered, "and Richard knows very well what they are. I've worked two years for this opportunity and I ain't going to miss it." Dippy looked determined and acted as if his presence at the race was a matter of life and death.

"If you hitch up to Atlanta now," Hobbs responded "you'll be there four or five days before the race starts. You'll have no place to sleep and no food. Here at least you might get a decent bed and some food."

"We'll feed you really good," Bill called from across the room. "I promise you that."

"Why don't you wait here and see what happens?" Hobbs asked Dippy. "If we win then we'll all get in like we usually do. If not, then we'll still have enough time to make it up there before the race, we won't have money, but we'll find a way in."

Dippy glanced at Bill. They had not eaten a decent meal in weeks and Hobbs knew the invitation for free food was a strong enticement for Dippy. Besides, Hobbs thought, if they missed the Atlanta race, Dippy would have enough ammunition to harass him and J.R for weeks to come.

"Okay," Dippy said. "But don't think I'm staying because I'm entertaining the thought that J.R. can win in that car. He'll be lucky to survive and when things go bad, you can't say I didn't tell you so."

"That settles it then," Bill exclaimed. He walked to where Hobbs, J.R. and Dippy stood. "You boys are gonna race the Green Ugly in this Friday's Central Georgia Championships, right?"

"It looks that way," Hobbs said as Bill took his hand and pumped it vigorously. "Just wait till the town hears about this," Bill said, hugging J.R. and Dippy.

He clapped his hands loudly and shuffled over to the door exit. Opening the door, he called out for Clarence. "Hey Clarence," he yelled out into the main garage.

"What?"

"These boys are gonna build up the Green Ugly and race her this Friday," Bill exclaimed.

"No, they ain't," shouted Clarence.

Bill closed the door and turned toward his new racing crew. His face beamed. "Oh yes they are," he sang.

Chapter 11

Dippy felt invigorated. It had been weeks since he'd eaten a decent meal and slept on a clean bed. But now, in a matter of hours, he'd done both. Were it not for old Bill Voyals and his ugly green car, Dippy would've once again dined on cold Vienna sausage and spent the cold, wet night tossing and turning in a tent along-side some dark Georgia state highway. The previous evening, old Bill Voyals had marched Dippy, Hobbs and J.R. up the road to Aunt Mae's Cafe and Boarding House where they were treated like royalty. They stuffed themselves on chicken and dumplings, fried okra, grits, and an assortment of greens; topped off with the best apple pie that Dippy had ever eaten. It was even better than the homemade pie that his grandmother made back home. Later, the boys retired to a room with two single beds and a cot. Richard, as usual, preferred the hard floor, so he folded up the cot and slept in his sleeping bag.

After a good night's rest, Dippy took his turn in the shower and discovered layers of grime on his frail body that he didn't know existed. Strolling back from the shower with a towel wrapped around his waist, Dippy looked two shades lighter.

Aunt Mae, bless her soul, was kind enough to wash and

press their worn-out clothing during the night; she even patched up a few stray holes. Dippy learned that Aunt Mae was Bill's wife and the two made a fine couple.

Now as Dippy combed his hair in the mirror, he admired his reflection. For the last several weeks he'd started to feel burned out with the day to day grind of living on the road. With a clean-shaven face, freshly scented clothing, and a good night's rest, he was ready to take on the day and set his worries aside for a few days. The first item on his agenda was an appointment in Aunt Mae's dining room. The kind old woman had promised a serving of her world-famous biscuits and gravy. Dippy Jordan never refused a meal and could eat twice the amount of Richard and J.R. combined. His mouth watered in anticipation of the fat-laden gravy that awaited him down stairs in the cafe.

"Come on J.R., you're holding up the gravy train," Dippy complained as he watched J.R. struggle into his work boots.

"Good thing you didn't hitch up to Atlanta last night," Hobbs said to Dippy.

Hobbs leaned his large body against the open-door frame, waiting patiently for J.R. He wore a clean set of clothes. "You'd be bumming leftover French fries from truckers instead of living high on the hog."

Richard was a loyal friend, but he always seemed to look for opportunities to question Dippy's judgement.

"I've woken up this morning in a fine disposition, Richard," Dippy replied. "I'll not let your disagreeable nature spoil it for me. By the way, what's that smell?" Dippy said, sniffing the air.

"What smell?" Hobbs asked.

"That smell, what is that?" Dippy walked slowly toward Hobbs, sniffing the air as he went.

"What are you talking about?"

"What a beautiful aroma, Richard. Is that daisy or lily? Roses perhaps? My oh my, aren't you a dandy?" Dippy batted his eyes at Hobbs.

"Get away from me," Hobbs said, smiling. A full stomach and sound rest had done wonders for Hobbs' crabby disposition.

J.R. on the other hand awoke irritated and uptight. Dippy knew J.R. had spent the night thinking about all the work that needed to be done on the Green Ugly. He'd eventually fallen asleep and slept two hours past his normal waking time. Dippy watched with an amused grin as J.R. tied on his work boots and marched out the door. "Let's go," he called and made his way down the hallway. He clearly wanted to get past breakfast and start work on the Green Ugly straight away.

Dippy followed J.R. around a hallway corner and down a solid oak staircase. He heard racket coming from the dining room that sounded like the bustle of a train station. *The room couldn't fit more than forty or fifty people*, Dippy told himself. But the hubbub sounded as if it was packed with at least a hundred people.

Dippy exchanged confused glances with J.R. and Hobbs. They hesitated before the swinging doors leading into the dining room. *Perhaps a private party's in session and we're not invited,* he thought.

"Aunt Mae said her biscuits and gravy were world famous, but I didn't expect the whole world to show up," Dippy said, staring dumbfounded at the oak wood door. The aroma of freshly cooked bacon tempted Dippy and his stomach growled. In his mind, he imagined a plate full of steaming hot biscuits, newly sliced open to reveal a soft, fluffy white interior. He imagined the gravy with large chunks of sausage and Aunt Mae pouring liberal helpings of the rich, delicious gravy over his biscuits. The chunks of sausage fell from the ladle in slow motion, landing softly on the pillow-like surface of the biscuits. His mouth watered and he felt drool forming at the corner of his mouth.

The loud commotion from the dining room interrupted

his revelry. "There's got to be a hundred people in there," he said to himself, dumfounded. He turned to Hobbs. "Do you think that one old lady can cook gravy for that many people?"

"It's hard to imagine," Hobbs said.

Aunt Mae had promised a generous portion of biscuits and gravy but now he considered the possibility that the crowd had eaten it all. Dippy turned angry.

"Get out of my way," Dippy exclaimed through clenched teeth as he rushed past J.R. and Hobbs. "I've got to get in there before they slurp down all the gravy." He rammed the swinging door with his shoulder and barged into the dining room.

"Where's the gravy!" he yelled.

Chapter 12

Hobbs watched Dippy disappear into the dining room. Immediately the clamor ceased, and the dining room fell quiet. The only noise was the thump, thump, thump of the swinging door as it closed. After a long moment the room remained still and quiet. Apparently Dippy's entrance has made a lasting impression, Hobbs thought.

"Shouldn't we go in there to help Dippy?" J.R. asked.

Hobbs shook his head. "You can't help a man like Dippy," Hobbs responded in a matter of fact tone as if he were an expert on the subject. "I've learned long ago that Dippy is prone to embarrassing situations and it takes a good amount of thick skin to partner around with him. The best you can hope for is that he lands on his feet in situations like this."

A Grandfather clock in the hallway ticked off the seconds as Hobbs and J.R. watched the door. When Dippy did not reappear, Hobbs slowly opened the door to peer inside. Dippy stood a few feet from the entrance, fixed and immobile. People jammed the cafe and a hundred pair of eyes glared at Dippy.

"What took you so long?" Dippy whispered from the side of his mouth as Hobbs and J.R. took positions on either side of him to survey the crowd.

"I guess we ain't as hungry as you, Dippy," J.R. answered.

Hobbs figured that there were at least one hundred people packed into the small cafe. From the youngest child to the oldest adult, they sat or stood expressionless and transfixed on the three men. The outside balcony held an overflow crowd and Hobbs detected faces smashed against the windowpanes, struggling to get a good view.

"Did I say something wrong?" Dippy whispered.

Before Hobbs could answer, a sprite old lady emerged from the kitchen area with a platter full of biscuits and a bowl of gravy. She moved rapidly and with an energy that belied her old age.

"Good morning," Aunt Mae declared with a beaming smile. "I trust you boys had a good night rest." She walked to a corner table and placed the platter down.

"I've reserved this table just for you. Come and eat," she said with an outstretched arm and bright smile.

The boys tentatively stepped toward the table and sat down. Heads in the cafe followed the trio and chairs scuttled on the hardwood floor as people struggled to get a better view.

"Now," Aunt Mae said, shoveling out the biscuits and pouring the gravy, "I want you boys to try some of my world-famous biscuits and gravy. Dippy, I know you're going to love them." Aunt Mae's soft voice sounded like it belonged to a woman thirty years younger. Her thick silver hair sat in a neat bun on top of her head and wrinkles formed on her cheeks when she smiled. Even in old age, she possessed the features of a beautiful woman.

Dippy offered Aunt Mae a half-hearted smile and looked down at his steaming hot breakfast. Hobbs had seen Dippy eat a half-dozen biscuits in one sitting and he suspected that today would be no different. But now, with one hundred pairs of eyes trained on his every move, Dippy no longer looked hungry.

Dippy picked up a fork and knife and prepared to cut

into a biscuit. He hesitated and glanced around to a nearby table where a group of men were watching.

"Go ahead, take a bite," Aunt Mae said. "I made them special just for you."

Dippy gave the sweet old lady a labored grin. "Yes ma'am," he said.

Tentatively, Dippy raised the fork to his mouth, prepared to bite down on the steaming mouthful, and then looked out the window. There, two feet from his open mouth was the face of a man; his nose and lips distorted and pressed tightly against the windowpane with one large eye peering in as if Dippy were a specimen under a microscope. Dippy dropped his fork and pushed away from the window.

"Get away from there, Earl," Aunt Mae retorted and she rapped the window pane with her knuckles. "Mind your manners." Earl backed away from the window leaving an oily smear.

"All of you mind your manners," Aunt Mae lectured to the crowd in the cafe. Her voice suddenly took on a harsh tone. "Can't you see that these boys are trying to eat?"

Slowly the crowd heeded Aunt Mae's admonitions and turned away from the three men. They talked quietly amongst themselves and only occasionally glanced at the corner table.

"Please excuse our rude behavior," Aunt Mae said to the boys, her soft and kind voice returning. "Whether you like it or not, you are celebrities in this town now. When the word got out that three mysterious men are in town to fix up and race our beloved car, well everybody wants to get a look at you. They've been gathering since before the sun came up. I suspect that once they've had their look, they'll head off."

"Now," Aunt Mae continued, "I've got some bacon on the stove and I don't want it to burn so I've got to get back to the kitchen. If you need anything just holler." She started to walk away and then turned around. "Dippy, I want to hear all about them biscuits and don't you never mind about peeping Toms. They won't bother you anymore." With that, she whisked away to the kitchen.

As Aunt Mae predicted, once the crowd got a good look at the strange visitors and realized there was nothing exciting about watching three men wolf down biscuits and gravy, they began to leave.

Hobbs had expected a few well-wishers in the crowd but there were none. The previous night, old Bill Voyals had mentioned that people would be delighted to know the Green Ugly was coming out of retirement. However, if anything, the town folk displayed hostility. The men glared a little too long, with looks much like the threatening stare Clarence had offered at the shop. Having received his full share of rejection throughout life, Hobbs knew hostility when he saw it. He cared little about these people's feelings, but physical intimidation underlined their prolonged glares and he'd have to remain vigil.

Chapter 13

As Hobbs stuffed the last forkful of syrup-covered pancake into his mouth he heard a commotion at the front entrance. People moved out of the way to let a large, bald man with overalls into the cafe. "Where are they at?" he bellowed. The man's voice carried across the room. He stood at the entrance with hands on his hips and scanned the room. His lower jaw jutted out and his brow furrowed into a stern and menacing glare.

A slight, red headed man directed the intruder to the far corner table where Hobbs wiped his mouth and gulped down orange juice.

A line of hard looking men filed into the room as the bald man marched, single mindedly towards Hobbs. In his hurry, the man knocked over a few empty chairs and the patrons scurried to get out of his way.

Hobbs picked at his teeth and measured the man's stature and build. He watched the man's tightly clenched fists with interest.

"What makes you think you can waltz into this town and race Jack Voyals' car?" the man demanded. He hovered over Dippy as half a dozen men took positions around the table.

J.R. looked down at his plate and glanced towards Hobbs

with a worried look.

"Are you hard of hearing? I asked you a question."

Hobbs took another swallow of orange juice and nudged J.R. "You'd better eat if you're hungry," he said calmly, ignoring the man.

Dippy appeared non-flustered at the arrogant man blathering over his shoulder. He eyed a leftover biscuit on Hobbs' plate.

"Hey," the bald man spat at Hobbs. "Answer the question."

Dippy looked up at the man with a perturbed look. "Listen," he said, "we're trying to eat here. Bill said we could race the car and he also said we could eat Aunt Mae's biscuits and gravy. This breakfast is the best I've had in a long time, even though you people are intent on spoiling it for me. I'm a serious gravy eater and I need my space so back off."

"Hey Richard," Dippy said, pleading. "Can I have that last biscuit on your plate?" Hobbs stuck a fork in the biscuit and plopped onto Dippy's outstretched plate.

The outraged man grabbed the plate from Dippy. "Bill Voyals don't speak for this town. He's got no right to let you race that damn car."

Dippy looked up at the man with astonishment. "Can't a man enjoy a simple breakfast of biscuits in this town?" He turned to Hobbs, irritated. "This whole town has aligned against me, Richard. They are determined to ruin my breakfast."

Hobbs stood slowly, keeping a wary eye on the belligerent stranger. The men surrounding the table gave Hobbs a wide berth.

"You ain't welcome here," the man said with a menacing sneer.

Dippy and J.R. followed Hobbs as he attempted nudge his way between two men blocking his exit.

"Wait, just one moment."

Hobbs looked up and saw a well-dressed, middle-aged man approach from the cafe entrance. He carried a notebook and wore thick, industrial strength eyeglasses. The glasses magnified his blue gray eyes two-fold. The bug-eyed man bumped into a few tables but eventually made his way to stand between Hobbs and the angry posse. The man was nervous as he turned to address the leader of the mob.

"I just have to say, Mr. Reynolds," he began with a tense crackle, "not all of the folks of Anna's Mill agree with your position and frankly sir, and with all due respect, you have no right to assume that you speak for us all."

"I speak for this group of men," Reynolds said. "And right here, right now, that's enough." He looked at Hobbs. "You and your friends need leave this town, boy. And I mean right now." Several men in the group grumbled their assent.

"Sir," the bi-speckled man said with a trembling but determined voice, "you have no authority to make that determination and if your threat to these men is followed through then I fear your actions will have serious consequences."

Hobbs watched as Reynolds struggled to contain his anger. He turned to address the bi-speckled man. "Reeves," he said, pausing to collect his thoughts and composure, "if we don't put an end to this right now, we'll all be sorry. There's honor at stake. Bill Voyals has no right to do this. He's out of his mind if he thinks we're going to let these drifters race that car."

"I understand your concerns, Mr. Reynolds," Reeves said, speaking more confidently. "And you'll have the opportunity to address your grievances at a town meeting that will be held later in the day."

Hobbs noticed movement and turned to see Aunt Mae standing at the entrance to the kitchen. She held a dishrag in her hands and looked at Reynolds with disappointment.

Hobbs realized she had witnessed the entire exchange, including Reynolds criticism of her husband.

Reynolds saw Aunt Mae and immediately regretted his comments. "Mae, I mean no harm against Bill, he's always been a good friend," Reynolds said in conciliatory tone. "But he's wrong to let this happen and you know I'm gonna speak my mind."

"You've said enough Bobby Lee Reynolds," Aunt Mae said. "I'd like you and these men to leave my restaurant."

"Bill can't do this," Reynolds said. "Not after what we've been through. Not after what has happened."

Hobbs detected a slight quiver in the man's lower-lip as he became distraught. He found it difficult to rationalize how one trivial racecar could elicit such emotion. Battle lines were being drawn and lifelong friendships were crumbling before his eyes. He began to reconsider his decision to let J.R. race the car. If men like Reynolds were reduced to the point of tears and desperate enough to end friendships simply because J.R. wanted to race the Green Ugly, maybe he and his friends should leave this crazy town and forget the whole deal. It wasn't worth it, and they could find work and money elsewhere.

When Aunt Mae made no response, Reynolds and his men started toward the exit. He stopped and turned back towards Reeves. "I'll be at that meeting," he said. He gave Hobbs a long, hateful glare and exited the cafe.

Once the men had left, Reeves turned to Aunt Mae. "I'm sorry you had to hear that," he said.

"It's okay, Reeves," Aunt Mae responded. "People like Bobby Lee have been grumbling about the Green Ugly for a while now. I know they've been doing it in secret and it's about time we get it out in the open." She smiled at Hobbs and his friends. "You'll find the people in this town to be a strange bunch. I hope you'll forgive the likes of Bobby Lee and those rude men. They are good men; good family men.

But by racing the Green Ugly you've touched a raw nerve."

"I've been thinking about not racing the car if it's going to stir up such passion," Hobbs said.

"Nonsense," Aunt Mae responded. "That car needs to be raced so that this town can move on. You'll help us do that, won't you? Please don't give in to Bobby Lee and his bunch."

Move on from what? Hobbs thought. He looked into Aunt Mae's pleading eyes for a long moment, wondering what type of misery surrounded the Green Ugly. "I can't promise; we'll see how things go."

"I'll walk you out," Reeves said. "I imagine you'll want to start work on the car right away."

"Yes sir," J.R. responded, enthusiastically.

The men thanked Aunt Mae for breakfast and walked out and onto the side walk. It had rained all night but now the sun shone brightly over the tall pines in the distance. The storm front had chased away the previous day's humidity and the air felt crisp and clean.

"My name's Reeves Carter," the man said. He shook Hobbs' hand. "I'm the postmaster in this town and I work right across the street." He pointed at the thin building across from Aunt Mae's. Several groups of people stood in front of the post office and along the sidewalks watching them. A truck drove slowly by; the driver gave Hobbs a long, curious look.

"When I saw Mr. Reynolds heading down the street towards Aunt Mae's I knew there'd be trouble and I rushed on over as fast as I could." There was an awkward silence. Perhaps the man wanted thanks, Hobbs thought. J.R. offered it.

"I also publish a weekly newspaper that's circulated throughout Bibb County. We don't make much money with the paper but it's enough to keep the post office running." After a pause, the man continued. "I've got an old printing press in the back of the post office. But don't tell the Postal Service, they wouldn't approve of such a thing." He grinned and winked at Dippy.

"I wouldn't fancy being a journalist in a town like this," Dippy said. "Ain't much to write about that I can see."

"I try to cover all of Bibb County, not just Anna's Mill," Reeves said in his defense. "You'd be surprised at how much there is to write about."

Silence followed and Hobbs noticed J.R. fidget. He was anxious to get to work on the car. "We best be going," he said to Reeves.

"I'd like to interview you boys," Reeves said abruptly as Hobbs turned to leave.

"The Green Ugly coming out of retirement is big news in the county and I want to be the first to write all about it. Will you give me some time?"

"Sure, mister," J.R. said with a smile and turned to follow Hobbs down the sidewalk. "Contact our publicist," Dippy said over his shoulder. "He'll work out the details."

Reeves watched Dippy leave with a confused look on his face.

Chapter 14

A small crowd had gathered to watch Hobbs and his friends make their way down the muddy road toward the auto shop. A few people smiled at Hobbs and he nodded.

"Do you think these people are crazy?" Dippy asked Hobbs as he kicked a stone down the road. The stone skipped into a puddle with a splash.

"I wouldn't call them crazy," Hobbs responded. "I think they've just got too much time on their hands."

Hobbs watched J.R turn around to look at the crowd. His friend looked worried and he wondered if J.R.'s enthusiasm for the race had diminished. The town folk had been extremely rude and J.R. had always been sensitive to such things.

"Do you still want to go through with this?" he asked.

"Yeah," J.R. answered as he looked over his shoulder again at the crowd. "But those people are making me nervous. I've got a case of the butterflies."

"Well I guess you've got the right to be nervous," Dippy responded. He kicked at another stone and frowned as it veered off his foot into a ditch. "Until this morning I would've thought that the most dangerous thing a man could do was race a stock car. But now, after watching that display at Aunt Mae's, I'd guess that racing cars comes in a distant second in the danger category. Driving *these* people's car is my new number one. If you manage to survive that race on Friday, you'll be lucky to escape the lynching that those people have in store for you. I don't care what Richard says; those people are crazy and when you don't win that race, you're gonna have a couple hundred people hunting you down. Shoot, from the way that bald guy was talking, you'll be lucky to survive the next twenty-four hours, never mind the race."

"Hush," Hobbs said as J.R. looked at Dippy in horror.

"I've heard that a favorite form of torture around these parts is being dragged behind a truck," Dippy continued. "Of course, in this loony town they'd probably drag you using that Green Ugly car. Wouldn't that be something?"

"Don't listen to him, J.R.," Hobbs said "He's just being ornery."

"Yeah J.R., don't listen to me. No one around here ever does and look where it's gotten us." Dippy picked up a stone and threw it as far as he could, a show of frustration.

"You know, Richard," Dippy said, anger in his voice, "I can't believe that you're allowing this to happen. J.R. ain't even got a driver's license and you're gonna help him to crawl into that deathtrap. I don't blame J.R. because he don't know any better. But you're a different matter. You do know better and you're gonna allow it."

They walked in silence for a long moment.

"Those other drivers won't go light on him either," Dippy continued. "They don't know he's simple minded. They'll take one look at him in that legendary car and take him as a threat. They'll drive him hard and if he don't harm himself, they will."

"I can take care of myself," J.R. said, unconvincingly.

"No, you can't, J.R.," Dippy shot back immediately.

J.R. winced at the sharp rebuke.

"That's Richard's job. Haven't you figured that out yet? I'm through giving advice to you boys," he said, looking at Hobbs. "You hear me? When J.R. hurts himself in this stupid race, and he will, you're responsible."

Dippy picked up his pace to put distance between himself and Hobbs. The three men walked in silence, contemplating Dippy's outburst.

"Richard?" J.R. asked tentatively.

"Yeah?"

"Tell me again where the gas petal is. Is it the one in the middle between the brake and clutch?"

Hobbs looked over at J.R. His friend looked confused. "Brakes are the middle; gas is to the right." He placed a hand on J.R.'s shoulder. "We'll work it out," he said.

"Lord help us all," Dippy prayed solemnly.

Chapter 15

Reeves Carter's cramped office reminded Dippy of his grandmother's small home in North Carolina where old things decorated every unoccupied space. Trinkets of all sorts sat upon shelving and desk space and old post office posters decorated the walls. Oddly, the scent of evergreens permeated the office and Dippy failed to detect its source.

He brought a dainty cup of tea to his lips and realized it was impossible to look manly when drinking tea in this manner. His pinky finger stuck up in the air and he gave it a side long glance, and then drained the cup. He rested the empty cup on the small saucer in his lap and looked for an empty space on Reeves' desk.

"Can I take that from you?" Reeves asked.

"Thanks," Dippy handed over the saucer and cup.

"Be right back," Reeves said and walked from the room.

Dippy studied the antique clock on the wall and thought of his grandmother. It had been two weeks since he'd last called her, and he wondered if she was okay. First chance he got, he'd call and check up on her.

Reeves returned. "I really appreciate you taking the time to answer some questions. The readers of my newspaper are going to love your insight regarding J.R.'s background and racing experience. If he gets a chance to race the Green Ugly, the readers will want to know all about the man behind the wheel."

"No problemo," Dippy said. "I got nothing else going on. Richard and J.R. are busy at the garage and I'm just sitting around twiddling my thumbs. I wish this town was a little more exciting."

Reeves reviewed the notes he had taken from the interview. "I would've never realized that J.R. has dreams of racing with the professional circuit."

"Sure," Dippy said. He'd fed Reeves a bunch of lies regarding J.R.'s experience as a driver and had not felt the least bit of guilt in doing so.

"And you say his nickname on the track is The Exterminator?" Reeves looked at Dippy through thick, round eyes glasses. Dippy felt like the man's eyes bored right through him.

"Did I say that?"

"It says it right here," Reeves said, consulting his notes. "They call J.R. 'The Exterminator' because of his aggressive racing tactics." Reeves looked at Dippy again. "That's a direct quote."

I guess I laid it on thick, Dippy thought. He knew Richard wouldn't be happy when he picked up tomorrow's newspaper and read that their simple-minded friend, J.R. Rentz, was a famous amateur racecar driver from South Georgia. "Yeah," Dippy said with a mischievous grin, "that sounds about right." *It'll serve them right for being so hard-headed about racing that green contraption in the first place,* he thought.

Reeves stashed the notes in a desk drawer and folded his hands. Dippy took it as a sign that the interview was over and that they had now entered the 'off the record' realm.

"What I find amazing," Reeves said, "is that you and your friends have traveled the country for the last couple years, attending professional stock car races. I never heard of such a thing."

Reeves looked at Dippy for several moments as if his statement deserved some type of response.

"Yep," Dippy said. "Say, listen, would you happen to have a few chores around here that might keep me busy? I know you work for the Postal Service but even the post office needs a few weeds pulled now and again. I'm handy with a paint brush too. I don't work for free, but it'll be worth the modest expense."

"What I find *most* amazing," Reeves said, ignoring Dippy's question, "is that you practically have a graduate degree in mathematics and yet you spend your time traveling from one race track to the next. I can understand that J.R. and Richard are motivated by a love of the sport, but you don't seem to have that same disposition. Why do you do it?"

Dippy looked at Reeves for a moment and decided that the man meant no offense. In fact, if anything, the comment complemented Dippy's achievements. The diploma on the wall indicated that Reeves had graduated from a college in Tifton and it had been many months since Dippy had conversed with an educated man.

"Well" Dippy said, "I suppose I've got my own reasons."

Reeves eyes lit up with curiosity. "Sounds mysterious," he said.

An uncomfortable silence fell on the room and Dippy could see Reeves' mind working; like he was searching for a different way to get Dippy to open-up. "There's nothing mysterious about it," Dippy said, "I just don't want to talk about it."

Reeves smiled. "I have a degree in education," he said, "and even though I'm not a teacher I always find a way to apply my training. For instance, I could be talking to a local farmer and before I know it, I'm teaching him about how lunar movements affect his crops. I seem to have a natural penchant for it. Do you ever find yourself applying mathematics to everyday things?"

You've also got a penchant for sticking your nose in other people's business, Dippy thought. "I use math at every opportunity," he said. "In fact, I don't relate to something unless numbers are involved."

"Fascinating," Reeves said. "Is that why you attend stock car races? It would seem to me that road racing provides an endless supply of formulations and numbers for someone like yourself."

Dippy looked at Reeves for a long moment. *You have no idea,* he thought.

"How do you apply mathematics to racing?" Reeves leaned forward and listened intently.

You are a nosey bugger, aren't you, Dippy thought. He leaned back and crossed his arms, studying Reeves' pleasant smile. He figured there'd be no harm in telling the man a little about his work.

"A couple years ago, when I started to attend races with Richard and J.R., I became interested in monitoring lap times on various cars. I was particularly interested in studying speed fluctuation. I actually developed analytical models that helped me to predict how drafting and new tires affected car speed." Dippy smiled and looked at the wall, reminiscing about his first experience with racing.

"After a while I got into the physics of stock car racing. I'd look at the effects of turn banking and aerodynamics. Racing physics is an entire discipline all by itself."

"I didn't know that," Reeves said, fascinated.

"Yeah, well anyway, for the last two years I've been recording lap speeds on specific cars. In fact, I've developed mathematical models that allow me to make predictions on how well a car will do in a race. I can predict how well a car will do based on its past performance."

"Wow," Reeves said. "That sounds very useful. I bet stock car officials could use that type of information. You know what I mean? It seems like they could use it to monitor cars to make sure nothing untoward happens. I'm sure they have controls to keep teams from cheating but a mathematical model like the one you just described would provide an extra level of control to ensure an even playing field."

Dippy nearly fell off his chair. He stared at Reeves, speechless. He wished Richard Hobbs was as easily convinced as Reeves had been regarding the significance of his work. Of course, Reeves was a journalist and Dippy dared not reveal his work for fear that it would be misrepresented. Besides, he figured, Richard had been right about one thing; no one in the press is going to believe a redneck fan that certain professional race teams cheat. No, there were better ways to reveal his work and in due course he intended to find a right time and place.

"Of course," Reeves said, "if that information got into the wrong hands, it could be used to predict race outcomes and thereby place wagers on the likely winner. I mean, I can understand how such a system would not work with horse racing since horses are not mechanical instruments and are therefore prone to greater unpredictability."

Dippy realized how much he missed conversing with educated people. Richard and J.R. provided no stimulation for his mind. Talking to them was like talking to two brick walls. Reeves, on the other hand, provided a refreshing break from the mundane. At the same time, Reeves' insight unnerved Dippy. He'd barely talked about his work and already Reeves had picked up on the salient points. *Have I revealed too much?* He felt like swearing the man to secrecy.

"Have you approached the stock car officials regarding your techniques?"

"Ah," Dippy said, reeling from the Reeves' insight, "no, I have not."

"Why not? You ought to."

"It's nothing that important. I was just fooling around with numbers," Dippy said, attempting to back-track. "I'm sure someone couldn't use my models in the way you just described."

"Well, you said that you can use the models to predict race outcomes. Can you do that or not? It would seem to me that such a tool would be a valuable resource."

Dippy felt like he was being deposed. "I'm sure I exaggerated," Dippy said, looking for a way to divert the conversation.

Reeves looked at him with expressionless eyes and Dippy wondered what he was thinking. Perhaps Reeves thought Dippy used the models to place bets on races. An uncomfortable silence fell on the room and Dippy suddenly felt like the accused.

"I guess I should be going," Dippy said as he stood. Reeves stood also. Dippy nodded his head and started for the exit.

"Dippy," Reeves said.

Dippy turned.

"It's been a while since someone's pulled the weeds out back," Reeves said. "And we've got some hedges that need trimming."

Dippy smiled pleasantly. "I'll get right on it," he said and walked from the office.

Chapter 16

Hobbs and J.R. stood at the open hood of the car and admired the newly built carburetor. They had worked deliberately throughout the day and Hobbs took a measure of pride in a job well done.

"There're still a few belts that will need to be tightened," J.R. said.

"Yeah, and we'll replace the fluids tomorrow. We've got three more days before the race and that's plenty of time."

When he and J.R. arrived earlier in the day, Hobbs was delighted to find that old Bill had stocked up on tools and parts. In fact, the old man had arranged and organized the supplies next to the Green Ugly. That way, Hobbs and J.R. weren't forced to scavenge from the cluttered main garage where Bill's grumpy nephew, Clarence, meandered about, ready to give insult at any opportunity.

The inner garage that held the Green Ugly seemed to provide a safe space where Clarence refused to enter. At one point during the day, Clarence stood at the open door and snickered as Hobbs and J.R. worked on the carburetor. "You think you can do better?" Hobbs had said and held a wrench in Clarence's direction. "Come on in, be my guest."

Clarence offered a smirk and walked back into the

main garage. It was as if the room was sacred territory and Clarence was too frightened or intimidated to enter. What did the man fear? Hobbs wondered.

"Let's clean up," Hobbs said and lowered the hood.

"I wonder what Dippy's been doing," J.R. said as he gathered tools.

"Getting himself into trouble I suspect."

Hobbs heard a door close and then footsteps in the main garage. After a moment, Bill shuffled into the inner garage with a long face. "Are you boys finished?" he asked. Hobbs noticed that Bill's cheerful demeanor was gone, replaced by a gloomy and foreboding countenance.

"We're just cleaning up," Hobbs said.

Bill scanned the garage. "You can clean up tomorrow. I want you to come with me. I've got something to show you."

"What's wrong, Bill?" J.R. asked.

Bill looked at J.R. for a moment. "I'll be waiting in my truck," he said and walked from the garage.

Hobbs and J.R. exchanged a worried glance and hurriedly gathered a few personal belongings before following Bill. When they opened the door to the parking lot, Hobbs noticed Aunt Mae sitting in the passenger seat of the truck while Dippy waited in the truck bed. Aunt Mae smiled wearily at Hobbs as he passed.

"What's going on?" Hobbs asked Dippy as he and J.R. crawled into the back of the truck.

"Don't ask me. I was down by the post office when Bill picked me up. The town is practically deserted. I was hoping that you'd know what this was all about."

The tall pines cast long shadows in the late afternoon sun and Hobbs struggled to get comfortable in the open bed of the truck as Bill sped down the uneven road toward town. Throughout the day he had found peace and contentment from his work at the garage. It had allowed him to forget the fiasco earlier in the day at Aunt Mae's Cafe. But now as the truck approached town, he remembered Aunt Mae's plea for help, *'That car needs to be raced so that this town can move on. You'll help us do that, won't you?'* Move on from what? He wondered.

And why had Bobby Lee Reynolds berated old Bill, saying he can't race the Green Ugly? 'Not after what we've been through. Not after what has happened.' He remembered the quiver in Reynolds lower lip and the desperate look in his eyes. *And what about Clarence?* The grumpy mechanic seemed to have an unending supply of fear; particularly for the race car in a back room of his garage.

For Hobbs, the day's events offered too much drama for his liking. He much preferred the mechanical workings of an engine to the unpredictable flow of human emotion. In the garage, he found comfort in knowing that parts fit together nicely and that the parts acted in concert to produce the desired effect. Not so with human relations; there was too much compromise, too much cajoling and molding. He despised the drama and unpredictability of human dealings and surely nothing good or worthwhile ever came of it. Other than his friendship with J.R., Hobbs carried around a life time of failure when it came to dealings with other people.

The truck entered Main Street and took a left-handed turn. He noticed that Anna's Mill was deserted, just as Dippy had said; an ominous sign.

A sick feeling entered his gut. He felt certain that wherever Bill was taking them, it had to do with their efforts to race the Green Ugly. *More drama,* he thought with dread.

The road that Bill traveled contained two neat rows of modest houses; each home packed closely to the next with picket fences, gardens and free-roaming chickens. The appearance was neat and organized; *and deserted,* Hobbs thought. It was as if the entire town had just walked away, leaving their belongings.

The truck took another left-handed turn and started up a gradual incline. He noticed a well-manicured lawn, dotted with massive oak trees and as they continued up the hill, he looked back at the town and was surprised at its beauty. In the distance he noticed Main Street with its tightly packed buildings and the residential areas fanning out in a wide circle. Close to Main Street he saw an expansive grassy park bisected by a meandering stream. Thick green pine trees enclosed the entire scene and Hobbs figured that if Anna's Mill ever wanted to produce a post card image of its town, this would be it.

"Will you take a look at that?" Dippy said.

"It sure is beautiful, ain't it?" J.R. responded, taking in the townscape.

"Not that you idiot," Dippy said. "Take a look up ahead."

Dippy stood at the front of the bed and held on to the cab with one hand and pointed at a large white church atop the hill. A massive throng of people surrounded the church and gathered in small groups on the grassy surroundings.

"This must be the town meeting," Dippy said.

Hobbs noticed that as Bill's truck approached, people began heading toward the entrance of the church. The town folk pointed his way and stared at the truck as it made the final climb.

"Those people don't look happy to see us," Dippy said. "In fact, I imagine there are three strong trees and a hang man's noose for each one of us."

Hobbs remembered the angry group of men at Aunt Mae's Diner and agreed with Dippy's assessment. These people were not happy that he and his friends were reviving the Green Ugly. For some unknown reason they appeared suspicious and offended that three drifters had come to town to race their car.

The truck traveled further up the hill and Dippy turned to Hobbs with a red, angry face. "This is your entire fault, Richard. If you hadn't agreed to let that dimwit race their cursed car, we'd be closer to Atlanta, working for pay, and not in this godforsaken scratch of a town."

"Calm down, Dippy," Hobbs said. He tried to show composure but the looks he was getting from the town folk made it difficult.

"Calm down?" Dippy screeched. "Can't you see we're not welcomed here? And worse, we ain't getting any pay for our hardships." Dippy turned back to the crowd and shook his head. "I'll tell you boys right now, if they pull out the hang man's noose, I'm gonna plead my case and you boys are on your own. It's every man for himself and I ain't letting you take me down."

"What's going on, Richard?" J.R. said. He sat across from Hobbs and stared out at the massive crowd as they jammed into the church sanctuary.

"It's nothing to worry about," he said unconvincingly. "I suppose they'll take a vote and we'll know the outcome. We'll race or not."

"There're gonna vote alright," Dippy said. "They'll vote to see who lives and who dies. In case you haven't noticed, there's been no police in this town since we arrived. This place is like some backwoods redneck encampment and it seems to me that they'll deliver justice any way they seem fit."

J.R. looked shocked at Dippy's comment and Hobbs reassured him with a nod of his head. The meeting promised to be a spirited affair.

Chapter 17

Bill directed the truck passed the church and toward a graveyard in the back. He parked and slowly stepped down onto the red clay road. "Follow me," he directed the boys and entered the graveyard, hand in hand with Aunt Mae.

Hobbs exchanged confused glances with his friends and obediently climbed down to follow Bill. He passed grave markers that were more than a hundred years old and wondered if any of the deceased were Bill's ancestors.

He kept a respectful distance and followed Bill along a winding path toward a newer section of the graveyard. Bill and Aunt Mae stopped at a gravesite and waited for Hobbs and his friends.

As Hobbs approached, he wondered why Bill would take them to a gravesite. *It's not like we know any of these people,* he thought to himself.

Hobbs walked up to Bill and looked down at the grave stone. It read, *Jackie Voyals, Rest in Peace.* He read the dates of birth and death and his heart sank.

"Jackie Voyals," Dippy said. He turned to Bill. "Is this your brother?" he asked.

No, look at the dates, Hobbs thought with trepidation. The grave site was small, and the deceased was ten years old when he died. He died three years ago.

The Green Ugly hasn't left this room in three years, Bill had said last night at the garage. *It was three years ago that Jack left us.*

"Jack is my brother and he's still alive, I think," Bill said solemnly, looking at the gravesite. "Jackie was my brother's grandson. He was Clarence's son."

The pieces of the puzzle began to fall into place for Hobbs as he recalled tidbits of conversation from the last couple of days.

"That car needs to be raced so that this town can move on."

"He can't race the Green Ugly; not after what we've been through. Not after what has happened."

Hobbs rued the day he set foot in Anna's Mill. He and his friends had walked right, smack-dab in the middle of an emotional tempest and had managed to push the one button that promised to send the small, isolated town over the edge. Aunt Mae looked at Hobbs with tender eyes, urging him to understand and to remain strong. *It's not my job to help you people move on from your grief,* Hobbs wanted to yell at her.

"Jackie died three years ago," Bill said. He nodded to the church. "When we go up to the meeting you might hear some people say cruel things about my family and the Green Ugly. But I want you to understand that no matter what is said, Jackie's death was a tragedy, nothing more and nothing less. It was an accident."

I ain't going up to that church, Hobbs thought. *No way I'm getting involved in any of this.*

"Do you understand?" Bill asked.

J.R. nodded his head and Bill started toward the church.

"Actually, Bill..." Hobbs said.

Bill and Aunt Mae turned, and Hobbs could see the strain in their faces. "I don't think we'll be getting involved. I understand what's going on here and we don't want any part of it."

Bill looked at him for a long moment with disappointment.

"I guess we'll be leaving now," Hobbs said.

Bill sighed and turned to the church. He leaned on Aunt Mae for extra support as he made his way up the path.

"You don't talk for me," J.R. said in a forceful manner that caused Hobbs to step back. J.R. looked at him for a long, glaring moment and turned to follow Bill.

Hobbs grabbed J.R.'s elbow. "You don't understand what's going on here," he said, trying to control his anger. "Something tragic has happened to cause the death of a boy and the people in this town blame the car we been fixing up. Bill's using us, J.R. He's using us to dig up the past and from what I can tell, the past, in this case, deserves to remain buried."

"I'm not a child, Richard. I know exactly what's going on here. These people need our help and you want to run off. Why don't you show some backbone? Maybe even a little compassion while you're at it." J.R. yanked his elbow from Hobbs' grip and jogged up the path toward the church.

Hobbs' jaw dropped at J.R.'s rebuke. He watched his friend run up the path and wondered where and when J.R. had suddenly become so determined and strong willed.

He felt Dippy at his elbow as J.R. entered a back door of the church. "I'd say we've got a reversal of roles here," Dippy said. "It's usually me barging through doors without thinking things through first." They watched the church door slam shut.

"I guess I've never been on the outside looking in," Dippy said. "What's the usual protocol for situations like this?"

"Dippy," Hobbs said as he squared his shoulders, "now we walk in after him and do the best we can to offer our support." He looked back at the gravesite for a moment and then started up the path with tentative strides. He felt like running in the opposite direction but J.R. needed his help.

Chapter 18

Hobbs entered the church sanctuary through a thin pastor's door. Tall pane-glass windows provided sunlight and a single aisle bisected two long rows of pews in which people sat shoulder to shoulder, packed in like sardines. They stood along the side walls; over a hundred people, Hobbs thought, and hundreds more waiting outside.

The crowd conversed in hushed tones as Hobbs and Dippy walked quickly to their assigned seat next to Bill and J.R. on the first pew. Reeves Carter, the bifocaled Postmaster stood behind a simple wooden lectern. He rapped a gavel twice, bringing the meeting to order.

Hobbs' heart pounded. In his darkest nightmare he could never have dreamed he would end up here, in this place, surrounded by such a hostile crowd. The place brimmed over with emotional tension and drama. He'd spent his life avoiding such situations. He wiped his sweaty palms on his jeans and took a deep breath, ready for the worst.

"I'd like to bring this town meeting to order," Reeves said with authority.

Hobbs spied Bobby Lee Reynolds sitting, stern and resolute, on the opposite set of pews. An elderly woman, perhaps his wife, sat to one side. On his other side, Reynolds wrapped an arm around a young woman in her early thirties. She looked as distressed and anxious on the outside as Hobbs felt on the inside. She held a handkerchief and looked as if she had recently been crying.

"The purpose of the meeting," Reeves continued, "is to discuss the matter involving the Green Ugly and Mr. Voyals' proposal to race her this Friday at the Central Georgia Championships."

Hobbs heard murmured disapproval in the crowd.

Reeves waited patiently for the crowd to grow quiet before continuing. "I realize there are positions on both sides of this proposition. It is our intention to allow everyone to speak. Please be considerate," he added.

The meeting lacked security and Hobbs anxiously eyed the nearest exit. He measured the distance and took notice of potential obstacles. On the first sign of trouble, he intended to grab J.R. by the arm and drag him from the building.

Reeves continued, "Before I ask Mr. Voyals to speak, I'd personally like to point out that Bill Voyals owns the Green Ugly. He has every right to race her at any time and at any place. He does not require our permission." A few people shouted divisive comments, but Reeves continued unfettered. "However, considering the emotional significance of this car, he is asking for your support." Now the rancor increased, and Reeves raised his voice to be heard. "Consequently, he has asked that a vote be taken." Mollified, the crowd quieted, and Reeves waited. "He will honor your decision," he said finally.

"Mr. Voyals?" Reeves motioned toward Bill and the old man stood to face the crowd.

Bill looked weary. His shoulders drooped and worry-filled creases crossed his normally cheerful face. He cleared his throat and looked out into the crowd.

"I know that many of you are disappointed in my decision." Bill looked directly at Bobby Lee Reynolds. "But I want you to know that whatever happens and however you feel I value the friendships I have with each of you. I don't race the Green Ugly because of personal reasons. Sure, I'm an old man and I'd like to see her compete one last time before I die, but my decision goes beyond that."

Bill looked at the crowd again and motioned toward Hobbs and his friends. "I believe that these boys here are heaven sent. They've been sent to help this town recover from a tragedy; a tragedy that cut deep into the soul of this town. I believe they can help if we let them." The crowd remained respectfully quiet as Bill spoke.

He placed a pair of reading glasses on his head and pulled a piece of paper from his shirt pocket. "Years ago, when my brother and I built a racing car," he said, reading from the prepared speech on the paper. "We never realized that it would play such an important role in civic pride and purpose. Throughout the years the Green Ugly has become part of the fabric of this town."

"I'd like to say something about that," Bobby Lee Reynolds bellowed, interrupting Bill. He stood at the pew with his hand raised.

Reeves rapped the gavel once. "Mr. Reynolds, everyone will have a chance to speak. Please let Bill continue."

Reynolds glared at Bill and reluctantly sat down.

Bill continued reading. "We are a modest town filled with hard-working and self-sufficient folks," Bill said, speaking confidently. "We don't ask for much, but what little we do have is cherished. We cherish our gathering spot at Aunt Mae's, we cherish the weekly newspaper Reeves publishes, we cherish our weekly worship in this church, and..."

"Joe's Gas Stop," someone yelled from the back. "We cherish Joe's Gas Stop." The crowd laughed and Hobbs turned to see the mean looking man he had encountered when they had driven into Anna's Mill. Joe stood at the back with a broad smile on his face.

"That's right, we cherish Joe's Gas Stop," Bill agreed. He looked encouraged and continued reading.

"Anna's Mill is surrounded by communities with high school football teams, peanut growing festivals and large cotton mills. The people in these small communities take pride in those things. As well they should because without them, they'd have nothing to pull them together, nothing to take pride in, and nothing to make them a community."

People in the crowd chatted quietly and nodded their heads in agreement.

Bill grew somber. He looked over his reading glasses into the crowd, took a deep breath and waited momentarily before continuing. "Three years ago, this small town was hit by a tragedy that brought us all to our knees. The events of that fateful day strained relationships and broke up families. We started pointing fingers at each other and making accusations. Rather than leaning in on each other, like most communities do when struck by tragedy, we all withdrew into our own little turtle shells. Because of that day, and our response to it, we lost the one thing that allows this dirt-poor town to hold its head high."

Bill took his glasses off and stored them in his front shirt pocket. He glanced at Aunt Mae as if to gain strength and then looked again to the crowd. "When we lost Jackie, we also lost our community pride and our identity. In many respects, we lost each other. We lost opportunities to gather on Green Ugly Day and to reconnect as a community and to show our support at the race track. When we cheered at the racetrack, we weren't cheering Jack and the Green Ugly, we were cheering for Anna's Mill. We were telling the rest of central Georgia that Anna's Mill has pride, and we're as good and maybe a little better than the rest."

A couple people shouted their agreement. "We were the

best," someone yelled.

Bill paused and turned to Bobby Lee Reynolds. "Bobby," he said as he looked at Reynolds square in the eye. "This Friday I'd like to see the Green Ugly roar down Main Street once again..."

"The hell you will," someone sitting close to Reynolds said.

Bill paused to gather himself and turned to the crowd. "I'd like us all to gather on Green Ugly Day and have pie baking contests." He smiled as if reminiscing on kinder days. "I want to see the boys chase down greased pigs and I'd like to see one of our pretty girls crowned Miss Green Ugly. I'd like to see our car tearing up the track at the Central Georgia Road Stock Championships. And I'd like to see all of you standing by my side once again, cheering on Anna's Mill."

Bill abruptly ended and started to his seat. A chorus of cheers and equal number of jeers followed him until he finally took his seat. Despite Bill's impassioned speech, the town remained divided. Many people stood and shouted encouragement, but others looked on impassively or else shouted derision. If Hobbs had to guess, he'd say that Bill's words carried a very slight majority.

Reeves attempted unsuccessfully to regain control of the meeting by pounding the gavel repeatedly against the lectern. For several long moments, the people in the crowd exchanged heated words. They cursed at each other across the aisle, red faced and spitting mad. The meeting quickly spiraled out of control. But suddenly the clamor abated as Bobby Lee Reynolds rose from his seat and walked across the aisle towards Hobbs. Reynolds stopped several feet in front of the pew, his eyes, stone cold, looking at Hobbs.

"What's your name, son?" he asked calmly.

Hobbs remained composed, although if given a chance, he would've bolted for the nearest door. "My name is Richard Hobbs," he croaked.

"Richard, my name is Bobby Lee Reynolds and this

woman," he said pointing to the young lady with the hand-kerchief, "is my daughter. Her name is Sally Voyals. She is married to Clarence Voyals. Although we don't see too much of Clarence these days, do we Bill?"

Reynolds looked down at Bill with contempt, but the old man stared straight ahead with a blank look. The crowd fidgeted and it was clear that some did not like to see one of their most respected citizens derided.

"Bill gave a fine speech, don't you think, Richard?" Reynolds asked. "I don't have a prepared speech to give like Bill did," he said patting his pockets. "But I don't need a prepared speech for what I'm about to tell you."

Reynolds paused and looked toward his family. Hobbs followed his momentary gaze and noticed that Sally, Reynolds' daughter, held her hands to her face. Whether she was extremely distraught or embarrassed, Hobbs couldn't tell. Regardless, Hobbs looked on and the pieces of the puzzle fell into place; Clarence and Sally, father and mother to Jackie, dead at age 10. *It was a tragedy, nothing more and nothing less,* Bill had said.

Hobbs looked at Reynolds, the grieving grandfather, with more empathy. The man looked mournful, but he also looked frustrated, conflicted between a sad reality and the inability to make things right.

Reynolds turned again towards Hobbs, resolute in his mission. The cold, impersonal stare returned. "I've got a story to tell you Richard and then I have a proposition for you."

Hobbs met Reynolds stare with composure but inside was turmoil. *I'm sorry you lost your grandson,* he wanted to yell. *I'm sorry we wanted to race your car and we'll leave right away. You'll never hear from us again.*

"Three years ago," Reynolds began. "I had a grandson; his name was Jackie. He was a fine boy, Richard; well-mannered and always respectful. There's not a soul in this room that didn't know Jackie. He was loved. Most days you'd find Jackie helping folks around town; doing odd chores, like going shopping for an old widow, helping a farmer paint a barn, helping around the school and at church.

"He loved to be around people, and he loved to give a helping hand. But more than anything else, that boy loved his granddaddy's car. You see, Jack Voyals, Clarence's father, was Jackie's other grandfather. He idolized that man for all he'd accomplished with the Green Ugly. Jackie use to say that when he grew up, he wanted to own the auto shop and race the Green Ugly, just like his granddaddy. I know Jack loved his Grandson, as we all did. But those two were inseparable.

"When Jackie wasn't busy helping around town, he'd be with his daddy and granddaddy at the auto shop. One Sunday afternoon, three years ago, Jackie was at the auto shop with his grandfather. Jack had a rule that Jackie was not allowed into the garage unless an adult was present. It was a sound rule I think, considering the hazards. But on this particular Sunday Jack broke his own rule and he let that little boy into the garage while he ran an errand in town."

"Only God knows why he did that," Reynolds said, striving to maintain composure. He bit his lip and looked toward his family. Sally still held her face.

You don't need to go on, Hobbs wanted to say. *I know the rest of the story.*

Reynolds looked back at Hobbs; his lower lip quivered, and his eyes began to moisten with tears. "That race car was lifted off the ground on supports and when Jackie crawled up under..." He paused, unable to continue. He pulled a handkerchief from his pocket and wiped his eyes. Hobbs heard several people sobbing.

Reynolds took a deep breath and looked down at Hobbs. For several long moments he stared, resignation on his face, but he also looked relieved because the hard part of the story was over, all that remained were the cold, hard facts. "The supports failed, and that car crushed Jackie. He died instantly." Other than the rustling of leaves outside an open window, the sanctuary fell quiet.

Reynolds turned to look at Bill. The old man seemed defeated and looked straight ahead at nothing. "Jack Voyals loved Jackie, we all know that," Reynolds said, still looking at Bill. For a long moment Reynolds seemed lost in thought as if he was not sure he should continue. Perhaps even regretting what he was about to say yet needing to say it.

"Let me ask you something, Richard," he said suddenly. "Let's say you love someone very much but because of some carelessness, you're responsible for their death. What would you do?" Hobbs ignored the rhetorical question. More than ever he felt like an actor in a supporting role with Reynolds in the lead.

"Would you grieve with the rest of us? Would you support your son, your family? At the very least, would you take responsibility and apologize?"

"Bobby Lee," someone said in a whisper, tinged with disappointment. Hobbs suspected the rebuke came from Aunt Mae who sat next to her husband. "Don't do this, not here." Few people heard Aunt Mae's plea and Reynolds glanced at her for a moment. Old Bill just stared straight ahead, emotionless.

Undeterred by Aunt Mae's pleas, Reynolds continued. "I suspect you're a better man than that," he said to Hobbs. "I suspect that you would own up and take responsibility. I suspect that you'd help your friends and family through the grieving process. After all, what kind of man would run off at a time like that?"

Hobbs noticed that Bill moved his head slightly and glared at Reynolds. *How dare you,* he might have said.

Reynolds met Bill's glare and he smiled. "Don't look at me like that, Bill," he said casually. "You know as well as I do, your brother is a coward. Jack Voyals and his car caused the death of Jackie. And what did he do? He ran away. Did he try to console his son Clarence, Jackie's father? No. He didn't even have the courtesy to stick around for the funeral."

Now Reynolds faced Hobbs who wanted to crawl under the pew to die a slow death.

"My daughter not only lost a son on that terrible day. She also lost a husband. Clarence was a good man, a good husband and father. I believe he'd have been a good husband still if Jack hadn't run away. But losing a son and a father on the same day was too much and the man broke. He's a recluse now and doesn't have the courage to... "

"That's enough," Reeves bellowed from the lectern.

Reynolds spun around in fury to face Reeves. "I didn't call this public meeting Reeves," he bellowed. "I'm not the one who's preaching civic pride and duty just so he can see that murderous car drive down Main Street. My grandson is dead because of that car. It has wrecked our lives."

An infant, distraught at the sound of Reynolds outburst, cried somewhere in the back of the church.

The cry distracted Reynolds and he took a moment to compose himself. "Here's my proposition to you, Richard," he said. He stood closer now and Hobbs could see the anguish and fury in his face. "I propose that you and I march down to the auto shop and burn that car. We'll burn it to the ground and place its remnants on Main Street for everyone to see. And we'll place a sign on top that reads 'Here lies Jack Voyals' Car. Jack Voyals ran away, but his car got what it deserved'. What do you say, Richard? Are you with me?"

Richard avoided the man's eyes. He looked at the ground between his feet and prayed that this nightmare would soon be over.

Reynolds regarded Hobbs for a moment. "I guess your answer is no and I suspect you'll be leaving this town straight away." Satisfied that he had made his point, Reynolds started toward his seat and then stopped midway to face Bill. The old man looked thoroughly drained and defeated.

"Bill, I know I've said a lot of hurtful things today," Reynolds said. "But you're trying to jam this down our throats and I'll have none of it. I don't apologize for what I said. It's how I feel and it's the truth. You should've talk to me first before calling this meeting. I would've fought you either way but at least it wouldn't have been so public. We've both suffered enough, don't you think?"

For the first time, Reynolds looked at the crowd. He looked surprised as if he'd forgotten they were present, witnessing the entire spectacle. He started to speak but thought better of it. He walked to his seat and placed an arm around his distraught daughter.

Chapter 19

The setting sun cast long shadows in the sanctuary and outside the gentle breeze brought the odor of freshly cut grass through an open window. Inside, the meeting stalled and no one, including Reeves, knew what to do next. Should they take a vote? Should they adjourn? *Surely no one else has anything of substance to say,* Hobbs thought. *Who could possibly follow Bobby Lee Reynolds after what he'd said?*

In the silence, Hobbs considered his options. He would leave Anna's Mill that very night. He would tie J.R. up and throw him in the back of his truck if he had to but there was no way he'd let J.R. race the Green Ugly.

Just then, Hobbs saw the long and lanky frame of J.R. Rentz stand and walk to the front of the altar. Meaning to stop his friend, Hobbs reached out too late. Mortified, Hobbs could only watch as J.R. turned to face the crowd. He would've rushed J.R. and dragged him off by the collar if he had not been scared stiff and motionless. *You've done it now J.R.,* Hobbs thought. *First, you drag us into this mess and now you're going to meddle in personal business where you don't belong.*

Hobbs heard Dippy chuckle. "You've got to hand it to J.R.," Dippy whispered in Hobbs' ear. "He's as dumb as a pinecone but at least he makes things interesting."

"My name is J.R. Rentz," he said in a low, lazy drawl. "I don't have much to say and I don't want to hurt anyone's feelings." He looked at Sally Voyals with compassion. "I know that you are very sad, and I am so sorry about what happened."

Sally no longer covered her face. She smiled ever so slightly, thanking J.R. for his acknowledgement.

"I've been sitting here thinking about what Bill said and then what Mr. Reynolds said," J.R. continued. "And while both had some points to make, I think they might've missed something that's very important. Bill says he wants to race the Green Ugly and Mr. Reynolds says that he wants to burn up the Green Ugly down there on Main Street. But neither one of them has asked what a ten-year-old boy might want. I realize that I'm not a smart man and that there are a lot of things I don't know but I do know something about ten-year-old boys."

Hobbs took a long, hard look at his friend. J.R. was not one to stand up in front of an entire town and argue a point. To be sure, Hobbs had never seen his friend shy away from large groups in order to make a friend or two, but always with meekness as if he didn't want to cause too much trouble. But now as J.R. faced the deeply divided town, Hobbs saw his friend in a new light. Gone was the submissive posture and gentle voice, rather he stood with shoulders squared and spoke with force and determination. *Unafraid,* Hobbs thought; *and passionate.*

"Have you ever seen a boy's face when a loud car engine is revved?" J.R. asked the crowd. "I have. I've seen their faces light up when a fast car takes off from a starting line, leaving nothing but piles of burnt rubber and smoke. They hoot and holler and they clap each other on the back because it is an awesome thing to watch. Boys love race cars and that's just a fact."

"Sometimes those boys grow up to become men and they never lose that love, not ever." J.R. turned to look at Sally. "I'm one of those men and I know of another not far from here. If you looked at this man, you'd think that he didn't care for anything. He's sad and mean. But at one time he must have loved cars because he built the most beautiful car I have ever seen. No man could have built such a car if he didn't love it first. If this man could somehow find it in himself to love that car again, I think that it could light a spark that would help him to love other things as well. If on the other hand, you take that car from him, it'd be like cutting the life line from a drowning man."

J.R. turned to the crowd and cleared his throat. "Jackie Voyals was a boy and he loved the car his daddy built," He said loudly. "I don't mean to be rude but if you think that Jackie would've liked to see the burnt-out hulk of the Green Ugly on Main Street then you ain't too bright. And if you want to crush his daddy's heart; if you want to destroy any chance that man has, then go ahead and drag his car onto Main Street and burn it to the ground."

As quickly as he had stood to address the crowd, J.R. sat. Hobbs stared at him with shock, trying to reconcile J.R.'s timid nature with his newly found strength. Bill patted J.R. on the knee and thanked him for his words.

Hobbs looked at Sally Voyals and her father, Bobby Lee. They conversed with each other from across the room in hushed tones. Sitting next to Sally, Hobbs saw, for the first time, a young girl. Probably Sally and Clarence's daughter, Hobbs thought; Jackie's sister. She looked to be nine or ten years old.

Reeves cleared his throat in preparation to speak. Now that J.R. had gotten the meeting back on course, Reeves felt in command once more. "Is there anyone else that would like to speak?" he asked, looking directly at Sally. Bill Voyals also looked at Sally, as did most everyone else in the crowd. Hobbs understood now that the decision rested on her. Sally's father had voiced his opinion and now it was her turn.

Sally took her father's face in her hands and kissed him lightly on the cheek. She smiled at him and wiped a tear from the corner of his eye. She turned in her seat and faced Bill across the aisle, folding her hands on her lap.

"Uncle Bill, what does Clarence say?" Sally looked at Bill with a longing on her face. Hobbs could tell that she yearned for her husband and wanted him back home. Hobbs wondered how long Clarence had neglected his family and whether he had even bothered to see his daughter. By the look on Sally's face, Hobbs figured it must have been years.

"He's afraid," Bill responded. "Afraid that if we resurrect the car that you and the rest of the town will have to relive the tragedy. He'd rather that everyone just forgot about him. He also wants us to forget about the car and his father."

Bill looked away from Sally, as if summoning the words to convince her. "I just know that if you; if all of us could support the Green Ugly once again, he'll be able to rise above the fear and shame. Sally, I know that deep in my heart.

"On the other hand, if we run these boys off, it'll confirm his fears and shame; it'll force him further away. We might never have another chance like this again to reach out to him."

Bill's eyes pleaded with Sally and his motives to revive the Green Ugly became clearer to Hobbs. Old Bill had been clever to recruit Hobbs and his friends. On their first meeting on that stormy night, Bill had been careful to avoid any mention of the car's tragic history. He had even lied about his brother Jack, saying that he was dead. He had played the innocent old man who wanted nothing more than to see his beloved car race once more. Hobbs and J.R. believed him. Had they known the truth, that Bill wanted the boys to race the Green Ugly to help his grieving nephew, Hobbs would surely have declined. But Bill was a wise old man and rather than shocking them with the truth, he had taken them under his wing and slowly revealed the tragic reality.

Sally looked into Bill's pleading eyes. Hobbs could tell that she wanted to believe Bill but remained skeptical. Perhaps she had seen too many entreaties to her estranged husband fail.

Sensing her doubt, Bill continued. "It cannot hurt," he said. "Although he pretends otherwise, Clarence loves that car. But because of what happened, he believes the entire town has aligned against him. He cannot believe that he will ever be forgiven.

"And Clarence is watching us. Today he was down at the shop watching Richard and J.R. work on the Green Ugly and I know he is wondering how we'll react. Let's not confirm his fears. Let's show Clarence that we want him back. Let's prove to him our love and forgiveness."

Sally smiled at Bill. "He does not need my forgiveness," she said. She turned to her father, seeking his support. He begrudgingly gave it and nodded his approval. "He doesn't need anyone's forgiveness," she said to the crowd. "But Bill is right, Clarence needs our love. I want him back."

Hobbs saw strength and determination in Sally Voyals as she stood to face Reeves. He saw fight in her eyes. "Reeves," she said in a loud voice that belied her slight stature, "I vote that we let J.R. race the Green Ugly."

"Who seconds that vote?" Reeves asked enthusiastically.

A large majority in the room came to their feet and shouted their consent. Hobbs noticed that even Bobby Lee Reynolds stood beside his daughter.

With no need to ask for dissenting votes, Reeves rapped the gavel once and declared that in a few days time, the Green

Ugly would race once more. The crowd erupted in applause, hoots and hollers. The flood gates opened and immediately Hobbs felt hands clapping him on the shoulder and rustling his hair. He saw Bill give J.R. a heart-felt embrace and then people crowded in on all sides to offer well wishes. They pumped his hands and grinned. Hobbs saw a large farmer bear-hug Dippy and raised him from the ground like a doll.

Bodies pressed against Hobbs and he listened to their exhortations. "You know the Green Ugly ain't ever lost that Championship," said one. "She ain't ever lost," another agreed. Strange hands pumped his and clapped his broad back. Now the advice and encouragement came fast and relentless. "I know you'll do great; it's a real honor; you can't help but win; tell Clarence we support him, we're behind him; the second turn is tight, don't go too wide; watch that Troy Mallard, he's a dirty driver."

The clamor and press of bodies continued and Hobbs lost track of Dippy.

In the bedlam, Hobbs sought after J.R. and saw him speaking to Sally Voyals. The loud commotion forced Sally to speak into J.R.'s ear and he held her hand, bending his ear to her. For a long time, they spoke, and Hobbs noticed her father, Bobby Lee Reynolds, standing to the side, alone, waiting on his daughter.

Reynolds did not offer his support, he remained aloof but not menacing. *Perhaps he remained skeptical and suspicious. Perhaps,* Hobbs thought, *Reynolds did not yet forgive. Perhaps he had said too much, and pride clouded his good nature.*

The press of bodies subsided gradually but the exhortation continued. Hobbs felt a tug on his arm and turned to face a slight man with yellow teeth. "Hey boy, you'll win, won't you?" He ignored the question and turned back to see J.R. crouching down to speak to Sally's young daughter. The girl smiled at J.R. and waved goodbye. She followed her mother and grandparents toward the exit.

Hobbs felt another tug on his arm. Dippy stood next to him with ruffled hair and wild eyes. "A man bear hugged me, Richard," he exclaimed in disbelief. "Somebody grabbed my backside."

"Don't exaggerate Dippy. You got patted on the backside, like athletes do to each other sometimes."

"It wasn't a pat it was a grab. I know the difference." Dippy looked violated. He glanced about suspiciously, giving the evil eye to anyone who attempted to approach.

"I've never known you to be so sensitive," Hobbs said, chuckling.

"I know the difference, Richard." He looked about wildly. "Where's J.R.? We need to grab him and blow this town."

Hobbs looked over at J.R. speaking to Bill and Aunt Mae. The town folks began filing out of the sanctuary and into the growing dusk.

"We ain't leaving," Hobbs said. "Didn't you hear? J.R. wants to help out."

Dippy let out an exasperated groan. "Well I don't want to help and neither do you. That's two against one so that means we're leaving."

"Who said I'm siding with you?" Hobbs said calmly, still looking at J.R.

"Since when did you ever care, Richard? Since when did you care about anything except getting to the next race? We have our own problems; let these people deal with theirs. You're always saying not to get involved."

"J.R.'s involved more than you and I know. And if J.R.'s involved, I'm involved. That's two against one so we're staying."

Dippy shook his head, frustrated. He pointed a skinny finger at Hobbs. "No more bear hugs," he said in an accusing manner as if Hobbs was responsible, "and my backside is off limits."

Hobbs held up both hands in submission. "I promise not to grab you, Dippy."

Dippy seemed satisfied with Hobbs' response. He marched over to where Aunt Mae stood, dinner called.

Chapter 20

Hobbs folded the newspaper and flung it onto the work-bench. "I can't believe you called J.R. The Exterminator," he said to Dippy, angrily.

"Hey," Dippy said, shrugging his shoulders. "I was just adding spice to the story. Would you rather I told the truth? That J.R. ain't got a driver's license and ain't ever driven a race car before? You and J.R. didn't want to give an interview yesterday to that newspaper man, so I did."

"His name's Reeves," J.R. called out from the garage floor under the Green Ugly. He searched the lines for a leak.

"Whatever," Dippy responded.

"He printed everything you said, Dippy," Hobbs exclaimed.

"Of course, he did," Dippy said with a touch of pride. "Who wouldn't, it's spicy commentary."

Hobbs picked up the paper and waved it in front of Dippy's face. "This paper was delivered today to thousands of people in this county. You told lies about J.R. You said he's a veteran driver and he's looking forward to showing central Georgia drivers how to race. J.R. ain't like that, he wouldn't ever say that neither."

"Oh...you don't talk to me about lies, Richard." Dippy

stood up and pushed the paper from his face. "You're the one letting everyone believe J.R. can race this car, never mind the fact that he doesn't even know where the brake is located."

"That ain't the same as a two-faced lie," Hobbs unfolded the paper, searching for the news article. "You say here that J.R.'s daddy raced professionally and that J.R. is in line for a professional contract. J.R.'s daddy left him when he was a baby you idiot."

"Idiot?" Dippy shot back. He took a step toward Hobbs and looked up at his towering frame. "You're the one that's risking J.R.'s life by letting him drive in that death trap and you're calling *me* an idiot?"

"It's gonna be hard enough for J.R. to race in a car like the Green Ugly," Hobbs said, his face growing redder by the minute. "But after what you said in the newspaper, drivers are gonna be gunning for him. You can't race with a name like 'The Exterminator' unless you plan on getting mixed up in trouble. Thanks to you..."

"I think you should stop yelling at each other," J.R. said, standing up next to the Green Ugly and patting dust from his pants. "What was said, was said."

"Good morning boys," Uncle Bill exclaimed, walking into the garage. A middle-aged man followed. "Are we interrupting?"

"No, sir," J.R. said.

"We were just talking about the news," Dippy said with a wise guy grin at Hobbs.

Bill introduced the stranger. Johnny Bullock raced road stock cars and wore a tee shirt that read 'Bullock Racing' with a number 55 on the left chest. His left forearm carried a tattoo that read 55 in black ink.

"When I read in the papers that the Green Ugly was coming out of retirement, I had to come down and see it for myself," Johnny said in a rough, husky voice. He walked around the car, checking on its condition. "It's been a long time, Bill."

"Too long," Bill agreed.

"She's looking fine." Johnny walked to J.R. "Are you the driver?"

"Yes, sir."

He appraised J.R. for a moment, taking measure. "You don't seem so mean like the paper says."

"He's a nice young man," Bill said. He looked at Dippy with a slight smile. "You can't believe everything you read in the paper these days."

"I'll be racing the number 55 car. You'll go easy on me, I hope," Johnny said to J.R. with an amused smile. "After all, I'm a friend of the family."

Johnny turned to the car again and placed a hand on the lettering above the driver side door. "Have you heard from your brother?" He asked Uncle Bill.

"It's been three years and not a word," Bill said with sadness.

"I was hoping to see Clarence. How's he holding up these days?"

"Well..." Bill said. "It's a long story and I know these boys have work to do. How about we go talk outside?"

When Johnny and Bill departed, Hobbs turned to Dippy. "No more interviews," he said. "Okay Dippy?"

Dippy zipped his mouth, locked it, and threw away the keys.

Throughout the morning, Uncle Bill interrupted work as several amateur drivers visited Voyals Auto Shop to get reacquainted with the legendary race car. The drivers tended to be older men who had raced against Jack Voyals for years. They showed respect by praising the Voyals' and their cars and reminisced with stories of encounters on the race track. Normally the encounters ended with the Green Ugly going on to victory.

Bill seemed energized by the visits. He took pride in showing off the Green Ugly. In particular, he enjoyed showing off seven older versions of the racecar that he stored behind the shop. The Voyals' had built fifteen versions and Bill had kept seven in pristine condition with full gas tanks and a thorough cleaning each month. All morning long, Hobbs heard the cars start up and reverberate the back wall. Clearly, old Bill was having a ball and he treated the older cars as if they were his children.

In the afternoon, after the visits had ended, Clarence finally arrived at the shop. He pulled a fold up chair into the inner garage and sat close to the door, watching Hobbs and J.R. work.

Uncle Bill arrived to offer lemonade, but Clarence declined. "Johnny Bullock and a lot of other drivers came around asking for you," Bill said to his nephew. "They wanted to know how you're doing."

Clarence did not respond. He looked at the Green Ugly with an expressionless stare, his hands folded.

"Suit yourself then," Bill said and left.

For several hours Clarence sat, oblivious to others in the room. At times he looked sad as if reliving the horrible moment when he found his dead son under the car. At other times he smiled, perhaps reliving happier times when Jackie lived and his father, the legendary driver Jack Voyals, stood tall and proud.

As the setting sun arced lower in the sky, Hobbs and his friends prepared to leave the shop. "We're leaving now, Clarence," J.R. said. "Do you want to come to dinner with us?"

Clarence ignored the invitation and looked at the car; lost in his thoughts and remembering happier times.

Chapter 21

As Hobbs, J.R. and Dippy walked into the garage lobby they found Uncle Bill facing the glass door and looking out at the parking lot. His hands gripped the door handle, white knuckled, like the claws of an eagle on its prey.

"What's wrong?" Hobbs asked.

"We've got trouble," Bill responded.

Hobbs stood behind Bill and looked over his head and into the parking lot. At the entrance of the lot, facing the auto shop door, sat a black 1978 Mach III. Hobbs heard the Mustang's engine open-up, shaking the glass panes in the lobby. Repeatedly the driver revved the engine and the car tensed and shook. Dust from the dry parking lot billowed behind the car as its double exhausts blew.

"It's that Troy Mallard boy, coming to show his respects," Bill said. "He's nothing but trouble."

"Why doesn't he come on in and say hello?" J.R. asked.

"It ain't like that," Bill responded. "That boy is the current champion in these parts, and he dislikes the Green Ugly. Before we stopped racing her, the Green Ugly whipped Troy at every race he competed in. We whipped his daddy before him. The Mallard's hold no fondness for us Voyals'."

The tinted front and side windows on the muscle car hid

the driver from view as he opened her up again in one long, tortuous howl. The back wheels turned hard and threw up dirt and pebbles. Like a raging bull, the car charged towards the glass door. Hobbs and the others ran from the door, looking for cover.

The car turned and spun out feet from the pane glass window and the driver pushed the car into tight donuts, throwing up thick billows of pebbles and dirt. Like a hail storm, the pebbles peppered the window pane in waves as Hobbs watched under cover.

Suddenly the storm ended, and the engine revved once and died. Bill ran to the glass door and checked to make sure it was locked while Hobbs cautiously approached and looked out at the dust-cloud-filled parking lot. Gradually, the dust settled, and the black form of the car revealed itself.

Seething with anger, Hobbs clenched his jaw and tightened his fists.

"Calm down Richard," J.R. said, knowing the damage Hobbs could cause when his anger went unchecked.

Three men emerged from the car with smirks on their face. The tall, thin driver wore a black tee shirt and sported a scraggly beard with a full complement of acne scars on his face.

"Unlock the door, Bill," Hobbs demanded, glaring at the driver.

Bill turned to Hobbs. "I don't want any more trouble, Richard. It won't do any good to rough that boy up. It'll just make things worse for all of us."

The three men approached the front of the car. The driver, Troy Mallard, dusted off the hood and sat. He folded his arms and smiled a toothy grin at Bill while his two burly friends stood on either side; *his protection,* Hobbs thought.

"Richard, promise me you'll cause no trouble," Bill

said. He waited until Hobbs nodded his consent. "You too Dippy," he said.

"Bill, I'm a harmless soul," Dippy responded.

Bill took one last look into the garage, perhaps checking for Clarence. He turned and opened the door and they walked out into the thick humidity, shading their eyes from the glaring sun.

"Well, well, well, here comes Old Bill Voyals with his three stooges," Troy said as Bill and the boys filed out of the shop. "Let me see," he said studying Hobbs and his friends. "You look like the dumb one," he said to J.R., "so you must be Curly. And you..." he said to Hobbs, pointing a finger. "You must be Mo because you look like the boss."

"The boss looks ready to blow," he said to his two companions. "Relax, boy. We're just having a little fun."

"You nearly destroyed the shop, Troy," Bill said. "You need to find your fun elsewhere."

"This place looks like it could use some renovation," Troy said, scanning the surroundings. "Looks like the Voyals family have fallen on hard times; what a shame," he said, mocking Bill.

"What do you want?" Bill asked.

"I want to see that ugly car of course."

"We're closing down. You'll see her on Friday at the track."

"Of course," Troy said. His expression became serious and he glared at J.R. for long moment. He stood and reached into his pocket and withdrew a clipped newspaper article.

"Which one of you is J.R. Rentz?"

"I'm J.R.," Hobbs said with a scowl. "If you got something to say, say it to me."

Troy regarded Hobbs for a moment. "Nah," he said. He turned back to J.R. "You're Rentz, aren't you?"

J.R. nodded, *yes*.

Troy unfolded the newspaper article, keeping J.R. in his gaze. He read the clipping, "J.R. Rentz comes from a long line of race car drivers. He has raced throughout the southern U.S. and is looking forward to showing off his skill to amateurs in central Georgia. To fans in his hometown of Valdosta, Georgia he is known as 'The Exterminator' for his aggressive driving style. Competitors in this Friday's Central Georgia Road Stock Championships should take notice that a new Sheriff is in town. His name is J.R. Rentz, The Exterminator, and come Friday night, he'll be taking names and serving up defeat to all pretenders. The Green Ugly has returned to reclaim its crown."

Troy stopped reading and glared at J.R. He folded the newspaper clipping, stepped up to J.R. and stuffed it into his shirt pocket. "You're afraid," he whispered. "I see it in your eyes."

Troy saw Hobbs approach and stepped away from J.R. while maintaining his threatening glare. "I came out here to introduce myself," he said to J.R. "I've won that champion-ship for three years now and I'll let no cocksure drifter get the better of me. You ain't Jack Voyals and this Friday night you're gonna know what it's like to crash into a wall at 80 miles an hour. I promise that."

"Watch what you say, Troy," Bill said.

"Shut up, old man."

As Troy headed for his car, the door to the shop opened and Clarence stepped out.

Troy locked his gaze onto to Clarence. He looked surprised and unsure.

"Clarence," Bill said to his nephew, "you don't need to be out here."

Clarence ignored Bill and glared at Troy.

"Get in," Troy said to his companions. They scampered into the car and Troy turned again to Clarence. "I heard you became a recluse after your car snuffed out Jackie," Troy said with his hand on the car door handle. "I think I saw your daddy begging for quarters in downtown Macon with the rest of the bums."

"You punk," Bill raged. He rushed forward as Troy laughed and quickly got behind the wheel and closed the door. The engine roared to life as Bill clawed at the driver side door. Hobbs and J.R. reached Bill too late as the car reversed and turned, throwing Bill face-first onto the hard gravel parking lot.

A brick, thrown by Clarence, crashed through the passenger side window.

"Child killer!" Troy yelled at Clarence through the broken window. He laughed wildly and his eyes looked insane. He placed the car in drive and sped toward Bill, turning at the last moment to avoid his head by inches.

Troy completed one donut in the parking lot, pelting the men with gravel. "You're next, J.R.," he yelled as he sped from the parking lot and onto the dirt road toward town.

J.R. and Hobbs helped Bill to his feet. His bifocals lay twisted and broken on the ground and blood seeped from his forehead and left cheek. Bill felt along his left collar bone, his face wincing in pain.

"You need to sit down," J.R. said.

"I'm fine. Let me rest for a moment." He sat down in a chair provided by Dippy and touched his forehead. When he pulled his hand back, he saw a thick mat of fresh blood and dirt. He chuckled. "Mae is gonna kill me," he said, "running around, mixing it up with boys fifty years younger. Sometimes I forget I got a seventy-year old body. I think my collar bone is broke. Oh, if I survive this, she'll kill me for sure."

Clarence rushed over to his uncle with a wet towel and fresh Kleenex. He washed the dirt from his face and blotted the wounds dry. Fortunately, the scrapes did not bleed profusely. "You'll have to get down to the doctor and get cleaned up," Clarence said. He turned to Hobbs, "Can you take him?"

"Yes, I can."

"Uncle Bill, I knew bringing back the Green Ugly was trouble," Clarence said, carefully tending Bill's wounds.

"You listen to me," Bill said, holding Clarence's wrists and looking into his eyes.

"Your father is no coward and neither are you. We can't let the likes of Troy Mallard bully us. He's afraid of you Clarence. Didn't you see that in his eyes? When he looks at you, he sees your father and that boy is afraid of Jack Voyals. His father was scared too. That's why he acted the way he did."

In the distance, toward town, they heard the Mach III revving its engines.

"He's in town now," Bill said looking in the direction of Anna's Mill. "He'll be leaving his mark."

"What do you mean?" J.R. asked.

"He knows we only allow one car to drag down Main Street and that's the Green Ugly. We allow it once a year on Green Ugly day. To humiliate us further, Troy's gonna leave his tire marks on Main Street." Bill shook his head in disgust.

The engine continued to rev in the distance.

"What's he waiting for?" Hobbs asked. He stood with J.R. and Dippy, looked toward town and imagined the black car lined up outside of Aunt Mae's with the sound of its engine reverberating off the buildings.

Bill stood up and joined the three men. "He's waiting for a crowd because he wants Anna's Mill to take notice. Twenty-five years ago, that boy's father tried the same stunt. A day before the Championship, his father dragged down Main Street. He was trying to intimidate my brother Jack. Well, Jack taught him a lesson at the race; he crashed him on the second lap. The man spent the night in the hospital."

In the distance, they heard booing from the town folk. It sounded like a rowdy crowd at a baseball game after a bad call by the umpire. Hobbs imagined folks lined up and down Main Street shouting and threatening Troy Mallard and Mallard sneering at them, perhaps raising his middle finger in salute.

Suddenly the car revved one last time and started down Main Street. Hobbs could not see the car spin out but the squeal from the churning wheels cut through the thick air like a dagger.

Anger returned to Bill's face. "Clarence, doesn't that make you spitting-mad?" But when Bill turned to look at Clarence, his nephew was gone.

"I don't think that man will ever come around," Bill said with a disappointed look on his face.

Hobbs walked up beside Bill. "We've got to get you to the doctor," he said.

Chapter 22

As Hobbs drove Bill to the small clinic above the barber shop, town folk gathered in front of Aunt Mae's to view the tire marks left by Troy Mallard. Hobbs was surprised at the number of people that had gathered. "That Mallard boy just raced down Main Street," a man yelled into the slow-moving truck as the crowd parted to let Hobbs pass.

"Hey, is that Bill Voyals in there bleeding?" another man asked.

"Mallard attacked him," Dippy exclaimed from the bed of the truck.

"Mallard beat up Bill," the man repeated to the crowd. The accusation spread like wild fire and expanded like a malignant growth until it was known, without a doubt, that skinny Troy Mallard had indeed attempted to take Bill Voyals' life.

As Hobbs parked in front of the clinic, the crowd followed to get a better view of Bill's wounds. "Make way," Hobbs exclaimed. He helped Bill from the truck and people gasped when they saw his skinned and bloodied head.

Hobbs and J.R. assisted Bill up the outside stairs leading to the clinic. "I'm fine," Bill stated repeatedly to all those that asked. He tried to mollify their concerns, but the town patriarch had been assaulted and battle lines had been drawn.

A young man dressed in camouflaged pants and a green tee shirt climbed onto Hobbs' truck bed to address the crowd. Dippy leaned against the cab, crossed his arms, and watched.

"This is a slap in the face," the man yelled. "It's bad enough that Mallard left his tire marks down Main Street. He might as well have lifted his leg and pissed on each and every one of us. Now we learn that he tried to kill old Bill. Something's got to be done about this!"

"Jody, let the sheriff deal with it," a woman responded.

"A lot of good that will do," Jody responded. "When's the last time you saw an Bibb County sheriff in this town. The sheriff is no good, we've got to take action ourselves."

The older, more mature people in the crowd argued for restraint. Jody urged for action and received enthusiastic support from a small minority of teenagers and young men, all of whom wore camouflaged pants and similar green tee shirts. The back of the shirts read *Official Member: Green Ugly Fan Club.*

"As president of The Green Uglies, I'm calling a meeting to decide how to respond to this atrocity," Jody declared.

"What do you mean?" a man asked. "You gonna form a posse and hunt down Troy and bring him to justice? Why don't you just hang 'em up from the nearest tree?" He asked sarcastically.

"I was thinking about a tar and feathering first," Jody responded seriously.

Dippy chuckled at Jody's nerve and wondered if the young man might have mental problems.

Several of the Green Uglies in the first row nodded their heads as if a good old fashion tar and feathering might be fun.

After several more outlandish remarks from Jody,

everyone in the crowd, except the Green Uglies, meandered away, commiserating the sad direction of the younger generation.

"Well Uglies," Jody exclaimed as the last of the old folk walked away, "looks like this town's honor rests on us alone. Are you with me?"

The five Green Uglies shouted their affirmation.

"Come on," Jody shouted, waving his arm. He jumped from the truck and strode down an alley. The Green Uglies obediently followed.

Dippy chuckled as he watched the green clad troops disappear into the alley. He looked up to the windows of the clinic and contemplated another sterile evening with J.R. and Hobbs. Crazy people interested Dippy and a night of harmless trouble-making with Jody and his friends might be fun. He jumped from the truck and hurried down the alley.

Chapter 23

Hobbs cleared away an old issue of Field and Stream from the examination table in the clinic and helped Bill climb up as J.R. fetched the doctor from the downstairs barber shop.

"The Doc's the town barber," Bill informed Hobbs. "He's also the pharmacist. His wife does manicures and pedicures on Wednesday otherwise she'd be up here to receive us."

"Was he a doctor first or a barber first?" Hobbs asked, trying to keep Bill's mind occupied.

"Doc became a certified doctor first. Then he opened the barber shop. He ain't much of a barber but he's a kind man and provides enough doctoring for this old town."

The doctor rushed through the door with a concerned look on his face. "My God Bill. J.R. says you broke a collar bone."

"It feels broke, Doc. I got bucked off a car into the gravel, if you can believe it."

"I heard about Troy Mallard," the doctor said, studying Bill's swollen face. "You better get your story straight before Mae gets here," he said as he felt along the abrasion. "It's likely she'll not understand why a man your age is getting thrown off cars onto a gravel parking lot."

Bill grunted.

"You've got small bits of stone embedded in your face." The doctor attached a small circular magnifying glass to his bifocals and retrieved a pair of tweezers. "I can give you a local anesthetic."

"No," Bill said. "Just pluck 'em out before she gets here."

The doctor stretched the skin on Bill's face and plucked out six small pieces of stone. He threw the debris into a waste paper basket.

The side door opened and Mae, grief stricken, rushed into the small examination room. She looked startled and relieved to see her husband sitting on the exam table and smiling.

"Oh Bill," she said, tenderly placing a hand on the undamaged side of Bill's face. "They said Troy Mallard tried to kill you. I was so worried I rushed right over."

"People exaggerate Mae; he didn't try to kill me. I got too close to his car, that's all. Docs cleaning my wounds and then I'll be good to go."

"Well, there's the collar bone too," Doc reminded Bill.

Bill looked at him, perturbed.

"What's wrong with it?" She asked.

"It might be broken."

Aunt Mae appraised her husband with a look of concern and compassion. "Bill?" she asked as the doctor sterilized the abrasions. Bill winced at each application of iodine. "What did he do to you? Why did he hurt you?"

"Well, things got heated between Troy and Clarence. Troy got in a hurry to leave and I was too close to his car," he said, not telling the whole story.

"He ran over you with his car?" She held onto his hand.

"More like he back up into me. I'll be alright, Mae. I got careless and now I got a broken collar bone and a torn-up face."

Aunt Mae looked over to Hobbs and JR. "Is Clarence okay?"

"He's fine," Bill responded as Doc applied bandages.

"Where's Dippy?" she asked Hobbs. "Is he okay?"

Hobbs looked out the window to the empty truck below. "Good question," he said.

"You boys can go," Bill said. "I'm in good hands here. Thank you for helping."

Hobbs and J.R. said goodbye and went in search of Dippy.

Chapter 24

Dippy stood under a tree and watched the Green Uglies traverse a large, well-tended field behind the buildings on Main Street. The field slanted downward into a thin creek and contained picnic tables and a large gazebo. Decorative green banners hung from the gazebo in preparation for Green Ugly Day. The group crossed an arched pedestrian bridge and headed toward a long line of tightly packed houses.

Dippy watched as they entered a gated enclosure surrounding a house and descended into a storm shelter. The odor of freshly turned soil drifted in the slight breeze and the western sky looked orange from the setting sun as Dippy headed across the grassy park in pursuit of Jody and his friends. When he arrived at the gate surrounding the home he turned once to make sure no one watched, and he stepped down into the cellar.

The ripping sound of masking tape ascended from the cellar and Dippy stopped midway to allow his eyes to adjust. He took another step and entered a small, dank room with a flickering light bulb dangling from a wire. A sturdy work table occupied the middle of the room and yard tools hung from the walls. A computer and printer in the corner looked misplaced.

The leader of the club, Jody, stood with one leg propped

up on the table and a roll of masking tape in his hands. The five other members of the club also held masking tape, apparently in the process of taping their knees. They stopped taping when they noticed Dippy's intrusion.

"You lost?" Jody said.

"No," Dippy responded. He wondered why everyone taped their knees.

"What do you want?"

"Well," Dippy said. "I'm a huge fan of irrational thought. It interests me. When I heard your speech out there by the truck, I recognized a rare opportunity. Besides, you invited people to this meeting. I guess I'm the only one who showed up."

"It's one of them drifters," a man said. The middle-aged man looked out of place in a room of young people. His eyes looked watery and glazed over like a man who drank too much. An adolescent boy, looking like an orphan from a Charles Dickens novel, squatted next to the man.

"You're with J.R., ain't you," Jody said.

"It's more like he's with me."

Jody regarded Dippy for a moment. "Are you saying that you want to be part of the Green Uglies?"

"Very much,"

"Well are you for Anna's Mill and the Green Ugly?"

"Yes."

"Are you against Troy Mallard?"

"I am."

"Then you're in the club," Jody said. "Give the man a shirt."

The boy reached into a box in the corner and threw Dippy a green tee shirt.

Jody began taping his knee and the others followed his lead while Dippy pulled the shirt over his head. He wondered what was next, *surely membership into this club wasn't this easy,* he thought.

"Ain't there some kind of initiation?" Dippy asked. "Aren't you gonna make me swallow a goldfish or something?"

"No wise crackers," Jody said. He stood up and Dippy noticed a one-foot long hunting knife in a scabbard tied to his lower leg. "What's your name?"

"Dippy Jordan."

Jody pointed to the older man with glazed eyes. "Dippy, that old man over there is Hank. We let him hang out with us because he's occasionally useful."

Hank gave Dippy an unfriendly glare.

Jody pointed to the boy. "That boy is Lester. He's my brother and he's allowed because he keeps his mouth shut. Besides, our parents ran off and he's got nowhere else to go so he's with me." Lester ignored Dippy and wrapped his wrists with tape for no apparent reason.

"Those two are identical twins," Jody said, pointing to two blond-haired men in their early twenties. "It ain't no use telling you their names because you can't tell them apart. Just call both of 'em Twin."

Dippy watched as one twin applied green paint to the others face. "Make it look like Indian war paint," one twin said to the other. "Don't forget to put the double zeros."

"This one is Gerald," Jody said as he walked to a teenager sitting at the computer terminal. Gerald remained active on the keyboard as Jody slapped him on the back. "How's it coming?" he asked. "Do you have the address yet?"

"Yeah," Gerald said. "I'm mapping it out now."

"We Googled Troy to find his address" Jody said. "There's a lot you can learn from the internet. Did you know that?"

Dippy nodded yes, he knew that.

Jody placed both hands on the table and surveyed the motley members of the club.

There's very little to work with here regarding human resources, Dippy thought but Jody seemed pleased nonetheless.

The twins still applied green face paint and to Dippy, the pattern looked more like The Mighty Hulk than it did Indian war paint. Close by, Hank tested a garden hoe for its strength and utility, swatting it in the air at an imaginary foe and Lester wrapped his knuckles with tape.

"Stop using all that tape, Lester," Jody scolded his brother. "You ain't in no boxing tournament. Besides, we might need that tape to tie Mallard up if we decide to kidnap him."

Kidnapping? No one said anything about kidnapping, Dippy thought with a touch of concern.

"Okay, Uglies, let's bring it together," Jody said. "We've got work to do. We've got to exact revenge on Troy Mallard for trying to kill Old Bill."

The Uglies gathered at the table and looked toward Jody. Hank glared at Dippy with suspicious eyes, apparently not prepared to welcome the new member.

"Gerald," Jody said, snapping his fingers. "Lay it on me. Give me the map to Mallard's Home." Jody measured Dippy with a glare, perhaps trying to determine if Dippy had the fortitude to do what needed to be done.

"I got it," Gerald said. He snapped up a piece of paper from the printer and handed it to Jody.

Jody examined the map for a moment and then slapped the paper on the table and pulled his hunting knife from its scabbard. He thrust the knife into the paper, securing it to the table surface. Dippy jumped and Hank, the middle-aged drunk grinned.

"Let's see what we've got here," Jody said, bending down to study the map as if he was a field commander in a battle zone. "It looks like his home is in a secluded spot, excellent." He traced his finger along a road on the map. "We'll park here and approach from the northwest."

"What do you plan to do when you get there?" Dippy asked. If things got too crazy, he'd bail out but for now he remained intrigued.

Jody looked up from the map. "You'll do good to listen and not talk. Understand?"

Hank grimaced at Dippy, silently warning him to keep his mouth shut.

Jody returned his attention to the map. "Eye for an eye," he said. "A broken collar bone for a broken collar bone and skinned-up face for a skinned-up face." He thought for a moment. "A collar bone might be hard to break," he said to himself. "It's not like a thumb where you just yank it back. At least if it were an arm, we could use a vise to hold it steady while we twisted on it. Can't get no vise around a collar bone." Jody scratched his head, dumbfounded.

"Give me your thoughts," Jody said to the others.

"Our dad has sledge hammer," Twin said.

Jody looked up at the twins. "Sledgehammer, huh?" He thought for a moment, scratching his chin. "Can't swing it too hard, it'll cave his chest in. I don't need murder on my rap sheet."

"Just hold it a few inches from the bone and let it drop," Twin said. "Keep lifting it higher and dropping it until the bone snaps."

"I like that," Jody exclaimed with a beaming smile. "A little torture won't kill him. Go get the hammer." Twin climbed the stairs and ran home.

"Now," Jody said, thoughtful again. "What about the face? I suppose we could rub it on the carpet. Although what's a carpet burn compared to what poor old Bill experienced."

"I've got an idea," Hank said, looking at Dippy in a sinister way. The drunk lifted an electrical sander and switched it on. The small motor whined as the frail man applied the sander to the wood table and sawdust filled the air. He moved it back and forth erratically, attempting to maintain control but failing.

Jody reached over and switched the motor off. He coughed and laughed, waving his hand to clear the dust.

"See I told you," Jody said to Dippy, coughing. "He has an occasional good thought that turns out to be genius. You get the honor of sanding Mallard's face," he said to Hank. Hank beamed.

Chapter 25

The first group arrived at the auto shop well after dark. Hobbs stood at the garage entrance and watched as the group, a family of four, walk down the dirt road. They used flashlights to guide their way. J.R. and Sally Voyals welcomed the family in the parking lot and invited them into the shop where Bill waited to assign duties. *A pitiful showing considering the mammoth task before them,* Hobbs thought.

In J.R.'s simple mind, the clandestine night operation represented a first step in a process he called "Operation Homecoming." J.R. mapped out the process to Hobbs on a piece of paper as if the rehabilitation of Clarence Voyals had a beginning, middle, and end. Hobbs doubted the rude man could be rehabilitated and even if it was possible, it wasn't going to happen in a few days and certainly not from a piece of paper like some instruction manual.

Hobbs tried to convince J.R. to concentrate on readying the Green Ugly for Friday's race and to stay out of the Voyals' personal problems. But J.R. connected the Green Ugly and Clarence Voyals in a way Hobbs failed to consider. "You can't fix one without fixing the other," he told Hobbs with an optimistic tone that grated on the nerves.

The first step in the healing process required the town

people to secretly clean and organize Voyals Auto and Repair Shop in a single night. Clarence departed earlier and sentries, posted close to his secluded cabin, provided a look out in the unlikely event of his return.

To Hobbs, J.R.'s grand scheme represented yet one more futile attempt by his friend to make a difference in a cruel world that cared nothing for the disadvantaged and outcast. Hobbs placed little faith in the people of Anna's Mill. He found it difficult enough to trust one person, never mind an entire town.

Hobbs kept close tabs on his friend, convinced that he would fail; convinced also that when failure came, it would be a hard blow. He needed to be there to pick up the pieces; explaining, once again, that people are cruel and can't be trusted.

Hobbs eavesdropped on J.R. as he spoke to Sally.

"Did you invite everyone?" J.R. asked.

"Yeah, I even posted notices all through town. I expected that more would show up," Sally responded, dejected.

"It seemed like they cared when we were at the meeting. Do you think they care Sally?"

Sally remained silent.

Operation Homecoming was already beginning to unravel, Hobbs thought. *Dead on arrival.*

Hobbs considered the overwhelming task of organizing and cleaning the neglected auto shop. For years Clarence littered the garage floor with unused auto parts. Over time the discarded parts formed a continuous pile that reached as high as a man's knee. In some areas the piles reached six feet or more and Clarence created narrow paths amongst the debris to allow limited movement.

The white paint on the walls chipped and looked brown after years of neglect. The windows, which at one time provided ample sunlight, were clouded with a thick layer of soot and grime. The overhead lights flickered and had become dim and nearly useless. Worse of all, a putrid odor emanated from a corner bathroom and Hobbs refused to investigate its source. Cleaning the mess would be monumental and Hobbs doubted it possible in a single night.

Even if the whole town showed up and cleaned the garage, Hobbs questioned the outcome. According to J.R., it would help Clarence realize that his town, family, and friends supported him and loved him. *Which of course is nonsense,* Hobbs thought. If anything, the plan might backfire. *What if too few people showed up to help?* With the job half completed, Clarence would know that only a few people cared.

Hobbs wandered into the garage. He expected to find the family of four wide mouthed and overwhelmed at the enormity of the task. Instead, he watched as the father and his adolescent son picked up a rusty muffler and tailpipe and walked it out of the garage and into the junk yard. The man smiled and nodded to Hobbs as he passed. The mother and her teenaged daughter got busy in the lobby area, cleaning cobwebs from the ceiling and trashing stacks of old magazines. *At this rate they might get the job done in a month,* he thought bitterly. It was like trying to kill an elephant with a fly swatter; a vain attempt but at least they showed spunk.

Hobbs returned to the garage entrance and leaned against the door jam. He turned his ear toward J.R. and Sally.

"Maybe we can try something else," J.R. said. "I've got a plan B if you'd like to hear it."

"Not now, J.R.," she said with a crestfallen voice. "You've done so much already. Maybe you shouldn't worry about Clarence and his problems. You've got so much on your plate as it is, with the race and all."

"I'd like to help."

"I just thought that more people would show up to-night," Sally said. "Maybe it's hopeless. Maybe Clarence will never come around." She wiped a tear from her cheek.

"Don't say that," J.R. said, placing an arm around her shoulder. "There's always hope."

Hobbs spat and shook his head in disgust. J.R. med-dled in the personal affairs of strangers again and now he'd caused more harm. He'd opened old wounds. *Why can't he just race the car, win some money and get on with his own messed up life? Didn't he have enough prob-lems of his own to deal with?*

He saw a light flicker amongst the pine trees in the di-rection of the road. *Another naive Good Samaritan with a swinging lantern coming to do a good deed,* Hobbs thought cynically; *another victim to J.R.'s scheming.* Several more flickers of light followed the first and he heard laughter. *At least they are cheerful about losing a full night sleep,* he thought.

Now he noticed a dull glow above the trees toward town. Hobbs wondered if he'd noticed it before and decided that he had not. The low clouds over the pines hung like a thick canopy and acted to reflect and amplify the glow. Cloud movement created an optical illusion as if the glow moved forward; increasing and diminishing with the undulating contours.

Hobbs heard more laughter and voices too, louder than before. He studied the pine forest and detected movement, slight but present. Shortly he noticed a multitude of twin-kling lights between the trees as if the forest filled with fire-flies on a summer night.

J.R. and Sally saw the lights and rushed toward the road to get a better view. Now the pine forest danced and glowed with light. Hobbs, curious, followed at a slower pace. Rounding the bend at the juncture between the auto shop parking lot and the dirt road, Hobbs got a good view all the way back towards town. The sight startled him. Town folks, in all shape and sizes, walked down the road toward the shop in a long, unorganized procession that extended all the way into town, a half mile away. Many carried lanterns or flash-lights. The procession contained hundreds of people.

Chapter 26

Sally Voyals cried out for joy at the sight of the masses walking down the road to offer help and J.R. rushed toward the closest person and heartily welcomed and thanked her. The people carried an assortment of tools and cleaning supplies including buckets, brooms, paint, and ladders. Several carried picnic baskets full of food and fold-up tables. One man struggled under the weight of two large drinking coolers and Hobbs hurried over to help him.

Hobbs walked back toward the shop with the heavy cooler over his shoulder and carefully sat the cooler down on a table. Old Bill emerged from the shop, his arm in a sling, with a beaming smile and began organizing teams of workers.

Hobbs stepped backward as more people filtered into the parking lot. The friendly banter on the road continued in the parking lot as men shook hands and helped each other with heavy loads of toolboxes and ladders. Women chatted loudly and began laying out tables for food and refreshments. Hobbs saw J.R. in the middle of it all, laughing heartily and making friends. Hobbs backed into a shadow along the junkyard fence and watched, unnoticed.

As more people streamed into the lot, Hobbs felt out of

place, as if he didn't belong. He didn't share their enthusiasm or their mission. He wished he did and that realization shocked and saddened him at the same time. He preferred loneliness to the alternative but now it troubled him to realize he might lack some basic nature that might allow him to have compassion for others, even strangers. *Do I lack the ability to care?* He asked.

In the crowd, J.R. patted a tall man on the back and when the man turned, his face lit up in recognition. He gave J.R. a hug, the type of hug a longtime friend gives and Hobbs suddenly envied J.R. for his ability to relate and belong. He'd always viewed J.R.'s friendliness as a weakness and vulnerability; something to be cured and corrected. But now, for the first time, Hobbs allowed that he may have been wrong. After all, J.R. sparked this sudden outpouring of support for Clarence, a man down for the count with no hope. Because of J.R., the man might have a chance to be reconciled with family and friends. *And that had to be a good thing,* Hobbs told himself.

He watched as Bill organized groups of people to remove junk from the garage. Others, he sent to the junkyard where large portable overhead lights with generators shone brightly on heaps of stripped-out cars and old, rusted refrigerators. Another group he sent into the garage with tall ladders to change out broken light bulbs. The town plumber arrived and immediately set to work on the dysfunctional toilet.

"Isn't this great," J.R. said to Hobbs. "All these people coming out to help Clarence."

Hobbs considered his friend. "Yes. It's hard to believe."

"Come on," J.R. said enthusiastically. "I want to introduce you to some friends."

"No," Hobbs exclaimed suddenly, out of fear. He recovered quickly, "I mean, I don't know these people."

"You can be friendly to people other than Dippy and me.

They're good people, Richard. They've made me feel like I belong, and they'll make you feel the same way if you open-up and let them in. Come on," he said, grabbing Hobbs' elbow.

Hobbs removed his elbow from JR.'s grasp. "You go on. I'm going to make myself useful." He left J.R. and mean-dered into the garage with his hands in pockets and saw several long lines of people removing junk. They stood side-by-side and passed each item of junk to the next person. Several small groups painted the walls while others with long ladders exchanged old light bulbs with new bulbs.

He looked for Dippy Jordan among the workers. Dippy had gone missing since they dropped Bill off at the clinic and Hobbs was perturbed that he hadn't even bothered to tell anyone what he was up to. He scanned the crowd but Dippy wasn't present. *Not surprising,* Hobbs thought, *Dippy wasn't the type of person to give out a helping hand either.* He wished his cranky friend hadn't weaseled his way out; he could have been useful at a time like this to of-fer some criticism that justified Hobbs' own thoughts.

Hobbs wanted to find a solitary chore; something to work on in private. But everywhere he looked, people worked as teams. Neighbors, friends and family, worked together, chatting loudly and laughing. *Maybe I'll just step into the inside garage and check in on the Green Ugly, its private enough,* he thought.

As Hobbs started toward the inner garage, he spotted a man in a line smiling at him. The man stood close by and passed a broken headlight to the next person in line. Hobbs held the man's gaze for a moment and looked away, uncom-fortable at the friendly gesture. He started to walk away.

"Excuse me," someone said from behind. Hobbs turned and saw the smiling stranger walking toward him, carrying an old car battery. "We sure could use some help in this line," the man said even though the line was sufficiently staffed.

The stranger placed the battery in Hobbs' hands. "Come on," he said walking back into the line. "There's a space right here, next to me." Others in the line looked at Hobbs, waiting for the next piece of junk.

"This line ain't gonna work unless the next person in line passes the junk. You're the next person," the stranger said with a smile.

Hobbs looked down at the old battery. He slowly took a position in the line and glanced down the length to see everyone watching him, waiting patiently. He passed the battery and watched it work down the line.

"Next piece," the stranger said, handing Hobbs a jumble of twisted wires. "My name is Travis and that guy on the other side of you is Tommy."

Hobbs turned to look at Tommy, a pudgy man about Hobbs' age. Tommy gave Hobbs a toothy grin and shook his hand.

"Isn't your name Richard?" Travis asked.

"Yeah."

"What do you like to do?" Travis asked, passing a torn and well used air filter.

"What?"

"In your spare time, what do you do for fun?"

Hobbs studied Travis with a critical eye. He wasn't used to small talk with strangers. It made him uncomfortable. But since he was trapped in this line with no place to hide, he begrudgingly played along. "I go to car races," he said mumbled.

"Burk got ripped off in that last race down in Miami. They should've black flagged Bobby Sother for pushing Burk into the wall." Travis passed a wheel rim.

Hobbs looked at Travis, amused. The stranger was a race fan. *Now you're talking*, he thought. "You're kidding, right?"

"About Bobby Sother?" Travis said. "No, he's a hot head

rooky that..."

"I was there," Hobbs interrupted. "Burke took a chance by going three-wide in turn one. No one goes three-wide on that track. He got careless and deserved to wreck."

On the other side of Hobbs, Tommy spoke, "I saw Skip Johnson on the Outdoor Channel last week hunting moose in Alaska."

"I like Skip Johnson," Travis said, passing piece of sheet metal. "He tells it like it is and he ain't afraid to mix it up on the track. He's from Macon, did you know that, Richard?"

"Yeah, I seen him race once in Valdosta." He liked Skip Johnson also.

"Jack Voyals raced against Johnson with the Green Ugly back in the 80s," Travis said, rolling an old tire to Hobbs.

"I didn't know that," Hobbs said, astounded.

"Jack beat him bad."

Hobbs thought about the Green Ugly racing against the legendary driver, Skip Johnson.

"Do you like to hunt?" Travis asked.

"No," Hobbs responded.

"Well then you'll have to go coon hunting with me and Tommy Thursday night. Okay? We go once a month."

Hobbs took a bicycle tire from Travis and passed it on to Tommy. *Hunting?* He thought. *With strangers?* "Why me? I ain't ever hunted before."

"Why you?" Travis said with an amused look. "Because it'll be fun. We'll talk about the Green Ugly and Skip Johnson."

"We don't see too many coons," Tommy said. "It's just an excuse for a bunch of guys to romp through the woods with our dogs."

"Bunch of guys?" Hobbs asked, concerned the conversation moved too fast.

"Yeah," Travis said. "We all get together once a month.

It's called the Coon Hunters Association of Anna's Mill; bunch of guys getting together, socializing, that sort of thing."

"I don't know. I ain't ever hunted." Hobbs winced at the thought of trudging through the dark woods with a bunch of men carrying deadly weapons, pointed every which way; hound dogs howling, fighting against leashes.

"Like Tommy says, we don't hunt that much. It'll give you a chance to make more friends."

More friends? Hobbs thought. He hadn't bargained for this.

"Anyway, you think about it," Travis said.

Travis passed Hobbs a large rusty can of nails and screws.

"I think it's great what you're doing for Clarence," Travis said.

"It's J.R.'s idea, not mine."

"Well your helping out now ain't you," Travis said. "Don't be so hard on yourself. Take some credit for yourself."

"Why do you say I'm being hard on myself?" Hobbs asked defensively but knowing the truth.

"All I'm saying is that it's okay to help people out and feel good about it."

"Ain't nothing wrong with that," Tommy agreed.

"You just seem bottled up," Travis continued. "All these people here are happy to help out. You ought to try it on for size, see if it fits," he said, smiling, passing a dented fold up chair.

Hobbs took the chair and passed it along. He looked about at the busy town folk and decided it did feel good to help. It also felt good to belong, even if temporarily. *Perhaps I should take Travis up on his invitation after all,* he thought to himself.

Chapter 27

The low clouds provided dark cover for Dippy and the Green Uglies as they trudged down the deserted red clay road toward Troy Mallard's house. Treeless farmland surrounded the house for miles and the moonless night and desolate location provided the only cover. A two-foot deep drainage ditch provided a hiding place if a passerby drove down the road.

Jody, the leader of the Green Uglies, decided to park his Honda Civic a half mile from the house. Dippy argued for a closer parking space but Jody insisted that the distance was essential. During the drive from Anna's Mill the Civic labored under the weight of six grown men, one child, and fourteen gallons of green paint. By the time Jody pulled the over-heated import into a soft and muddy field it promptly got stuck. It took merely fifteen seconds of rigorous back and forth acceleration by Jody to sink the car to its floor board. The Green Uglies exited the car through the windows and quickly concluded that no one had ever seen a car planted so deeply into the ground. Dippy claimed he'd never seen a car ridden so hard in such a short period of time.

After leaving the club house cellar, the Green Uglies were intent on breaking Mallards collar bone. But Dippy had argued against torture and had convinced Jody and the others that a good dose of vandalism would do the trick. "A couple gallons of the right colored paint can go a long way to send the right signal," Dippy had said. Thankfully his argument had prevailed.

Jody established a brutal pace in his march toward Troy Mallard's house and each of the Green Uglies carried two gallons of green paint. Ten-year-old Lester lagged somewhere in the dark distance and Hank set his own leisurely pace, stopping every hundred yards or so to take a swig of whisky from a squirt bottle tied around his neck. At one point in the grueling march Dippy turned to see Hank stagger and drop the paint cans in the road. He squirted whiskey onto his face as if it were water and headed off in a dark field, evidently calling it a night.

Dippy kept pace with Jody and the remaining Green Uglies. In the distance he saw the lights of Mallard's home, but the lights seemed to taunt him, moving further away the longer he walked. Contrary to Jody's claim, Dippy believed they had parked more than two miles away, not a half mile.

When Dippy spotted the headlights from an approaching truck, he quickly ran to the shallow ditch and hid.

"Don't move," Jody commanded to everyone.

"Get off the road," Dippy said from the ditch. "You'll be spotted."

"No one move," Jody repeated. "They won't expect a thing."

"What are you, some kind of an idiot?" Dippy exclaimed. "Your faces are painted green and you're carrying cans of paint down a deserted road in the middle of the night. They'll think you're up to no good, which incidentally is the truth. Save yourself and crawl into a ditch."

"Everybody standstill and don't move," Jody ordered.

"Do you think they won't see you?" Dippy yelled.

"That's the plan," Jody said.

Dippy marveled at Jody's stupidity.

The approaching headlights slowed as it neared the men. Jody stood still as a statue, one foot in front of the other, one-gallon cans of green paint held in each hand. The other three Uglies adopted the same posture, in single file.

Jody suddenly realized the merit of Dippy's observation. "Okay, change of plan," Jody said suddenly. "Just act natural like we're going fishing," he said. "Move out." The men marched forward in unison, right, left, right. Their buckets swung back and forth.

The truck, carrying a man and woman, slowed and stopped as the men marched passed. The couple sat silently, their faces illuminated by the green interior lighting of the dashboard. They watched with curiosity at the four men with painted faces.

The truck moved on and Jody picked up the pace. "I don't think they noticed us," he said. He and the other Green Uglies jogged and Dippy ran after them. They drew closer to the house.

Moments later the truck approached again from the opposite direction. Dippy saw the lights approach from behind and dove into the ditch. Jody and the others slowed to a casual walk as the truck coasted alongside. The window on the truck lowered.

"Let me do the talking," Jody said to the others.

"What're you boys up to?" the man in the truck asked.

When Jody and the others ignored the question, the man asked again.

"We're going fishing," Jody said, still walking and looking straight ahead.

"Fishing? At this late hour? Where's your rod and how come you're carrying cans of paint?"

Jody stopped and looked at the man in the truck. He said,

"We're going to help paint a friend's house up this road."

"The only places up this road are the Mallard house and mine. If you plan on showing up at my house with that ugly shade of green, I'll fill you full of buckshot."

"Yes sir," Jody said, respectful. "We ain't going to paint your house. We're here to paint the Mallard house." Jody turned and started again up the road. The truck coasted alongside.

"You say you're going to paint Mallard's house?"

"Yes sir," Jody said, still walking. The Green Uglies followed him.

"Mallard has a brick house and I doubt he wants you to paint it green," the man said. "You're up to no good, ain't you?"

Jody stopped and looked at the man again. "Actually," he said. "We're going to paint his car."

"And he wants you to paint his car with that green house paint?"

"Yes sir," Jody said. "Honest."

"I'm calling the sheriff," the man said. He dialed the Sheriff on his cell phone.

"Let's make a run for it, boys," Jody shouted. He ran toward the Mallard house with the heavy buckets of paint pumping back and forth. The others followed.

"Sheriff?" the man said loudly into the cell phone. "This is Dewey Simms out here on County Road 203. I've spotted four hooligans running toward Troy Mallard's house with cans of green paint. I got them in my headlights, and I'm following close behind. They're running along the road and up to no good I can tell you."

Dippy figured he was too far in to turn back so he emerged from the ditch and sprinted after the Green Uglies.

"Make that five hooligans," Dewey Simms said into the phone. "A skinny one just popped up from the ditch. There's no telling how many trouble makers we've got in the fields out here tonight. I saw a green-painted drunk wandering in the dark and a couple miles from here and I saw an import half buried in one of my cotton fields. You need to send some boys out here pronto."

Chapter 28

When Dippy finally reached Troy Mallard's home, he heard punk rock blaring from the house. It seemed every light in the house shone through the windows and illuminated the front yard where Mallard's 78 Mach III sat. Jody had already splashed one can of green paint onto the car and was extracting the lid off another. One of the twins painted the back panel of the car and managed to splatter Dippy with a good dose. They heard police sirens in the distance.

"Great idea, Dippy," Jody said sarcastically. He poured half a gallon of paint onto the rear seats. "Because of you and this stupid idea, you've put me in a sticky spot. I need the law after me like I need a hole in my head."

"I told you to park closer," Dippy said. He threw a gallon of paint in a high arcing stream over the top of the car. "But no, you had to park ten miles from here and force marched us down that road. There's no telling where Lester's at, and Hank's face down in the mud a mile back. You're a lunatic."

Jody reached into the car and poured another half-gallon onto the dash board. He threw the empty can at the car and it ricocheted and hit him in the knee. "Lester can take care of himself and I don't care much about Hank. It's the car I'm concerned about. I know it's just an import but it's the only wheels I got. Now I've got to walk back home."

One of the twins struggled with a can of paint and so Jody pushed him out of the way and pried the can open. He stood with the open can of paint and looked back at the road where the man from the truck stood, watching the vandalism take place.

"If it weren't for that nosey neighbor this operation wouldn't have been so messed up." He splashed the can of paint onto the chrome grill of the Mach III. "Look at him over there," Jody said, nodding toward the man. "He sounds like a sports commentator at a football game, giving a play by play."

The neighbor stood a few yards from the melee and relayed all the action over the phone to the Sheriff's Department. "It's worse than my five-year-old grand-daughters art class. There's paint flying every which way. I don't know what's got these boys so fired up but they're going after it with gusto." Paint splattered close to his feet and he took a step back.

"I got to tell you though," he said into the phone, "I don't mind seeing this. That Mallard boy has been racing this car up and down my road for four years now. Every time I call you to complain, your deputy gets here too late. It's about time something's being done about it."

As Dippy struggled to open his remaining can of paint, Jody soaked the wind shield and the sirens grew closer. "Okay Uglies," he said. "You get back to home base the best you can and don't follow me. It's every man for himself from here on out. If the law nabs you don't spill your guts. Especially don't tell them you were with Jody Spencer."

Jody turned and sprinted through Troy Mallard's front yard and into the fields beyond. The other Green Uglies ran off in every direction. Dippy continued to struggle with the can. Lights from the police cars swirled in the distance, approaching fast.

"That's right," the neighbor said into the phone. "The leaders name is Jody Spencer. The idiot blabbed it out right in front of me. There one left here and he's struggling with the top on his last can." He turned to watch the approaching sheriff deputy. "What's that Sheriff?" he said into the phone. "You want me to grab him before he runs off? I don't think I'll do that Sheriff. He's a little guy and I could handle him easy. But the more I watch these boys go to work on that cursed car, the more sympathetic I feel. Hold on..."

The man placed the cell phone onto the hood of his truck and walked over to Dippy. "Let me have that," he said to Dippy. "Go on and run off. The sheriff deputy's going to be here in a minute. I'll take care of this."

Dippy **looked** at man, stunned. He stood up and glanced at the fast approaching police car, sirens blaring, lights flashing. He nodded at the man and sprinted into a field.

Dewey reached into his pocket and extracted a pocket knife. He knelt, flipped the lid off the can and causally walked to the car. He found a clean section and carefully poured paint on it.

The punk rock inside the Mallard house turned off as the sirens got **louder**. Troy Mallard emerged from the house in his underwear. He stood on the front porch and watched his neighbor splash green paint onto his beloved car. Paint cans littered the ground and his once **beautiful** black car looked sticky green. Large gobs of green paint oozed and dropped to the ground to form puddles.

"What the hell, Dewey?" Troy said.

"I didn't start it," Dewey said to Troy with a defiant look, "but by God, I finished it."

The Sheriff's Deputy skidded to a stop and turned off the

siren. Dewey dropped the can of paint and walked to his cell phone. "It's finished Sheriff. Your Deputy got here too late again. But the good news is that the perpetrators got away and that car won't be racing up and down my road for a while. Troy Mallard is standing out here in his skivvies. He looks ready to cry."

Dewey nodded to the Deputy and climbed into his truck. "By the way Sheriff," he said into the phone. "If Mallard says that I took part in painting his car, he's telling the truth. If you want to do something about it, you know where I live. Also, on recollection I can't be certain that I heard the leaders name correctly. The sirens were so loud I couldn't make it out. Good night Sheriff." Dewey closed his flip phone and drove away, a smile on his face.

Chapter 29

Hobbs and J.R. finished cleaning the auto shop just be-fore sunrise and staggered into bed for a couple hours of sleep. Dippy had gone missing the previous evening and a concerned Hobbs found the room empty at sunrise. But a few hours later Hobbs awoke to find Dippy snoring loudly and peacefully. Hobbs decided to let Dippy sleep while he and J.R. went to work. They hoped to put the finishing touches on the Green Ugly.

After a late breakfast at Aunt Mae's, they hurried to the auto shop. Walking onto the auto shop parking lot, Hobbs and J.R. surveyed the scene. They had seen the improve-ments earlier in the day, but the scene took on a whole new look in the bright light of the day. The cinderblock build-ing looked sharp and handsome with a fresh coat of grey paint with blue trim. The fresh grey gravel on the resurfaced parking lot crunched under their feet.

"Before last night, I would have never believed you could clean a junk yard," Hobbs said, viewing the fenced area beside the auto shop. Wide pathways bisected rows of old cars like the grid of a well-ordered town.

"Bill had a couple hundred people and five tow trucks working all night in there," J.R. responded.

They walked under the frame of a 1973 Corvette that belonged to Clarence and had been a gift from his father. Over the years Clarence had stripped the car of parts and had abandoned it in a far corner of the junk yard. Last night Bill extracted it, applied a fresh coat of red paint, and had it secured to the display pole in front of the shop. Hobbs considered it a thoughtful gesture. Normally he looked upon display poles as a tacky form of advertisement but in this case the display added a nice touch.

They stepped to the front door and looked upon the large glass pane window. The window had been scrubbed clean and a local artist had repainted the words "We Do It Right the First Time." Under these words, the artist added, "Home of the Green Ugly." He also painted the consecutive years that the Voyals' had won the Central Georgia Road Stock Championships. He left plenty of room for additional years. Hopefully Clarence would get the message.

Hobbs discovered the shop unlocked and entered the lobby. They stepped onto new carpet and immediately noticed a beautiful oaken counter, constructed by a skilled cabinet maker, standing between the lobby and garage entrance. Gone were the naked and flickering light bulbs, replaced by fresh banks of ceiling mounted fixtures. The soft interior lighting directed attention to the newly painted walls where framed photographs of the Green Ugly hung proudly. Hobbs noticed that Bill had installed double and triple chairs with oak frame and charcoal grey fabric. Recent editions of Popular Mechanics sat upon a coffee table.

"This is a major improvement," Hobbs said.

"Yeah, but let's check out the garage," J.R. responded, walking behind the counter and through the door to the garage area.

The garage sparkled from morning sunlight streaming through a bank of two-story high windows. The previous day Hobbs found the space dim and depressing. The murky windows provided modest transparency but now, after a rigorous cleaning, the eastern sun shone brightly and illuminated the freshly painted walls and floor to provide a friendly and warm feel. With all the junk removed from the floors, the garage looked cavernous. Widow Bakers 1985 Chevy Impala waited for Clarence in the same open spot he had left it the previous day. The car, along with the tools he had been using, were the only items left untouched. Other tools and supplies had been neatly organized into heavy tool boxes along the wall.

Hobbs noticed an office close to the garage entrance. The office had been Jack Voyals' and had been unoccupied for three years since his departure. Sally Voyals had spent much of the night redecorating the office for Clarence. She placed photographs of family on the walls and organized the business files. Other memorabilia, once cherished by Clarence but long forgotten, filled the office. If Clarence would allow it, she planned to work as the business manager for the shop until Clarence could get back on his feet again.

Triple overhead doors stood open and industrial-strength fans expelled paint fumes out of the garage. Fresh air from open windows drifted into the space and Hobbs could barely smell the noxious paint fumes that were present only a few hours earlier.

"So," Hobbs said to J.R., taking it all in. "I guess the plan is that when Clarence arrives today, he'll see what the town folk have done, and he'll improve his ways. Is that it?" His hostility toward J.R.'s overly optimistic plan had diminished somewhat overnight but doubts remained.

"I don't know about that," J.R. said. "I guess we'll have to wait and see."

"Step two, huh?" Hobbs asked. He remembered J.R.'s step-by-step plan to rehabilitate Clarence.

"Maybe," J.R. said hopefully.

"Don't forget, you've got to race the Green Ugly tomorrow night. You've got to get your mind right about that. You ain't here to fix up Clarence Voyals' life. You've got a race to win so that we can earn some money for the race in Atlanta."

"Yeah, we've got to do that too."

"It's not that too, J.R.," Hobbs said, perturbed. "The race is all there is." He noticed movement at the door to the interior garage where the Green Ugly was stored. He turned to see Sally Voyals and a little girl, hand in hand.

"Who's that little girl?" Hobbs asked.

"Maybe, that's step two," J.R. responded, walking past Hobbs. He waved and the little girl waved back.

Chapter 30

Hobbs stood in a corner of the inner garage and cleaned tools. He watched J.R. squatting in front of the open hood of the Green Ugly, tutoring the little girl on the basics of internal combustion engines. The girl was Clarence and Sally Voyals' daughter, Maggie. Pink ribbons decorated Maggie Voyals' long blond hair and she wore a flowery dress. Like her father, Maggie had a round face with fair skin and a good dose of freckles on her nose and cheeks. At nine years of age, she would have been six years old when her brother died on the very spot she stood. Hobbs wondered if Maggie resembled her brother.

Hobbs felt tense as they waited for Clarence to enter the shop. It was just past noon, his normal arrival time. Maggie, on the other hand, did not seem nervous. *And why should she,* Hobbs thought. It had probably been three years since she had last seen her father. He represented only vague memories to the little girl. In addition, J.R. put the girl at ease.

She laughed at J.R.'s antics as he made funny noises that supposedly simulated a running motor. To Hobbs they sounded like a dying moose. J.R. loved children and he related to them in a caring and loving way that Hobbs could not.

"Have you ever owned a BB gun?" J.R. asked Maggie. He crouched to get at her level. His intent gaze let Maggie know that she was the only person in the world.

"No sir. But my friend Kyle owns one. But it's not a real gun cause he's got to pump it first to make it work."

"That's right," J.R. responded with a smile. "Do you know why he pumps it?"

"Yeah, every time he pumps, he's pushing air into the gun and when he pulls the trigger, the air pushes the BB out. He pretends like he's in a war, but Kyle wouldn't have a chance with that gun in a real war. He'd be shot down before he'd get two pumps in."

J.R. chuckled. "Kyle's gun works by compressing air in the firing chamber. Do you know what compression means?"

"Yes sir. It means to press something real tight."

"That's right. Did you know that this engine works the same way as Kyle's BB gun?"

"Nope, I didn't," Maggie said, amazed.

"Sure, it does." J.R. pointed at the engine. "Do you see that cylinder there?"

"Yes sir."

"Well that's like the firing chamber on Kyle's gun. Except it not only compresses air, it compresses gasoline."

"Just like Kyle's gun?" Maggie engaged J.R. playfully in wide-eyed surprise.

"That's right. There's something called a piston in there and it compresses air and a drop of gasoline together. When it's tightly compressed," J.R. said, using his clasped hands to simulate the process, "there's a spark and the gas explodes, driving the piston down. The engine takes all the energy from the explosion and turns the wheels on the car."

J.R. smiled at Maggie as she explored other parts of the engine. She had his full attention and meant to keep it. "What's this?" she asked, pointing to the flat carburetor.

Just then, a door in the main garage opened slowly and then closed. Uneasy footsteps echoed. J.R. paused for a moment and looked at the open door. Maggie followed his gaze.

"Is that my father?" Maggie asked. "Is he going to come home today?"

J.R. smiled. "We'll see," he said. "Now, you asked about the carburetor. Let me tell you about that. It's one of my favorite parts."

Hobbs directed his attention toward the main garage and let his gaze fall upon the far wall. Yesterday the wall had been covered in empty boxes and junk but now it was clear of all clutter. He listened intently and tried to imagine the surprise Clarence must be feeling. Several town folks had wanted to greet Clarence with a surprise party, but Sally felt that his first time back into the refurbished garage should be a personal and quiet affair. Close family only. J.R. and Hobbs were also invited.

Sally Voyals, along with Bill and Aunt Mae, stood close to the car. Sally looked her best with a cheerful green dress that brought out the color of her hazel-green eyes. She watched the open door to the main garage with a look of determination, waiting for Clarence. Bill looked nervous and Aunt Mae held a steady arm around his waist.

Above J.R.'s quiet lesson on carburetors, Hobbs heard a pair of shuffling feet.

Clarence mumbled something incomprehensible. Hobbs heard the clattering of tools as Clarence rummaged through a tool box. A tool fell and clattered on the cement floor. J.R. stood and placed a hand on Maggie's shoulder. They faced the open door.

"Bill? Are you here Bill?" Clarence asked. His words echoed off the walls of the empty garage. "Where are you?" Clarence walked toward them.

"In here, Clarence," Bill said with a dry and crackled voice.

"What's going on?" Clarence asked as he rounded the corner and stepped into the interior garage. "Who cleaned the garage...," his voice trailed off as he saw Sally.

Clarence looked presentable with a fresh pair of jeans and tee shirt. His face went white when he saw his estranged wife. For a long moment he met Sally's gaze. Her eyes were overflowing with compassion and hope while his were full of confusion. He took a step back and turned to leave.

"Clarence," Sally called after him.

As Clarence turned back, he saw Maggie standing by the open hood of the Green Ugly and his confusion turned to fear. He reached out to her. "Get away from that car, Darling," he said, his arms urging her to move back. "It ain't safe. Please move back," he pleaded.

Maggie looked at her father and in a moment of indecision she turned to her mother for direction.

"Maggie is safe," Sally said to Clarence. "Stop this nonsense. Nothing is going to happen to her."

"But Jackie... "

"Jackie died. It was an accident. That was... "

"Get away from that car," Clarence bellowed at Maggie. Maggie, frightened by the outburst, ran to her mother's arms.

"I don't want her here," Clarence exclaimed to Sally. "Don't you understand? I don't want any of you here."

"She's your daughter," Sally responded tearfully. "I'm your wife. You have responsibilities."

"I'm no good to you anymore," Clarence said. He turned and left hurriedly.

"Clarence," Sally exclaimed. "Wait." She started after him, but Aunt Mae placed a hand on her arm.

"Let him go," Aunt Mae said. "It'll do no good to run after him."

Sally placed her hands on her face and sobbed on Aunt Mae's shoulder.

Bill watched Sally with anguish, his face flushed with anger. He charged into the garage. "How dare you treat your family in this way," Hobbs heard him yell at Clarence. "After all we've done for you."

Hobbs followed Bill into the main garage. Bill's words echoed off the walls as Clarence retreated toward the exit. "The whole town spent all night fixing up your garage and now you deny your wife and child."

"I don't want anyone's charity," Clarence cried, turning to face Bill. "What I want is for people to leave me alone."

Bill stuttered some incomprehensible words, anger paralyzing his speech.

Clarence hurried from the garage, slamming the door shut as he went. Bill did not follow. He stood, shaking, with hands to his sides, staring at the closed door. When Bill did not move Hobbs turned to look in on Sally. She continued to sob on Aunt Mae's shoulder. Maggie buried her head between the two women.

J.R. stood with one hand on the open hood of the car and with the other hand he messaged his eyes; his head held low. Hobbs stared at his friend with a disgusted look. He walked over and stood close, facing him.

"You're tearing these people apart," he said to J.R. over Sally's quiet and muffled sobs.

J.R. dropped his hand from his face. He kept his head low, eyes pointed at his feet. "I don't know..." He looked up at Hobbs with a defeated look; his eyes red with fatigue and raw emotion. "That man is in a lot of pain."

"What makes you think you know anything about that man? You've never walked in his shoes," Hobbs said in a low but angry voice. "You don't know what he's been through these last several years. Did you think you could just waltz in here and fix his problems in a couple of days?"

J.R. didn't respond. He looked over at Sally as she cried. Aunt Mae rubbed her back and whispered soothingly into her ear.

"You know," Hobbs said to J.R. "I was beginning to admire your determination and confidence but now I see it was only arrogance."

J.R. looked at Hobbs. "Please don't say that, Richard. I didn't mean no harm. I was only trying to help."

"Tell that to the mother and child over there," Hobbs said pointing to Sally. "Or how about telling it to the old man out there standing in an empty garage and staring at the wall? And while you're at it," he said with anger rising further, "explain it the father who lost a son and is wandering about in the woods bawling his eyes out."

J.R. looked at Hobbs with a mix of confusion and hurt. "But I didn't mean no harm," he repeated, more desperately.

"Of course, you didn't mean no harm. You never do but that don't mean you can't cause it. You almost had me believing you were doing a good thing here, helping that poor man out. But in the end, you only caused more harm."

J.R. turned and leaned his weight on the frame of the car and folded his arms. He did not face Hobbs, but he listened.

"You're always trying to give a helping hand to strangers, J.R. But maybe you should pay more attention to yourself or your friends. You can't trust strangers. I've been telling you that for years, ain't you ever going to listen?"

J.R. turned his head to Hobbs and smiled wearily, his eyes full of sadness. "I remember a time when you helped out a stranger," he said. "Do you remember? Has it been so long ago that you've forgotten?"

J.R.'s words disarmed Hobbs. "That's different."

"It ain't different," J.R. responded. His eyes moistened and he stood to face Hobbs. "You helped me when no one else would."

"You would've made it without my help, J.R.," Hobbs responded. He looked away, embarrassed.

"You know that ain't true. You saved my life."

Hobbs and J.R. looked at each other in silence. Hobbs remembered his first meeting with J.R. in the fourth grade of Eli Jackson Elementary School. J.R. was a new student from special education and was badly bullied. Hobbs defended J.R. and the two became lifelong friends. He also remembered that fateful Christmas night in his sixteenth year when he had driven to J.R.'s trailer home to show off the old Ford he had refurbished.

Hobbs was living in a foster home at the time and had worked in secret on the car for months, hoping to surprise his friend on Christmas. But when Hobbs arrived, he found J.R. had been badly beaten by his step-father. The severe beating was only one in a long line of abuses J.R. received at the hands of neglectful parents. On that night, J.R. cried and pleaded for help and Hobbs responded. He and J.R. ran off that very night with thirty dollars in gas money and the shirts on their backs. They did not return.

"I was a stranger and you helped me out," J.R. said. "You taught me how to care, Richard. Even for strangers, you taught me to care."

As Hobbs looked at J.R. now he still remembered the skinny and frail kid with a black eye. He also remembered the bloody nosed teenager kicked down the front steps of his step father's trailer home on a frigid December night. And he was reminded that through it all, J.R. never lost faith in himself and the good nature of others. He was a well-versed student in the hard knocks of life, yet he never disparaged himself or anyone else.

"I can't ever stay mad at you, J.R.," Hobbs said with touch of frustration and a rare smile.

"That's because you're a good man. You act like a tough guy but deep down you're kind. You want to see Clarence back on his feet as bad as I do. You're just upset because you don't like to see Bill or Sally get hurt in the process."

"What I want J.R., is to make some money so that we can make it to the Atlanta race this weekend," Hobbs said.

"We all want that, and we'll make it there somehow," J.R. said. "But life goes on don't it? If we don't help when we see people in trouble, then we're no better than all the people that have done us wrong."

Hobbs glanced over to Sally and noticed that she dabbed her eyes with tissue and was preparing to leave.

"I better go and talk to her," J.R. said.

"Better you than me. I'm no good around crying women," Hobbs said, looking over his shoulder at Sally.

"I'm no good at it either," J.R. said. "But I've got to see this through." J.R. walked over to Sally and took her hand. He said a few supportive words and escorted Sally and Maggie from the garage. Sally smiled at Hobbs as she exited. Hobbs gave her a feeble wave.

Hobbs noticed Aunt Mae making her way toward him. He pretended to be busy with the car engine.

"I want you to know that we appreciate all that you are doing for us and for Clarence," Aunt Mae said to Hobbs. Despite spending the last five minutes with a distraught Sally Voyals, Aunt Mae seemed resilient and fresh.

"From what I saw, it doesn't seem like we're doing much good to help the situation," Hobbs said.

"That's poppy cot," Aunt Mae said, rebuking Hobbs. "Clarence is grieving, and he needs a little more time. What we have done here today will help him."

Hobbs looked into Aunt Mae's steadfast eyes. Hobbs felt uncomfortable and once again pretended to work on the engine.

"Another thing, Richard," Aunt Mae said, "J.R. needs your support. It's going to be hard on him tomorrow night when he's racing the Green Ugly and on top of all that pressure, he's willing to help Clarence. You've got to support him, Richard," Aunt Mae said in a demanding voice.

"I will," he said.

She placed a hand on Hobbs' hand and smiled. "We'll all get through this and be better for it."

"I hope you're right," Hobbs responded wearily. Aunt Mae smiled again and left the garage.

Hobbs turned his attention to the engine and began double checking fluid levels.

Aunt Mae's words echoed in his mind. *You've got to support him, Richard,* she had said. He felt helpless and ashamed. Helpless because the best he could do for his friend was to make sure the engine didn't fail during the race. He felt shame because of the harsh criticism he had leveled against J.R. in his efforts to help Clarence. J.R. deserved better and Hobbs was determined to provide it.

Hobbs had seen men die in crashes on race tracks, professional and amateur. He walked to the driver side door to check on the seat harness. He had checked the harness many times; tugging on the latches and studying the seams for weakness. He'd be unable to protect J.R. from the likes of dangerous drivers such as Troy Mallard but he could at least ensure that his friend had a secure harness.

Chapter 31

Troy Mallard sat on the front porch of his three room shack and considered the vandalized car parked in the yard. He wore black pants and boots with a tightly fitted tank top. Katydids sang in the dark cotton fields and moths circled a lone street light. Greasy perspiration ran from his hairline down to his long, pointed chin.

The blotched green paint on the car exterior didn't concern him much. A detail man owed him a favor and a new paint job could be easily had. The paint in the gas tank was no major problem either. He stored several gas tanks at the shop and the exchange would be a job of only a couple hours; no big deal. The real damage had been to the interior where paint had dried in thick-caked layers on the leather seats and console. The repair job promised to be an expensive ordeal. In fact, he decided after all, the car was useless to him now. He'd have to trade it out for another.

No matter, he told himself. The Mach III was an errand car; the car he used to get from one place to the next and the car he used to impress girls on the drag in Macon. He'd had his eye on a 1978 Trans Am as his new run around car anyway. The real prize was the 2002 Monte Carlo parked in a secure shop in the city. He had won three Central Georgia Road

Stock Championships with the modified Monte Carlo and if the degenerates in Anna's Mill had vandalized it, he would have gone ballistic.

He knew that lunatics lived in Anna's Mill. He'd seen evidence of their existence every year when the town invaded the Bibb County race track. With their green banners and waving pom-poms, they acted like the race was as important as a state football championship. They even had a musical band for God's sake.

Looking at the vandalized Mach III, he should've expected no less from the people in that crazy town. No doubt they had a rip-roaring time at his expense, trashing his car while he listened to music just a few yards away. Troy imagined that skinny drifter, J.R. Rentz, in the middle of it all. That's okay, he thought to himself; he knew the score. He'd get his revenge and then some.

Headlights twinkled in the distance and Troy checked the time on his watch. He wondered if the paint smeared all over the Mach III was the same paint the Voyals' used on their car. No, he decided, the paint looked like common interior paint; probably bought right off the shelf at some hardware store between Anna's Mill and Macon. It wasn't the paint they used on the Green Ugly. The God-awful color haunted his dreams at night, and he would know it if he saw it.

As a child he'd watched the Green Ugly race and one of his earliest memories was that of a raging fit his father threw after losing to Jack Voyals. Every year he crossed his fingers and wished that the Voyals' wouldn't show up at the championship so that his father could have a chance at a win. Every year he was disappointed when the Voyals' rolled up to the track, hauling their cursed car. He remembered rolling his eyes at the sight, knowing full well that it would be a horrible night.

He hated his father for losing to the Voyals'. Later in life, as his old man accepted defeat and even became friends with his rival, Troy lost all respect. He turned eighteen, stepped out of his dear old Pops shadow, and began racing his own car. It was the year of Jackie's death and the year Jack Voyals retired from racing. Troy celebrated on hearing the news and got rip-roaring drunk. Naturally, when the Voyals' didn't show up at the track, Troy's father figured to have a lock on the elusive championship. But Troy had other designs and on mile ninety-seven of a one-hundred-mile race, Mr. Mallard careened into the front stretch wall thanks to a well-placed nudge from his son.

A Dodge Ram truck pulled into the yard and two men nodded silently to Troy. He stood and walked from the porch to the truck. "Did you bring the fuel?" he asked.

He received an affirmative nod from the driver.

"Move over," Troy said to passenger. The passenger complied and Troy climbed into the truck. *Payback time,* he thought to himself, smiling.

Chapter 32

Antique figurines and Voyals family photographs stared down at Hobbs as he carefully laid out his sleeping bag onto the hard wood floor of his sleeping quarters. Light from a full moon glowed through drawn lace curtains and the faint tic of a pendulum clock kept pace with Dippy's incessant snoring. As he had done since youth, Hobbs folded his pants and shirt and placed them neatly at the foot of the sleeping bag. He slipped into the cool covering and rested his head.

"Some day, huh?" J.R. said quietly. He lay on the bed next to Hobbs, propped up by an elbow, looking down at Hobbs.

Hobbs grunted in agreement and thought of the coming day. "Tomorrow will be bigger still," he said, watching the ceiling fan make its slow rotation. "Are you sure you want to go through with this?" he asked J.R. for the tenth time in three days.

"I'm sure," J.R. responded.

Hobbs had not expected sleep to come so quickly. It caressed his sore joints and mind even as J.R. answered.

"Good night," J.R. said as Hobbs breathed heavily.

Hobbs slept as the amber moon light softened to grey and awoke with a startle to a darkened room. He felt hot and sweaty and kicked off the cover of the sleeping bag. A Grandfather clock chimed twelve times in the downstairs hallway and Hobbs remembered that today was race day. Apprehension settled into the pit of his stomach. He placed his forearm over his brow and tried to banish the images in his mind that had caused him to wake; images of J.R. racing the Green Ugly against Troy Mallard in his menacing black car. The black car bashed into J.R. repeatedly and when the driver turned it was not Troy Mallard's face that glowered at J.R., but the face of Mr. Rentz, J.R.'s abusive stepfather.

The dream had been terrible and sinister. Yet there was something else in the dream that he'd lost after waking; some other presence that he couldn't wrap his mind around. Whatever it was, it made J.R. smile and there was comfort in that. Reassured, Hobbs nodded off to sleep.

He awoke to the sound of running feet and frantic shouts of terror. He sat upright and looked into the darkness with uncomprehending eyes. Light from the hallway shone into the bedroom. He tried to understand why the door stood ajar, knowing full well he had locked it earlier. Another shout from downstairs brought Hobbs to his feet. Dippy lay on the bed and shielded his eyes from the intruding light. "What's going on?" he asked Hobbs with a cracked voice. J.R. was gone from the room.

Suddenly a flash of light from the dark window filled the room. An instant later a loud explosion shook the floor. "My God!" Dippy exclaimed and jumped from the bed.

Throwing on his clothes, Hobbs sprinted from the room and bounded down the stairs and into the street. "J.R.!" he yelled. A man, half dressed and bare footed, ran down the street toward the dirt road. A pickup truck with two men standing in the bed and holding on for dear life sped by dangerously, nearly hitting the half-naked man but swerving at the last moment. The truck bounded down the dark road toward the auto shop.

Hobbs jumped from the sidewalk and looked down the dirt road. In the distance an orange glow radiated above the pine trees. As he watched the glimmer fade and strengthen, a loud booming explosion split the night air and flames licked the sky. Hobbs threw his weight forward and raced toward the auto shop with Dippy on his heals.

Shouts, curses and strange popping noises greeted Hobbs when he neared the shop. The air smelled of burnt rubber. Balls of flame sprang forth from the backyard area, sending up thick, oily soot. The cinderblock building appeared untouched.

Pandemonium greeted Hobbs when he rounded the building. Two large mounts blazed against the back wall of the shop, giving off black clouds of ash that saturated the air and made breathing difficult. Hobbs coughed and staggered under the intense heat.

The cinder block wall smoldered, and a thick metal awning melted against the heat, curling up like the opened top of a sardine can. Waves of heat battered the awning, forcing it to resound loudly against supports. Further away from the fire, amidst the junk yard itself, Hobbs saw half a dozen men engaged in a furious battle to quench fires on a car that had been dragged from the wall. Other cars, emitting traces of smoke, dotted the yard.

Hobbs searched the crowd of men fighting the fire for the lanky frame of J.R. He saw dozens of men in various stages of dress, their skin blackened by the ash. He did not see J.R.

Hobbs watched in astonishment as a tow truck backed up to within twenty yards of the fiery masses. A man, draped with a thick wetted mat, staggered up to the wall holding the hooked end of a tow cable. The man crawled on the ground and disappeared on the other side of the fire. The blaze raged and Hobbs could not fathom an act of such desperation. He took a step back as the fire seemed to gain strength and still the man did not reemerge. After long moments of tension, the man appeared, his clothing steaming and smoking like a burnt casserole. He stumbled into helpful hands even as the tow truck lurched forward dragging another burning car from the far side of the flaming mounds.

The truck roared and threw up streams of dirt from all four wheels. Initially the car resisted but eventually the power of the truck caused it to lurch ahead. It hopped forward on locked and burning wheels, bouncing and stuttering across the yard.

Hobbs saw double zeros emblazoned on the side panels of the burning car. The sight brought the unsettling realization that this car was no ordinary junked car, it was a trophy stock car; one of seven versions of the Green Ugly that made up Bill Voyals' beloved stable. The other six cars of the stable were either fully alight or partially smoldering. Hobbs guessed that the two flaming hulks close to the wall were the two oldest and valued of the Green Ugly versions.

With a saddened heart, Hobbs watched the car being dragged by the tow truck. He recognized it as the 1971 Ford Thunderbird that he'd seen in the photograph in the auto shop lobby. He remembered the car as it appeared in the photo; driving the backstretch of the Valdosta speedway all those years ago; racing as if flying on air. The car owned the speedway record and he wondered how many other track records this car had broken in small towns across the south.

Yet here it was, throwing up flames and leaving melted rubber smears on the ground as it sputtered and sizzled, dragged mercilessly across a backwoods junk yard. Hobbs wondered if any of the racing fans in all those small towns gave two hoots about this old car. *No,* he decided; *only the people of Anna's Mill remembered and cared enough to risk life and limb. A valiant but vain attempt,* Hobbs thought as flames consumed the engine and interior. The car would burn for many long hours, he realized. Like a beached whale, it would be a slow agonizing death.

Several men approached the Thunderbird with buckets of water and sand. "Back away," Bill Voyals yelled, waving his hands frantically. The white in his eyes contrasted the blackened, tear-streaked skin on his face.

Hobbs saw the reason for Bill's concern. Flames licked the undercarriage of the car, close to the gas tank. Men backed away and the tow truck operator dropped the cable and accelerated to safety. Hobbs retreated to Bill's side and watched the sad spectacle.

The Thunderbird had been raced during a time in Jack Voyals' career when he had been especially aggressive. As a result, it bore the scars of many battles. Prominent among these were several round tire marks along the side panels where competitors had driven too close. Bill had scrubbed the tire marks but to no avail; they were deep and permanent reminders that the car had been driven hard. They could have been painted over but Bill preferred the battle scars. *Fond memories for an old man*, Hobbs thought.

Hobbs summarized the losses. Of the seven stock cars in the stable, only four had survived. The four survivors would require attention, but Hobbs was sure that Bill and the others would restore them to their former glory. The same could not be said for the two flaming hunks next to the wall or the Thunderbird that sat in the yard, crackling and sizzling.

Two dozen men stood in the shadows of the fire. In a wide semicircle they watched in silence. Other than the clanging of the metal canopy and fizzing sounds of the melting cars, no other sound could be heard. Hobbs watched as the green paint on the Thunderbird boiled, bubbled and turn black.

He looked down at Bill. The old man gazed at the fire forlornly and wiped his nose on the sleeve of his shirt as a large tear rolled down his cheek. For years Bill had cared for these cars. They were the best the Voyals' had to offer and Bill took special pride in each one, supplying them with fresh tune ups and full tanks of gas. Hobbs placed a caring hand on Bill's frail shoulder and felt the man shake under his grip. Bill did not respond.

The flame fully engulfed the car now so that the only distinguishable parts were the four tires that supported the fiery frame. The tires shook slightly as if unsteady and then gave way. An explosion rocked the car and forced the hood eschew. Just as Hobbs was thinking that the fuel tank explosion was milder than expected, a massive detonation blew the car into the air. Men retreated further as the car nose-dived into the dirt and settled back onto the ground with heavy thud. A fire ball billowed high over the trees.

Hobbs saw the crowd grow as more town folks rushed to the scene.

They streamed into the yard with bewildered looks, stealing concerned glances at Bill and Aunt Mae. Now that the fuel tank had exploded, the fire fighters could venture closer.

They began to apply water as soot-covered men expressed condolences to Bill. As the fires diminished, the crowd thinned, and Hobbs searched for J.R.

A group of five or six men huddled on the far side of the perimeter and Hobbs saw J.R. in the middle. He approached and heard the men speaking in anguished voices.

"You know who did this, don't you, J.R.?" one man said. "It was that Mallard boy."

"Look," said another, placing a hand on J.R.'s shoulder and pointing to the auto shop. A large number "13" had been spray painted on the back wall. "That's Mallard's number, J.R. He burned up our cars and left his calling card." The man's face was blackened with soot.

"You've got to take revenge on Mallard in today's race,"

the man said desperately. "Justice is required and don't expect the law to hand it out. A jail cell would be too good for the likes of Troy Mallard. He'll receive Anna Mill's response tonight at the track when he and his car are mangled and crippled along the race track wall. Ain't that right, J.R.?"

J.R. managed a tentative smile and nod. He looked over the men toward the dark recesses of the junk yard as if looking for something or someone.

Another man began speaking harshly and Hobbs nudged through the group and took J.R.'s elbow. "He needs to rest," Hobbs told the men and escorted J.R. away.

Hobbs noticed burns on J.R.'s hands and realized that while he had slept, J.R. had probably rushed to the scene. He had been amongst the hottest spots of the fiery battle. As Hobbs escorted his friend to the exit of the yard, J.R. continued to look to the long line of cars at the edge of the junk yard. He stopped abruptly. "There he is," he said.

Hobbs followed J.R. glance. Along the far chain-linked fence he saw a lone figure, barely distinguishable in the dark night.

"I noticed him about fifteen minutes ago, right before the car blew."

"Who is it?" Hobbs said, squinting to see more.

"Clarence," J.R. responded. "There's no telling how long he's been there. When the fires started, he must have rushed over from his cabin."

As Hobbs and J.R. watched, the figure shimmied through a hole in the fence and vanished into the thick pine woods. Hobbs could not imagine the horrible anguish that Clarence must have gone through, watching the cars consumed by fire. At least Bill had the support of family and friends in town. Clarence had no one to turn to. He'd return to his desolate shack or wander the woods, alone with his thoughts.

J.R. walked toward Bill and Aunt Mae. Hobbs followed.

A thin smile crossed Bill's lips when he saw them approach. Dippy had joined them now and all three offered their regrets.

"Boys," Bill said, looking at J.R. "When you came to town and said that you'd race the Green Ugly, I was overjoyed. I figured that by resurrecting the car, Clarence would finally come around. I thought he'd come back to us." Bill looked exhausted. Fleshy white streaks ran down his dirty cheeks and blood caked his cracked lips. Aunt Mae held him with a look of concern.

"But I can see now that it ain't going to happen. Clarence ain't going to come around after all." Bill looked at the smoldering wrecks against the wall. "Troy Mallard is a dangerous man," he said looking up at J.R. "Any man who would commit a crime like this is desperate and unpredictable. I believe that Jack could have handled him on the track, Clarence too."

Bill took his sad eyes from J.R. and looked at the large number thirteen painted on the wall of the shop. For several long moments they waited. "I'm afraid for you, J.R. This..." he said waving a hand across the carnage in the yard, "ain't worth it. I don't want you caught up in all this."

Bill smiled slightly at J.R. and then turned to Hobbs. "You boys have been so kind. You've worked hard and I owe you. I'll pay you for the work that you've done and then you can get on your way."

"No sir," J.R. said.

Bill appraised J.R. for a long moment. "You've never raced a car, have you son?" The question was delivered with kindness, but it cut through any pretenses.

Hobbs lowered his head as J.R. hesitated and stammered.

"But I can race the Green Ugly," J.R. said. "You have to let me. I can do this."

"It'll be enough money to get you to your race in

Atlanta," Bill said to Hobbs, ignoring J.R. "That's what you came here for isn't it?"

"That's very kind of you Bill," Dippy said, smiling.

Bill reached up and placed a hand on J.R.'s shoulder. "I'm sorry, J.R."

J.R. looked disappointed and hurt. Bill acted as if he would like to say more but he appeared too exhausted. He turned and walked away, Aunt Mae supporting his elbow.

"You shook my hand," J.R. said to Bill's back. "You shook my hand and we made a deal." J.R. squared his shoulders, a determined look on his face.

Bill stopped. His frail shoulders drooped slightly.

"Hold on there," Dippy said to J.R. "The man said he'd pay us and then we'll be on our way, just like we planned. Ain't that right, Richard?"

Hobbs ignored Dippy as he watched Bill. The events in Anna's Mill had gotten totally out of control but J.R. was emotionally mired in the saga. In truth, he too felt committed to the end. Somehow, with the burnt remains of ruined stock cars all around, the race in Atlanta no longer seemed as important as it once had. In this instance, Hobbs decided to trust J.R.'s instincts.

Bill turned slowly to face J.R., a harsh look on his face. "What are you holding out for son? Do you think you can actually win the race tonight? If that's it then don't even bother, I've done told you, you can have the money."

"This ain't about money," J.R. responded.

"Oh...," Bill said, faking surprise. He looked at town people milling about. "Then you must be some kind of champion, here to defend the honor of our good town."

Hobbs was surprised at the sarcasm in Bill's voice.

"That's a heavy burden, J.R.," Bill continued. "Believe me, I know."

"I'm no champion," J.R. said. He admitted it without shame.

"What is it then, J.R.?"

"If I don't race the car, no one else will," J.R. said. "It's like I said when I first laid eyes on the Green Ugly, it's a shame she's holed up in a garage."

"She?" Bill said. "You talk like the car is alive. It ain't. It's a machine J.R., it's got no feelings. Just like these burnt out hulks here…" Bill nodded to the smoldering remains of his cars. "They've got no feelings and when they burned to the ground, I didn't hear no cries of anguish. Did you?"

"No, I didn't. But I cried and I wasn't the only one. Call me stupid if you'd like, but I think when someone puts in so much effort to make the car what it is, then there's a part of it that's alive." J.R. and Bill looked at each other for a long time, neither speaking.

"The Green Ugly has a part of you in it," J.R. said to Bill. "It's got your brother Jack in it and right now it's got a big part of Clarence in it." He paused and searched Bill for any indication of understanding. "Like I said, you can call me stupid, but I haven't lost hope. I haven't lost hope that something good is going to come of this tragedy. I know it in my bones. Something good is going to happen today, and I want to be a part of it."

Bill appeared too exhausted to respond. "What do you have to say?" he asked Hobbs.

"I don't mind a good fight now and then," Hobbs said.

Any objection Bill may have had gave way to an apathetic glare. He gave J.R. a weary nod and walked away.

"There goes any chance we had to make it to the Atlanta race," Dippy said bitterly.

Hobbs placed a hand on J.R.'s shoulder. "Let's get some rest," he said. They walked from the junk yard and headed back to town.

Chapter 33

Walking through the deserted rooms of the auto shop, Hobbs felt unsettled as if the old place had undergone an irreversible change. Clarence and Bill Voyals used to occupy the garage and work on cars but now the rooms had an eerie, lonely feel. He fretted the shop might remain deserted even after he and his friends moved on and a small part of him wondered if he and J.R. had corrupted the place. The smell of smoke and burnt rubber from the previous night's carnage only validated his troubled thoughts.

To soothe his uneasy mind, Hobbs busied himself with pre-race preparations. Naturally, J.R. appeared jittery before the race and Hobbs was determined to distract his friend from the unpleasant chore that awaited him later that night. And so, Hobbs involved J.R. in the pre-race diagnostics. They worked quietly and happily on the Green Ugly for several hours until finally, only the leakage test remained.

Hobbs attached the leakage tester to the cylinder heads and J.R. scrambled into the driver's seat. Even though he had not detected worn valves or cracked cylinder walls, Hobbs considered the test an essential step in the checklist. Hobbs and J.R. had performed the test numerous times for local drivers back home. With J.R. driving, this run through carried that much more significance.

From behind the wheel, J.R. placed a finger on the **ignition** switch and gave Hobbs a thumbs-up. Hobbs confirmed the fit on the leakage tester and returned the gesture.

Suddenly the super-powered engine roared to life sounding like a giant monster from an old Godzilla movie. J.R. let the car idle as Hobbs studied the valve. After a few moments Hobbs pumped his fists and J.R. throttled the engine.

Hobbs had experienced fully throttled stock car engines but as J.R. released gas into the cylinders of the Green Ugly, he felt **like holding** on to something. The deafening sound and vibrations of the engine shook the ground like the blows of a jack hammer.

Fighting the urge to cup his ears, Hobbs checked the valve again. The engine sucked the surrounding air through the intake manifold like a high-powered vacuum; extracting combustible oxygen as if it could **not** get enough.

Hobbs saw no leakage within the cylinders; the car was ready to race. He released the tester and signaled for J.R. to cut the engine. Mercifully, the reverberating engine died and Hobbs momentarily lost hearing. "All systems go" he yelled to J.R. He stowed the **leakage** tester and joined J.R. at the open **hood** to appraise the engine one last time. "This car is ready to race," Hobbs said, closing the hood.

"It's **not** quite ready," J.R. responded. He pointed to the twisted rear **bumper**. The bumper had been damaged when the car fell from the support jacks, killing Jackie Voyals. That was one piece of morbid information that Hobbs could have lived without knowing.

Hobbs emitted a disappointed sigh. "We're engine mechanics, not body men," Hobbs said to J.R. His solution to non-aerodynamic pieces involved a torch or sheet metal cutters. "Besides, we ain't got an extra bumper. If we had an extra bumper, we could replace it." Mending a bent bumper on the day of a race was not in his skill set.

Hobbs and J.R. walked to the back of the car to evaluate the back end and summarize their options. Looking more closely, the damage did not appear severe. In Hobbs' opinion the slightly damaged bumper could fulfill its function. Namely, it could stave off serious damage to the back end of the car. "It doesn't look too bad to me."

"Me neither," J.R. agreed. "I've seen worse. It's barely twisted."

"Well then," Hobbs said, relieved, "let's leave it the way it is. Nobody will care one way or another."

As the two men turned to tidy up the shop, they noticed Clarence Voyals standing in the doorway. Even though he probably hadn't slept in days, Clarence looked presentable with neatly combed hair. His long, scraggly beard was gone, and Hobbs had to study the man for a moment to make sure it was Clarence. He smiled pleasantly and nodded.

"I hope you boys don't think you're gonna race the car with a bent bumper," he said.

Hobbs took a quick glance in J.R.'s direction. His friend was slack-jawed and bewildered at the transformation in Clarence. His demeanor and friendly tone were a major shock when compared to the cranky and bearded drunk they had met four day previous.

"It's barely twisted," Hobbs managed to say after a long moment. He noticed a wedding ring where before it had been missing.

"I hate to say this, and I know it's on short notice with the race only a few hours away, but we'll have to fix it," Clarence said. He looked at the car, already calculating how the damage could be repaired.

"Ah...," Hobbs stammered. "Did you say we?"

"I did," Clarence replied.

Hobbs and J.R. exchanged glances. "There are no spare

bumpers," J.R. said.

"We'll take it off and mend it," Clarence said as if he'd done it hundreds of times, which probably he had, Hobbs thought.

Clarence walked to a tool bench along the wall. He assembled a welding torch and other tools onto a metal cart while Hobbs and J.R. watched silently from a distance. Once the tools were assembled, Clarence grasped the cart. He hesitated and looked at the Green Ugly. For a moment he looked apprehensive as if rolling the cart to the car required more courage. Clarence had not worked on the car since the death of his son and Hobbs could tell that the twisted back bumper brought the tragedy into clear focus.

Clarence gave Hobbs a tentative smile. "Well then...," Clarence said with broken and halted speech, "I guess we should get started." He looked at the back bumper once more and did not advance.

Hobbs suddenly felt like an intruder. Perhaps Clarence needed privacy and some time to come to grips with the mangled bumper that had crushed his son. It was an emotional moment that Hobbs preferred not to witness. "If you'd like," he said, "we can leave."

"No," Clarence said as he took a step forward. "Please... stay." The wheels on the cart squeaked as Clarence made his way tentatively toward the car. Hobbs and J.R. followed slowly, unsure if Clarence would bolt for the door at any moment.

Clarence pushed the cart beside the car and picked up the blow torch. Methodically, he grasped the face guard and stepped to the back end of the car, forcing his eyes to the ground and away from the damaged bumper. He knelt and kept his gaze directed at the ground. Slowly he lifted his head to look at the dent.

For several minutes Clarence knelt, holding the unlit torch and face shield in his lap.

Hobbs could not imagine the thoughts rolling through his mind. *Was he thinking of the moment when he found Jackie's lifeless and mangled body lying under the car? Did he think of his father? Was he regretting the wasted years he'd not spent with his wife and daughter?*

J.R. slowly approached and knelt next to Clarence. "Once we take the bumper off, how are we going to straighten it?" he asked him, hoping to force Clarence passed his hesitation.

Clarence ignored the question and placed his hand on the bent metal. *The last time he touched the car was when he lifted it off Jackie, no doubt crying and cursing in anguish,* Hobbs thought. Clarence turned to J.R. with a dazed look. After a moment of confusion, he gave J.R. a thin smile of recognition. He used J.R.'s shoulder to stand.

Clarence stepped around J.R. and walked next to the car, slowly running his hand over its contours, as if getting reacquainted. When he reached the driver side window, Clarence held both hands over the etched lettering of his father's name. He felt the etching as if reading brail and when he looked to Hobbs and J.R. his eyes looked red and moistened.

"Last night I saw you battling the fire," Clarence said to J.R. in halting speech. "Others were there also, and I came to realize, I guess for the first time, that the people around here still care." He looked down at the hood of the car. "Not only for the cars but for me and my father also."

He wiped a tear from his eye. "Even after Jackie's death they still care," Clarence added.

"I've gotten to know your family and friends," J.R. said. "And based on what I've seen and heard these past few days, I'd say they care for you more and especially because of Jackie's death."

Clarence considered J.R. for a moment. He looked down at the bandages on his hands and gave him an appreciating smile. "Thank you for what you've done; not only for last night but for fixing up the shop and for supporting me at the town meeting. Uncle Bill told me what you said."

"Sally loves you and wants you back home," J.R. said.

A contemplative frown crossed Clarence lips. "I don't understand that," he said. "How can she love me again after what I've done? I was responsible for Jackie and look what happened."

"Sally doesn't blame you," J.R. said, a little too harshly, Hobbs thought. "You might believe you're responsible but that's something you'll have to work through. Right now, Sally and Maggie need a husband and father."

Clarence looked at J.R. for a long moment. "I've spent three long years without them," he said as a tear fell from his cheek. "I'd like to go home now. I hope they'll have me back."

"You have no idea how much they want you back, Clarence," J.R. said, sounding relieved as if a huge weight had been lifted. He placed an arm around Clarence's stocky shoulders and escorted him to the damaged bumper. "Now, let's talk about how we're going to replace this bumper."

Clarence considered the back end of the car for a long moment. "After were done, I'll give you a crash course on how to race her."

"I don't think 'crash course' is the right wording," Hobbs said to Clarence. "I mean, under the circumstances."

Clarence turned to Hobbs with a smile. "I guess I could've chosen better," he said with a chuckle. "Don't worry J.R., I'll get you all set up. You'll be fine."

Hobbs and J.R. exchanged relieved glances. With Clarence on the team now, maybe they had a fighting chance.

Chapter 34

Dippy entered Aunt Mae's Diner refreshed from a late morning wakeup call and a hot shower. Surprisingly he found the diner empty. When he entered the dark kitchen, he remembered Aunt Mae's had closed for Green Ugly Day.

Was it Friday already? Regrettably, his brief stay at Aunt Mae's was coming to an end. He and his friends had the cold and hard infield of the Atlanta Speedway to look forward to. Tomorrow they'd be eating hot dogs instead of roast beef.

Dippy rummaged through the pantry for food. He prepared toasted bread with a thick application of strawberry jam and poured himself a large glass of orange juice. With plate and glass in hand, Dippy kicked open the front door to the diner and walked out onto the sidewalk. He walked to the edge of the raised sidewalk and sat with his legs dangling. The morning air felt clear and warm; a few billowy clouds dotted the sky. *It will be a fine day for the celebrations,* he thought as he took a bite from the toast and looked around.

Large green banners and checkered flags decorated the store fronts up and down Main Street. He took a bite of toast and watched festive, green clad fans stream down the road and into a large park. Barriers blocked both ends

of Main Street and Dippy noticed a long line of cars driving into town and directed into a large field. He suspected
the population of Anna's Mill would likely double as out of
town fans joined in on the celebration.

Dippy washed down a mouthful of bread and jam with
a gulp of juice. He noticed small aluminum bleachers on
the elevated sidewalks along both sides of the road. Apart
from Aunt Mae's Cafe and the post office across the street,
bleachers lined the sidewalks, providing seating for thousands of people. He wondered if a parade was expected.

On the road under his feet, Dippy saw a freshly painted
white line. He followed the two-foot wide line with his eyes
and saw it ended on the other side of the road where two
men applied the last strokes of paint.

"Hey," Dippy called out.

The two men turned, paint brushes in hand.

"What's the line for?" he asked.

The men exchanged glances as if they'd never heard
such a stupid question.

"It's for the Green Ugly of course," one said.

Oh, that explains things, Dippy thought sarcastically. He
saw the two ugly skid marks on the road left by Troy Mallard's
Mach III and remembered Bill Voyals' comment that Anna's
Mill only allowed the Green Ugly to drag down Main Street.
Dippy looked again at the bleachers and then at the white line.
My God, he thought with dread; *the town's not set up for a
parade, it's a darn drag way and J.R.'s the driver.*

"You mean to tell me that J.R.'s got to race that car down
this street?" Dippy exclaimed. The two rows of bleachers
provided a dangerously thin drag way.

The men stared at Dippy with amused looks. "He's a
race car driver, ain't he?" one asked.

Dippy ignored the question and scrambled to his feet.
Juice dribbled down his chin as he gulped in large mouth-
fuls. He opened the diner door and stowed the plate and

glass on the nearest table and raced to the auto shop where he knew Hobbs and J.R. would be working. Someone had to talk J.R. out of this foolishness.

As he reached the dirt road leading to the auto shop, Dippy slowed to a walk and then stopped. He looked down the long road and remembered how stubborn J.R. had been about racing the Green Ugly. He'd advised against it at least ten times in the last few days and still J.R. wanted to race. With Hobbs supporting J.R.'s decision, Dippy could do nothing. "Bullheaded fools," Dippy said to himself. He turned to face the large park where the festivities were in full swing.

From his position, the land sloped downward so that Dippy could see the entire festival. At the far end of the park, sporting fields filled with competitors and blue grass music played from a large gazebo. On the far side of the gazebo, smoke rose from a large barbeque pit and Dippy counted twenty pigs turning slowly on spits. In the foreground, large canopies, decorated in bright green colors, lined the park. Each tent carried a placard and Dippy read each one in turn: *Arts and Crafts, Face Painting, First Aid, Refreshments, Tee Shirts, Kissing Booth, Pie Tasting Contest, Antiques.*

"Pie Tasting Contest?" Dippy said aloud, looking back at the spacious tent where a large group of people had gathered. *Two pieces of dry toast and a few gulps of juice could hardly be called a meal,* he thought to himself. He took one last look down the dirt road. He'd given ample warning to J.R. and if he hadn't listened to reason yet, he never would. Besides, he reasoned, the pies were calling his name, he made a bee-line for the tent.

Dippy's eyes widened as he entered the tent and saw large tables full of mouth-watering pies of all varieties: apple, peach, blueberry, raspberry, lemon, boysenberry, banana cream, and much more. The tent looked like a circus tent with a high center pole. Crowds of people, talking loud-ly, walked along the aisles of pies, eating and talking with the proud cooks. With the judging completed, the event had become a come one, come all sampling. Dippy's eyes fell on a blueberry-filled pie and he headed in its direction.

"Dippy," someone yelled.

He turned and saw Aunt Mae calling him over to her table. He edged past a few idlers and arrived next to Aunt Mae.

"Good morning sleepy head," Aunt Mae said with a big smile. "I was worried that you'd sleep too late and miss the pie contest." Bill stood close to his wife. He looked rested and cheerful considering the horrible events of the previous night.

"I can see I haven't missed the sampling," Dippy said. He looked with envy at others around the table stuffing their mouths.

"Try the apple," Bill said. "It'll melt in your mouth." He cut out two large pieces of pie, placed them on a paper plate and lifted it to Dippy's outstretched hands. Steam drifted from the pie and chunks of delicious apples oozed from its corners. Dippy grabbed a fork and cut out a piece. He placed it in his mouth and closed his eyes, savoring the de-lectable flavors.

"Umm...I guess you won first prize," Dippy mumbled with a full mouth.

"I wish," Aunt Mae said. "Martha Baker's been winning this contest for years. Some people say she makes the best peach pie in all of Georgia."

"There's no shame in coming second to Martha," Bill said.

"Well you still make the best biscuits and gravy," Dippy said between bites. Aunt Mae smiled at the compliment.

Dippy heard tapping on a microphone. "Is this thing working," someone said into the microphone. Dippy turned to the front of the tent where a small elevated stage stood. A bald man with a white beard and large pot belly stood on the stage and tapped the microphone again.

"It's time to announce the results of our annual pie contest," the man said. The large crowd grew silent as Dippy shoveled another scoop into his mouth and looked up to the stage.

"Third place goes to Betsy Folsom for her yummy blueberry pie," the announcer said. The crowd clapped and Dippy looked to the far side of the tent where a thin, bird-like woman squealed and placed her hand to her mouth in embarrassment. She received congratulations from people close by and her husband held up the pie with pride on his face. "Bufford don't hog that pie," the announcer said jokingly. "You get plenty at home so share this one." Several men shouted agreement and the man looked sufficiently chastised. He placed the pie on the table and offered a slice to the nearest guest.

"Our second-place award," the announcer continued, "goes to Mae Voyals for her world-famous apple pie." The crowd cheered and Aunt Mae waved to the judges in appreciation. "Folks don't worry if you're unable to sample Mae's apple pie today. She serves pies every day at the diner and there's plenty to go around. For you folks from out of town, Aunt Mae's diner is at the end on Main Street. She's opened all day long and closes at eight o'clock."

"The check's in the mail, Jim," Bill yelled to the announcer. The crowd laughed.

"Finally, we come to the first-place award," the announcer called out. "Once again the judges have awarded the prize to Martha Baker for her peach pie, the best in all of Georgia."

The crowd cheered and Dippy looked to see a heavy-set woman receive congratulations two tables from where he stood. Dippy gobbled down the last of Aunt Mae's apple pie and eyed Martha's table only to find that all the pies had been eaten.

Martha edged passed Dippy on her way to the front table to receive her award. A slight, grumpy-looking man followed. Martha shook hands with the announcer and received a blue ribbon. "How about a little speech," the announcer said. Martha took the microphone and addressed the crowd.

"I'm just so happy that we can all meet again to celebrate Green Ugly Day," she said. "Thank you so much for all of the wonderful compliments." She turned to the smiling judges. "Thank you," she said.

The announcer retrieved the microphone while Dippy scooped up a slice of peach pie from a close by table. "Gerald, do you have anything to say?" the announcer asked the grumpy man standing next to Martha. "I think everybody would like to know what it's like to be married to the best pie cook in all of Georgia."

Dippy held the pie-filled plate close to his face and scooped a piece into his mouth. He turned to the front stage. He too would like to know what it's like to be married to the best pie cook in Georgia.

Gerald grabbed the microphone. "I don't know what the big deal is," he said. "There's a lady up in Waycross that makes a pie that's ten times better than Martha's."

Stunned silence settled over the crowd. Dippy nearly dropped his plate. He stood motionless, eyeing the stage with a scoop of pie suspended in front of a gaping mouth.

Martha whacked Gerald over the head with her purse. He covered his head and Martha punched him three times on the shoulder.

The crowd recovered and a chorus of boos fell upon the beleaguered old grump. Gerald blocked his wife's blows as if well practiced and made his way to the exit. Martha delivered a swift kick to his back end to send him on his way as a slice of blueberry pie, thrown from somewhere in the crowd, splattered on the back of his bald head.

"Good riddance," the announcer said to Gerald as the grumpy man looked back at the angry crowd with a wounded look on his face. "I guess we know who'll be sleeping in the dog house for the next two months." Gerald waved a hand at the announcer and staggered out of view. "You make sure that you tell that lady up in Waycross to bring her best pie next year," the announcer called out to Gerald. "You tell her that we not only have the best race car in Georgia, we've got the best cooks too. Also, we don't take kindly to criticism so mind your manners next time."

"Folks," the announcer said to the crowd, "let's hear it one more time for Martha Baker." The crowd erupted in a wild cheer and Martha clasped her hands high in the air like a champion boxer.

Chapter 35

The announcer thanked everyone for participating in the pie tasting contest and closed the competition. Dippy bade farewell to Aunt Mae and Bill and fell in line as the crowd streamed from the tent. He followed the boisterous crowd through the festival and ended up at a large half acre pigpen. Spectators streamed into the grand stands surrounding the pen and Dippy found an open space along a wood fence. He rested his elbows on the rail and inspected the muddy pen.

Approximately thirty young men stretched their muscles in preparation for a competition of some sort and a large swine fought against its tether on the far side. Dippy figured a greased pig contest was in the offing. He'd heard about this event from patrons at Aunt Mae's. Due to the violent nature of the sport, youngsters under the age of thirteen were prohibited and broken bones were expected. Dippy noticed the doctor and his wife laying out several splints on the ground behind the fence.

"Hey, buddy."

Dippy turned to see Jody Spencer, leader of the Green Ugly Fan Club, standing inside the pen. Naturally he wore camouflaged paints and a Green Ugly tee shirt; thankfully the foot-long hunting knife was absent.

"I ain't seen you since that night we painted Troy Mallard's car," Jody said. "Have you been trying to avoid the Green Uglies or something?"

"I wouldn't think of it," Dippy said apathetically. In fact, every time he saw Jody in town, he purposely tried to avoid the lunatic.

"You're a member of the club," Jody reminded him as if membership carried certain obligations. "We've had three meetings and you've missed them all."

Dippy avoided eye contact. "I've been busy."

Jody appraised Dippy for several moments. "Since you're J.R.'s friend and part of the race team, I'll forgive your absence this one time, but you're required to wear the green tee shirt."

Dippy looked down at his Duke University tee shirt. "I'll try to remember that," he said flippantly.

Jody glared at Dippy. After a long moment he dismissed Dippy's smart aleck grin and leaned into the fence. He looked past the mud pit to the greased pig. "The winner gets that fat pig over there," he said.

Dippy thought the pig looked more like a wild boar. He noticed small white tusks jutting up from its lower jaw.

"I'm gonna smoke it and eat it after I win," Jody said, looking down at Dippy. "The Green Uglies are invited, even you buddy."

Dippy wondered if Jody even remembered his name. He looked closely at the pig. Bristles extended from its back. *That ain't no pig,* he thought, *it's a razor back boar; maybe part pig, part boar.*

"I said you're invited," Jody said more loudly.

Dippy gave Jody a disinterested glare. After the fiasco at Troy Mallard's house, he wouldn't be caught dead with the Green Uglies. He was surprised they all hadn't been carted off by the police. "I heard you," he said.

Jody leaned back again and appraised his competition. "The only guy I've got to worry about is that pretty boy with the muscles over there." Jody pointed to the crowd of wild-eyed young men limbering up for the competition. The gathered youth looked motley and wore a hodgepodge of protection; football helmets, shoulder pads, bicycle helmets. Dippy noticed one young man with a hockey helmet and goalie pads attached to his legs. Another frail looking fellow wore a two-inch thick helmet of masking tape about his head.

"His names Johnny Banks and he's already won first place in archery and horse shoes," Jody said. "He wins at everything and all the other boys look up to him like he's some god."

Dippy noticed a handsome and strapping man in his early twenties towering above the other competitors. The man waved to a group of girls in the stands. The girls giggled and waved back flirtatiously as he took off his shirt and flexed his muscles.

"Will you look at that?" Jody said. "He's got no class."

You're one to talk, Dippy thought.

Jody took a moment to look up at the google-eyed girls in the stands. "Johnny might have muscle and good looks, but he lacks the intelligence needed to develop strategy. Sure, he might impress the girls with his skill at the individual events, but the pig chase requires a game plan." He looked to Dippy. "It requires strategic alliances to defeat your enemies, do you hear me, buddy?"

Intrigued, Dippy smiled at Jody. He liked the way this harebrained redneck thought. "Sure, I hear you. A smart guy like you will have a game plan. Am I right?"

Jody appraised Dippy for a moment as if trying to determine if he could be trusted. "You're a Green Ugly," Jody said. "You're bound to secrecy, but can I trust you to keep a secret?"

"Sure," Dippy said. "I won't tell anyone." Dippy didn't remember any obligation to secrecy but he went along with the idea anyway.

Jody turned and called the twins over. Dippy remembered

the two brothers from his misadventures with the Green Uglies. They slogged through the ankle deep mud and nodded to Dippy. "Where've you been?" one of the twins asked. "We've already had three meetings without you," the other said. "We keep attendance, did you know that?"

"Never mind that; he's been busy," Jody said. "Now tell him what our game plan is."

Looking at the twins, Dippy stifled a laugh. One wore a baseball catcher's mask with body pads while the other sported an old leather football helmet that looked like it'd been stolen from a trophy case.

"The plan is for me to hit Johnny below the right knee," catcher mask said.

"And I'm gonna hit him above the same knee at the same time," leather head said.

"We're gonna twist him up like a pretzel," catcher mask said. The twins grinned and exchanged high-fives.

"With Johnny out of the competition," Jody said with a beaming smile. "Lester over there is gonna latch on to that pig like bees on honey."

Dippy looked at Jody's brother, Lester. He loitered a few feet from the twins with thick bindings of masking tape on his arms and body. The tape had been turned inside-out so that the sticky side faced outward. He looked like a human fly trap.

Lester seemed fascinated with his garb. He touched his hands to his body to test the adhesive.

"Stop testing that tape," Jody scolded his brother. "If you keep testing it like that, you'll have no stick left for the pig. And keep your arms and legs stretched out so they don't get stuck on each other."

Lester looked up at his brother with a perturbed look.

"Ain't that boy just ten years old?" Dippy asked as he watched Lester waddle away, stiff-legged, like a mummy. "I thought there was an age limit."

"No one but us knows Lester's age," Jody responded. "Besides, who's gonna deny a starving kid like Lester; that boy's hungry. By the time he gets done with that pig, they'll have to pry him off with a crow bar."

Jody's words reminded Dippy of why he had been attracted to the Green Uglies in the first place. Their bizarre and senseless behavior were matchless even when compared to his own eccentricities. Dippy had the urge to throw on a helmet of some sort and join the melee.

"So, the plan is for the twins to take out Johnny Banks and then Lester chases down the pig," Dippy said to Jody. "What part do you play?"

"Me?" Jody asked as if he hadn't thought about it. "I suppose I'll direct the action and help out if I see an opportunity."

An overhead intercom called all competitors to one side of the pen.

"Got to go," Jody said. "See you around, buddy."

Dippy watched the Green Uglies take their positions in the throng of competitors; the twins close behind Johnny Banks and Lester off to the side.

Spectators packed the wooden stands along the full length of the pigpen, shouting encouragement and well-wishes to the young men in the ring. As the moment of truth approached, Dippy saw fear and apprehension on the faces of the young men. *This ain't no county fair greased pig contest where children chase a squealing piglet around a grassy enclosure*, Dippy thought. *These men are about to engage a wild animal that doesn't squeal, it growls; it has teeth and knows how to use them.*

A man entered from the far side of the pen with a long pruning clipper in his hands. He approached the tethered boar slowly, his rubber boots making loud sucking noises in the deep mud and manure. The crowd grew quiet as the man neared the boar.

The animal was the size of a large wolf. It looked up at the approaching man with a confident, menacing glare. The man said a few harsh words to the boar, cursing it and promising a swift death if it should charge and gore him. After a few hesitant tries, the man clipped the strap, releasing the boar. The man scampered from the ring.

The beast strolled to the center of the ring. It meandered about, sniffing the air for danger. It circled toward the tightly packed group of men, sniffing more than seeing. Suddenly the animal froze, its eyes firmly locked on the intruders. The large head dropped and bristles on the back of its neck stood on end.

"Let us say a quick prayer," the announcer said over the intercom. "Pastor Jones is here to offer a prayer of protection for our brave boys," the man said.

The spectators lowered their heads. The boys in the ring kept a wary eye on the beast.

The deep resonating voice of the pastor came over the intercom. "God, we thank you for this fine day and we ask your favor on the boys down there in the mud. We've all committed foolish acts as youngsters, and we ask that you'll not look too harshly on these boys. Protect and deliver them from their foolishness. We ask that none of the injuries will be of a serious nature. We'll accept a few broken bones here and there as payment for their fool nature; and perhaps some serious lacerations that will require attention from the good doctor. But we intend to draw the line when it comes to paralyzing injuries and certainly, we won't accept any unfortunate deaths. Thank you, Lord, and Amen."

The announcer's voice came back over the intercom. "Boys," he said. "If you're not absolutely certain that you've got the heart for this competition, now is your chance to crawl over the fence to safety. There's no shame in leaving a competition like this."

The boys in the ring looked at each other suspiciously, wondering who among them would bolt for the exit. Suddenly a pimply-faced teenager ran from the pack and climbed the fence. His dash over the fence attracted ridicule and a few well thrown clumps of mud from the remaining competitors. They clapped each other on shoulder pads and helmets; girding up courage for the violent conflict to follow.

"Is there anyone else that would like to exit the competition?" the announcer said. He waited but there were no takers. "Alright then, you can begin now boys and be careful."

Johnny Banks emerged from the pack and took a few steps toward the boar. He stopped and rested his hands on his hips, appraising the beast as if contemplating a solution to a problem.

"Show him whose boss Johnny," someone yelled from the crowd.

Johnny turned and pointed to a small fellow wearing a white football helmet. The boy pointed at himself with a question on his face. The other competitors took a step back. Johnny nodded. "That's right, you," he said loudly. "Get out there and attract his attention."

The boy gulped and took a hesitant step. Others patted him on the shoulders for encouragement. "Be brave, Eugene," someone shouted from the stands.

Eugene stepped to Johnny for direction. *Move right straight at him,* Johnny indicated. Eugene protested but Johnny insisted. With a pathetic look on his face, Eugene searched the spectators for help. Finding none, the boy walked slowly into the center.

Eugene walked like a doomed man and Dippy wondered if roles between man and beast in this contest hadn't been reversed where the beast did the chasing and the man ran for his life. The boar sensed a threat from Eugene and its eyes narrowed. With lowered head, the animal stepped forward in stalking fashion. Dippy had never seen anything like it; the boar moved low and swift like a lioness on an African prairie.

Eugene glanced back for support, but Johnny and the other boys had retreated against the fence. He was alone with the approaching beast. "Run for your life," a man yelled.

Eugene sprinted for the far side fence. The boar leapt toward the fleeing boy with a snort and growl.

The crowd erupted in a cheer. Dippy saw the boy had no chance, the animal moved too quickly. Ten feet from the fence, the boar overwhelmed Eugene. It knocked him into the mud. Before the animal could root through Eugene like a sack of potatoes, the leading edge of competitors pounced on it.

The frightened animal bolted from the pack, its powerful hind legs digging deep into the mud. Now the roar from the crowd intensified and the chase was on. Johnny Banks led the pack of boys through the mud. The boar reached the opposite side of the pen and threw itself against the fence. Johnny grabbed a leg and lifted the boar's hind quarters into the air. The animal kicked hard into his stomach and retrieved its leg. With surprising swiftness and agility, the boar dodged flying bodies and arms and raced back to the center of the pen.

Johnny emerged from the ruckus with an angry look on his face. His eyes locked onto the boar and he sprinted after it. The other competitors seemed happy to let Johnny lead the charge. Evidently everyone expected Johnny to win.

Dippy looked for the twins in the crowd of competitors. Johnny's speed and power had almost overwhelmed the boar on the first chase, if Jody and the Green Uglies didn't act now the contest would be over before they could execute their strategy. He noticed young Lester standing close to the fence, watching the action from a distance.

The boar slowed as it approached the opposite fence and Johnny slowed into a jog, maneuvering to cut off escape. Dippy finally saw the twins emerge from the pack, eyeing Johnny as they moved in unison. They traversed wide arcs and as Johnny sprang into a sprint toward the boar, one twin hit above his knee while the other hit below it. Dippy heard the sickening pop of ligaments as Johnny crumpled into the mud. The girls in the stands screamed in horror as Johnny wallowed in agony in the mud. The twins exchanged high fives.

"That's a completely legal move," the announcer reminded the crowd. "All is fair game in this sport and it looks like Johnny Banks is down for the count. It's anybody's pig now."

The boar trotted close to the fence, looking for a hole large enough to crawl through while the competitors gathered around Johnny. The angry boar attacked a lone boy; throwing him into the fence and continuing its lap around the pen.

With Johnny Banks injured, the pack lost cohesion and the contest degenerated into a full out riot. For twenty long minutes the competition raged as a mass of muddied bodies sprinted, dodged, and dove after the confused and wide-eyed creature. The young men of Anna's Mill could not bring the pig down and Dippy heard older folk commiserate about the lack of talented youth. Dippy agreed it was a pitiful display as fist fights broke out and cheap shots abounded. The doctor stayed busy.

Eventually the boar grew tired and Dippy watched Lester make his move. The boy waddled to the center of the pen and waited. When the exhausted boar cut in his direction, Lester pounced, head first into the hog's neck. The animal gave a wild, ear-screeching yell and bounded around the pen like a bucking horse. The adhesive provided no grip on the slick boar and Dippy marveled at how the boy stayed attached to the pig with his arms and legs flailing about like ribbons in a strong wind. When the boar reached the end of the arena it stopped and lay down, screaming bloody murder. The exhausted animal, its tongue lolling from its mouth, lay on its back and a ten-year-old boy received first prize. The crowd erupted in cheers.

Dippy rushed toward the gate to offer congratulations. When he arrived next to Lester and Jody, he found Johnny Banks and several other contestants in a heated exchange with the judges.

"That boy cheated by latching on to the boar's neck," Johnny exclaimed. He stood on two crutches with a large brace on his leg. Johnny leaned on a crutch and bent to pluck a tooth from the whimpering pig's hide. "Look," he said, holding the tooth in the air, "here the evidence."

The judge smiled and took the broken tooth from Johnny and handed it to Lester. "A man is born with two arms and two legs," the judge said in retrospect, "but sometimes even that's not enough to bring down a greased pig." The judge fastened a rope around the pig's neck and handed it to Lester. "Son," he said, "here's your prize." Lester smiled a toothless grin. "Thank you, sir. I believe we'll eat him tomorrow."

Chapter 36

As the crowd dispersed from the greased pig contest, Dippy congratulated Lester and declined Jody's invitation to the Green Ugly Fan Club pig roast. "I'll be at the race in Atlanta," he said. He wished the Green Uglies good luck and walked away.

He meandered through the festival, stopping to watch an obnoxious clown get dunked in the baseball target throw and paid fifty cents to kiss a pretty brunette at the kissing booth. As the afternoon wore on, he made his way to the gazebo and found a seat next to Reeves Carter, the town postmaster and newspaper man. A politician of some sort gave a patriotic speech from the gazebo platform.

"Are you enjoying yourself at the festival, Dippy?" Reeves asked pleasantly; a camera hung from his neck.

Dippy nodded. "Are you taking notes of this speech?" he asked, looking down at an open notebook in his lap.

Reeves looked up at the pudgy man on the podium speaking through a blow horn. The man dressed like Colonel Sanders and vocalized like a Baptist preacher. He wiped incessantly at his sweaty and bald head with a hand-kerchief. He spoke of plans to pave the dirt road leading to town and promised renewed efforts to win state subsidies for poor farmers. Judging by the small crowd, most town folks didn't care.

"That's our mayor," Reeves said. "Mayor Jack Sweeny."

Reeves looked down at the scribbles on his notebook. "I don't know why I bother with these notes," he said. "Mayor Sweeny has been giving the same speech for thirty-two years. I've got it memorized by now." He closed the notebook and crossed his legs.

"Every four years we hold an election for mayor and a hundred people or so show up at the polls to elect Jack every time. I don't know why Jack runs because there's no stipend and there's no responsibility either. County Commissioners oversee the basic needs of the town. I suppose he just likes the title." Reeves closed his eyes and held his face to the warm sun.

"If there's no official mayor how come he has an opponent? Who would run for a position that didn't exist?" Dippy asked.

"Mayor Sweeny likes the show," Reeves said with closed eyes. "He likes to give speeches and act the part of mayor. And every four years he likes to run against an opponent." He opened his eyes and looked at Dippy. "So, the Mayor pays someone to run against him."

Dippy was not surprised. Nothing in this quirky town surprised him.

"I heard he gave Hank Townsend a milk cow to run against him this year," Reeves said.

"Is that the same Hank whose drunk all the time and hangs out with the Green Uglies?" Dippy asked.

"The very same," Reeves said.

The last time he'd seen Hank, the man was drinking whisky from a squirt bottle in a cotton field beside Troy Mallard's home.

"This was supposed to be a debate between the Mayor and Hank for the upcoming election. But Hank's passed out behind the Post Office." Reeves nodded toward the podium. "As you can see, the mayor is undeterred."

Dippy sat back and listened. As the speech reached its conclusion, a man on the front row stood and accused the mayor of infringing on his property with a fence line.

"That's Pete Jenkins," Reeves said, waking from his stupor. He checked the film in his camera. "This should be interesting," he said and stood to take a few pictures.

Initially stunned by the public confrontation, the mayor quickly regained composure. With blow horn in hand, Mayor Sweeny delivered a vicious serious of personal rebukes aimed at Mr. Jenkins and his wife.

"I guess the mayor got his debate after all," Dippy said, stepping next to Reeves.

Reeves clicked away on his camera as Jenkins crawled up on stage to confront the mayor. The two were separated before fisticuffs commenced.

"This can't be good for the mayor's re-election hopes," Dippy said. He watched as the mayor misstepped and rolled from the stage. He stood with grass stains on his white trousers and threw more curses at Pete Jenkins.

Reeves lowered his camera. "I'll admit it's a distasteful show, but he'll be reelected in spite of it all," he said. "Come on Dippy, let's go for a walk."

Dippy fell in beside Reeves and they joined a throng of people heading toward Main Street. A fine layer of dust rose from the trampled path. They stopped at a concession stand for fresh squeezed lemonade.

"So, what do you think about our Green Ugly Day Festival?" Reeves asked.

"It's like an old-time carnival without the noisy mechanical rides. It's hard to believe so many people are here just to celebrate a race car."

Reeves chuckled. "I like to think Green Ugly Day is the one day of the year that we gather and celebrate everything that is unique and special about Anna's Mill. On Green Ugly Day we get to forget about our poverty."

They walked slowly, sipping cool lemonade.

"I wouldn't call the neighboring towns rich by any means, but they've got it a lot better than we do," Reeves said. "Did you know that Anna's Mill is not on any official map from the state?"

Dippy shrugged.

"It's like the State of Georgia has forgotten that a couple thousand people live down here and I guess we generate so little tax revenue that we don't count."

Reeves waved to a passerby. "Some of our neighbors think it's trivial for Anna's Mill to make such a fuss about a race car. Meanwhile they celebrate cotton harvests and peanut-growing seasons. But we've got nothing to celebrate but an ugly green Ford Thunderbird. I suppose the Green Ugly allows us to remind the rest of Georgia that we're still alive and kicking. That's why we take so much pride in that car. It helps us feel relevant." He turned to Dippy. "Does that make any sense?"

Dippy said that it did.

"That's why this dirt-poor town owes you and your friends a huge debt of gratitude," Reeves said. "Without you boys, there'd be no celebration."

"I guess I haven't helped much," Dippy said. "If it were up to me, we would be up in Atlanta by now."

"Well you're still here, aren't you?"

Dippy didn't respond. He thought of J.R. and the race. He wondered what Reeves and the rest of Anna's Mill will think when they learn the truth that J.R. has no driving skills. When J.R. wrecks their precious car, he doubted they'd be so grateful.

Dippy and Reeves rounded the post office and looked down the length of Main Street. Hordes of fans lined both sides of the street and packed the stands and rafters making the buildings indistinguishable. The thin black corridor of the paved street ran through the multitude, separating both sides by a mere car length.

"My God..." Dippy said, finding it difficult to breathe. The crowd stretched past the buildings and into the pine woods on both sides of the dirt road. It looked like two opposite walls of humanity.

All eyes of the rambunctious crowd focused on the empty dirt road leading to the Auto Shop.

"Does J.R. have to drive down this street?" Dippy asked with astonishment.

"No," Reeves said. "He's gonna drag down this street. Then we're all gonna pack up and follow him and the Green Ugly to the race track in Macon. This is what Green Ugly Day is all about. When she drags through town, it gives us a chance to show our appreciation. It's like the ultimate pep rally; nothing gets the blood up like a three-hundred and fifty one horse powered engine roaring past at a hundred miles an hour."

"A hundred miles per hour?" Dippy asked in disbelief.

"He'll have her at one hundred miles an hour easy by the time he reaches the dirt road."

"I think I need to sit down," Dippy said with a stricken voice.

Reeves looked at Dippy with worry. "You shouldn't be so concerned," Reeves said. "We ain't ever had any accidents and with an experienced driver like J.R., there's nothing to worry about."

Dippy looked at Reeves. He winked several times and swallowed the bile rising in his throat. "I'd prefer a seat that's as far away from the road as possible, please," he said.

Chapter 37

Dippy found a shaded bench outside Aunt Mae's Cafe. He sat and wiped sweat from his forehead.

"You don't look so good, son," Bill Voyals said as he passed by.

"Too much heat," Dippy replied. He fanned his face with his hand.

"Well," Bill said, "you look green like you just saw a ghost." He looked up at the awning casting a shadow over Dippy. "This shade should cool you off. When you feel better come on over and join us by the street. You won't be able to see the show from this bench." He patted Dippy on the knee and joined Aunt Mae and Sally Voyals at the edge of the walk. Sally knelt next to her daughter, Maggie, and wiped ice cream from her chin.

Dippy also saw Bobby Lee Reynolds and his wife. Bobby Lee exchanged pleasantries with Bill and hugged his daughter, Sally. He pinched Maggie's cheek and magically pulled a candy from behind her ear. Bobby Lee's mood had improved greatly since the town meeting at the church.

A teenager walked from the cafe carrying folded chairs. He set the chairs close to the sidewalk edge and the Voyals' and Reynold's sat. The teenager placed a fold out chair directly behind Bill and Bill waved to Dippy to join them. He begrudgingly complied.

When Dippy took his seat, he looked upon the restless crowd of onlookers and waited for the Green Ugly to appear.

The crowd pounded the stands with their feet and cheered while a blue grass band played *Togary Mountain* outside the post office doors. Venders sold steamed corn on the cob from metal pots and children played freeze tag on the street.

"I don't think the town's ever been this excited to see the Green Ugly," Dippy heard Bobby Lee yell over the crowd noise to Bill. His granddaughter, Maggie, sat on his lap and Sally sat between him and Bill.

"It's been a long three years," Bill responded.

"It's been too long," Bobby Lee Reynolds said. The two men exchanged friendly glances. "I never apologized to you for what I said at the town meeting. I…"

"No apology is needed," Bill said.

Bobby Lee nodded his head in appreciation. "I wish that Clarence could be here," he said.

"Maybe someday," Bill said sadly.

Bobby Lee reached across Sally and grasped Bill's hand in a strong embrace. "It's not right what that Mallard boy did to your cars," he said.

Bill nodded and smiled bravely. Evidently the tragedy was too fresh, and Bill managed to say thanks before looking away.

Suddenly the festive mood exploded into wild cheering when the crowd saw a cloud of dust moving rapidly down the dirt road from the auto shop. The band broke into a frenzied rendition of *Foggy Mountain Breakdown* and everyone stood, straining their necks to get a view of the famed race car. Dippy stood also.

The cloud approached and Richard Hobbs' truck cleared

a strand of trees and bounded onto Main Street. An audible moan emanated from the crowd and the band stopped playing. The truck turned and screeched to a halt beside Aunt Mae's Cafe. Hobbs and J.R. slid from the truck and hurried to Bill's side. J.R. looked down the stretch of Main Street at the horde of fans; his face turned white with fear at the immense gathering.

"Boys," Bill exclaimed to Hobbs and J.R. as the crowd sat down. "You've got it all wrong. You're supposed to race the Green Ugly down Main Street." The silent crowd gave the boys confused looks. "She can't race down Main Street by herself. J.R., you'll have to go back to the shop and drive the car down here to race her. There's nobody at the shop..."

Suddenly a loud and powerful rumble from a car engine emanated from the distant auto shop. Bill looked bewildered as Dippy cast his eyes into the dark pine forest. A cloud of dust hung low to the ground like a mist and the revving engine of the distant car sounded like a primal call from a prehistoric beast. He stepped to the edge of the sidewalk and looked further into the pine woods, searching out the car.

"What in the world?" Bill exclaimed with a mystified glance at Hobbs.

Hobbs smiled back and a trace of hope flashed across Bill's face. He turned to Sally Voyals and took her hand. "Stand up next to me, Darling," he said.

"What's going on Uncle Bill?" Sally said. She looked to J.R. for help. "Shh...," Bill said, holding her close. "Let's just wait and see."

The silent crowd stood in unison as the low rumble approached from the dust-filled road. Like an approaching thunderstorm, the reverberating engine echoed from the dark recesses of the forest and a stand of frightened quail flew high above the trees as the car passed.

Bill held Sally close and looked over his shoulder at

Hobbs once more. A question formed on his face and Hobbs nodded with a smile. Tears welled up in the old man's eyes and he extracted a handkerchief from his back pocket. He wiped his eyes with shaking hands and turned back toward the rumble. Aunt Mae looked to her husband and Bill wrapped an arm around her shoulder. Huddled together like frightened and fragile children, Bill, Sally, and Aunt Mae awaited the arrival of the Green Ugly.

Dippy nudged Hobbs with his elbow. "What's going on?" he asked in a whisper.

"Wait and see," Hobbs replied.

The first sighting appeared like a dark shadow, hugging the dusty road like a foggy mist that's gone in an instant. Yet still, the low beat of its engine approached and suddenly a dark form appeared, like a black hole in a mist of red dust. Slowly, as if materializing from deep within the earth, the Green Ugly emerged for the first time in years and the citizens of Anna's Mill beheld their pride and glory. The dull green finish of the car gave off a hazy glow in the afternoon sun as it glided to the white line at the edge of Main Street.

The car rumbled for a moment and then cut off. An awkward silence followed. Birds chirped in the distance and a brief wind rustled the tops of pine trees.

Sally bent slightly and shaded her eyes to peer into the driver compartment but the nylon netting over the window blocked her view. A hand reached to latches on the window and released the netting. At once, she recognized the wedding ring and the thick, burly hands. She stepped onto the street mindlessly and walked toward the car. She caught a glimpse of the driver's profile and stopped, placing a trembling hand over her mouth.

Dippy watched, astounded, as Clarence Voyals grabbed the window frame and heaved himself from the car in one swift motion. He turned and looked at his wife with tears in his eyes. She rushed to him and fell into his arms.

"It's Clarence," someone exclaimed from the crowd.

Bill and Aunt Mae hurried to Clarence's side with Maggie in tow. Bobby Lee Reynolds and his wife also hurried to join the embrace. Clarence lifted his daughter to the crook of his arm and kissed her. He held on to his wife and daughter as if nothing could separate them.

Chapter 38

The Voyals and Reynolds families surrounded Clarence like a protective shield, allowing him to shed overdue tears for his dead son. He cried also for the wasted years he wallowed in self-pity. "I'm so sorry," he told his wife.

Richard Hobbs watched Clarence's family gathered next to the Green Ugly. He thought of the painful efforts that brought Clarence to this moment; the emotional speech by J.R. at the town meeting, the all-night cleaning session at the auto shop, the awkward confrontation in the garage, the tragic fire. And he remembered J.R.'s words. *'If we don't help out when we see people in trouble then we're no better than all the people that have done us wrong.'*

Hobbs turned to his friend on the sidewalk. J.R. crossed his arms and smiled as he watched Clarence's friends crowd from the stands to welcome back a long-lost companion. They swarmed the street in front of the cafe and shouted encouragement.

He noticed Hobbs looking his way. "Some scene, huh?" J.R. asked.

"I wanted to high-tail it from this old town when I learned the truth about Clarence and his family," Hobbs remarked. "I was a coward."

J.R. regarded him for a moment and then turned back to watch Clarence embrace a long procession of friends and family. "You ain't no coward," he said.

"Then what's wrong with me?" Hobbs said. "How come I can't seem to connect with people like you do? It's like I don't care or something."

"You're the most caring person I know," J.R. said. "Afterall, who in their right mind would put up with the likes of Dippy and me?"

Dippy joined Hobbs and J.R. "It ain't cool to talk about people behind their back," he said to J.R., "where's your manners?"

"I was just telling Richard that it takes a lot of patience to put up with me and you," J.R. said.

"Speak for yourself," Dippy said to J.R. "He should count it a blessing and an honor to associate with someone of my intelligence and charisma."

Dippy looked down at the horde of town folk in the street. "Well, I'd say this ended well," he said. "You boys fixed up the race car and you did a pretty good job on that poor man too. The town has their Green Ugly and the Voyals' get Clarence back. All that remains is for us to collect our payment and then ride off into the sunset like heroes."

"It ain't over yet," J.R said.

Dippy ignored J.R and turned to Hobbs. "Did you collect the money so that we can get on up to Atlanta?"

"We'll collect our money when J.R. wins the race tonight," Hobbs said. He looked out at the crowd with a stern face.

Dippy turned to Hobbs and chuckled. "You two boys beat all," he said. "You've got to be the two most ignorant people on the face of this earth."

Hobbs and J.R shifted uncomfortably and avoided Dippy's gaze.

"Here's a news flash," Dippy said, getting animated.

"Clarence is back! Do you hear me? He's a race car driver and a good one from what I've heard. You don't have to race. Clarence can race that death trap now."

"Clarence ain't in any condition to race," Hobbs said.

"And J.R. is?" Dippy exclaimed with bugging eyes.

"I told Bill I'd race tonight, and I don't want to break my promise," J.R. said.

Dippy grabbed J.R.'s elbow and briskly turned him to face the line of stands along Main Street. "Do you see that narrow strip of pavement down there?" he asked harshly. "You've got to race the car down that strip without killing yourself and others. Do you think you can manage that Mr. Race Car Driver?"

"I've been praying about that ever since I saw it," J.R said.

"It'll take more than prayers," Dippy exclaimed. "The Lord helps those who help themselves. I say we help ourselves to the money Bill offered and skedaddle."

J.R. gently retrieved his elbow from Dippy's grip. "I shook Bill's hand and made a promise. Besides, I want to see this to the end. I'm gonna race the Green Ugly tonight."

Dippy glared at J.R., incredulous. He turned his attention to Hobbs. "So, you're just going to stand by while J.R. risks his life because of a handshake?"

"You heard the man," Hobbs said. "He said he's gonna race tonight. There's nothing you or I can do about it."

Dippy stared up at Hobbs with a dumbfounded look. He slowly turned and walked back to his seat.

"I think that's the first time that Dippy didn't get the last word," Hobbs whispered to J.R. with a chuckle.

"It ain't polite to whisper," Dippy said from the bench, getting the last word.

Down on the street the festive reunion continued. Clarence held Maggie in his arms and shook hands with long-time friends. Sally stood close by, an arm around his waist.

Bill scampered up the steps with a blow horn in his hands and a huge smile on his face. He gave J.R. and Hobbs a hearty bear hug and thanked them. "My offer from last night still stands," he said to J.R. "I'll pay you for the work you've done, and you don't have to race."

"I intend to race," J.R. responded.

Bill smiled. "I can never repay you," he said. He turned to the crowd and lifted the blow horn to his lips. "Who wants to go racing?" he asked the assembly.

The crowd erupted in a chorus of cheers.

"Then let's clear a way for J.R. and the Green Ugly," he said. "They've got an appointment to keep in Macon and time's-a-wasting."

The crowd began to disperse into the stands.

Bill placed the blow horn aside. "I want you to be safe," he said to J.R. "I don't care if you come in last place. You've done so much for my family already."

"I'm gonna try my best and I'll be careful."

Sally and Aunt Mae walked from the street and smothered J.R. in kisses and hugs. He blushed as they thanked him for never losing faith in Clarence. J.R. gave credit to others and looked to Hobbs for help.

Hobbs placed a hand on J.R.'s shoulder. "Let's go and get you set up," he said. He sounded like a death row jail guard talking to a condemned man. *Any last words before they throw the switch J.R.,* he might have said.

Chapter 39

J.R. walked onto the street, his face somber and heart pounding. Clarence stood alone next to the Green Ugly and waited. The car waited also, like some sleeping beast about to be woken. J.R. knew the explosive power under its hood; as a mechanic he appreciated that power, as a novice driver he feared it. He forced a brief look down the thin street and the multitude crowding both sides. The crowd cheered when they saw J.R. He looked away in fear. "Exterminator" they chanted in unison.

"Are you ready for this?" Clarence said, handing J.R. a helmet and goggles.

J.R. nodded. He felt reassured by Hobbs' hand on his shoulder.

"Just remember what Clarence taught you back at the shop," Hobbs said. His voice sounded nervous. "This is a standard transmission, so you've got to work the clutch and stick. When you apply the gas, ease off the clutch and hold on tight. When the engine feels like it's about to explode, engage the clutch and shift gears. Don't let go of the wheel no matter how rough it gets."

J.R. looked down at the tire marks left by Troy Mallard. "I hope I can lay down tracks as long as Troy did," he said.

"Everyone expects that."

"Don't worry about that," Clarence said. "You'll be at the other side of town before you know it. When you get to the dirt road don't try to avoid the potholes. Go straight over them; you'll be going so fast you won't even feel them. It's a dead straight run so just hold her in the center and apply the brakes when you've cleared the crowd. You won't believe how quick this will be over; ten seconds, fifteen seconds at the most."

J.R. strapped the goggles onto his head. "A lot can happen in ten seconds," he said to Clarence.

Clarence fixed the helmet to J.R.'s head. "You've earned this ride J.R. Only two people have dragged the Green Ugly; that's me and my daddy. There're several hundred people in those stands that would love to trade places with you. So, enjoy the ride. Have fun with it." Clarence gave J.R. an encouraging smile. He patted him on the helmet and helped him through the car window and into the driver's seat.

"You floor that gas pedal, J.R." Clarence commanded. "We'll see you on the other side." Clarence patted J.R.'s helmet and joined his family on the sidewalk.

Hobbs leaned into the window and secured J.R. into the harness. "Look at you now," he said, smiling. "Who would've ever thought you'd be a stockcar driver?"

"Yeah, look at me," J.R. said. "I feel like my hero, Skip Johnson, getting ready to race in Daytona."

"You're much better than Johnson," Hobbs said. "You are J.R. Rentz, the Exterminator, and all those people in the stands love you."

"Let's hope I don't mess that up in the next few minutes."

Hobbs stood back from the car. "You look mighty fine in this car, J.R." He patted the top of the car. "Just remember what Clarence said and you'll do just fine."

J.R. nodded and gave Hobbs a thumb up. "I guess I'll see you later."

"Not later," Hobbs said. "Soon, I'll see you real soon." Hobbs turned toward the sidewalk.

"Hey Richard," J.R. said. Hobbs turned back. "Have you said a prayer for me yet?" he asked.

"No, not yet," Hobbs responded.

"Well don't dally. I still got the butterflies and it ain't getting any better."

"Shoot J.R., the hard part is sitting here talking. Once you start her up and head off the line, you'll start feeling much better."

J.R. thought about that for a moment. "I guess you're right," he said and started the engine. "I expect that prayer," he yelled over the engine noise to Hobbs.

The crowd erupted in a frenzied shout at the sound of the Green Ugly. Banners waved from the stands and rooftops while a final few stragglers hurried off the street.

Inside the Green Ugly, J.R.'s head bobbed with the rhythmic beat of the idle engine. His heart raced and he looked down the narrow path of Main Street where fragile human bodies represented out-of-bounds markers. Heads turned in his direction, straining to get a better view of the legendary car. To J.R., the scene looked like an ocean of human faces.

He applied a white-knuckled grip to the steering wheel and closed his eyes for a quick prayer. With the clutched firmly engaged, J.R. floored the gas and the engine roared with a force that startled the driver. Nearby onlookers took a step back and covered their ears. The windows along Main Street rattled as the explosive noise reverberated off the closely aligned buildings. Like echoes in a deep canyon, the noise built to an ear-splitting crescendo.

J.R. mercifully let off the gas and released his grip on the steering wheel. The noise from the engine left his ears numb and ringing. The crowd yelled but he heard nothing. He looked to Hobbs for help. *Get me out of this death trap,* he wanted to yell.

Clarence rushed out to a frightened J.R. and stuck his head into the driver's compartment. "Aim her straight J.R. and let her go," he said.

"What? I can't hear," J.R. responded.

"Aim her straight and don't hit anybody," Clarence yelled as he pointed down Main Street.

"I don't know if I can," J.R. yelled back.

"She'll go straight if you let her. Now release the clutch and give her gas. It's now or never." He gave J.R. a look as if to say, *if you don't do it, I will.*

J.R. nodded bravely and Clarence hurried back to the sidewalk.

J.R. applied grip to the steering wheel and engaged first gear while the car idled, shaking his head and body. *I feel like I'm tied to a rocket,* he thought to himself. He watched his left leg twitched from holding down the clutch and understood that it was probably the only thing keeping him and others from certain death.

He thanked God for his life and prayed for Hobbs and Dippy. "Watch out after 'em if I should pass," he said to God. "And forgive me if I take out a few of these people that line this street. I didn't put 'em there Lord, so please don't hold it against me. Thank You and Amen."

J.R. looked down the narrow course and feathered the gas. The car tensed and the engine shook with each successive burst of power. Slowly, the Green Ugly inched forward, straining against J.R.'s hold. The crowd looked on with wide-eyed anticipation.

J.R. floored the gas petal and the car responded with an angry howl. He released the clutch and power surged through the engine and drive shaft, commanding the tires to spin. Rubber melted from the rear tires as the car fought to gain traction and for several long moments the Green Ugly shuttered, making slow progress in a thick cloud of black smoke.

Behind the steering wheel, the leisurely progress of the car seemed like a slow-motion dream and J.R. felt a sense of calm before the storm. The sickness in his stomach vanished and for a fleeting moment, J.R relaxed.

But then, in an instant, the tires found purchase and the car exploded from the line. J.R.'s head and shoulders slammed violently against the seat and his hands momentarily lost the steering wheel. Adrenaline surged through his body.

Immediately the engine felt ready to explode and J.R. shifted gears leaving fresh tire marks on the pavement. He caught erratic images of people on both sides of the car, dangerously close, their faces a collection of frenzied screams. When he shifted into third gear the landscape ahead blurred into a collage of bright, indiscernible colors. Panicked and disoriented, J.R closed his eyes and let out a fearful, panic-stricken squeal. "Here I come, Lord. Welcome me home," he yelled. He imagined a light in the distance and thought surely this jaunt down Main Street had turned into a trip to heaven.

Chapter 40

J.R. opened his eyes and found himself on a lonely dirt road with thick pines screaming by on either side. He released the gas petal and the Green Ugly glided to a bumpy stop. The car stalled and J.R. exhaled with a shudder. He pulled off his helmet with quivering hands and released the harness.

The distant cheer of the crowd seemed far and remote. He pulled himself from the driver's seat and leaned, weak-kneed, against the car. Alone in the forest, J.R. rested his forehead on top of the car and thanked God for his life. He contemplated the brutal power of the car and saw it as a small sampling of what awaited him at the race track.

A large pickup truck with a covered trailer sped toward him and Hobbs' truck followed close behind. J.R. lumbered toward the speeding trucks, amazed at the distance he had traveled from town.

The truck pulled to a stop next to J.R. "Shoot, J.R.," Clarence yelled from the driver's seat. "I couldn't have done any better myself."

"Did I hit anyone?"

"No but you traveled a mile down the road. We didn't expect you to go so far. I was beginning to think you were going to race to the track without us," Clarence said.

J.R. smiled tentatively and noticed Bill in the passenger seat. Sally, Aunt Mae and Maggie occupied the back seat.

"You drove her like a pro," Aunt Mae said. "The mark you left was twice as long as Troy Mallard's mark."

"She's powerful," J.R. said, looking back at the Green Ugly.

Hobbs and Dippy ran to J.R.'s side. "You okay?" Hobbs asked. He studied his friend with a concerned look.

"Yeah, just a little shook," he responded. "She's powerful, Richard. You ought to give her a try."

"Not now, boys," Bill called from the passenger seat. "We've got to load up and head out to the track. It's getting late."

A long line of vehicles, flags waving and horns blaring, rumbled down the road from Anna's Mill.

"Here comes the town," Clarence said, looking back at the procession. "I'm gonna pull the trailer up. Richard will help me with the car. J.R., you need to go rest in your truck."

As Dippy and J.R. walked back to Hobbs' truck, fans streamed from their vehicles and swarmed J.R. Men grasped his hand and women hugged his neck, offering their support and expressing hopes of victory. J.R. greeted the town folks warmly and signed autographs. He felt love and acceptance and found strength and resolve in their support.

"You're gonna teach that Mallard boy a lesson tonight," a man shouted from the crowd.

"He'll know not to mess with Anna's Mill after you're finished with him," another said.

"Do your best, J.R.," a woman said.

J.R. smiled and continued to sign autographs until Bill pushed the crowd back so that J.R. could get some peace. As the crowd scampered back into their vehicles, J.R. joined

Dippy in the truck.

"I know you're determined to race but I just got to say that when you went off the line back there it didn't look like you were in complete control of the situation," Dippy said.

J.R. ignored the comment and watched Hobbs and Clarence drive the car onto the trailer.

"I mean the way your head shot-back and your arms flailed about, it's a wonder you made it down the road."

"I'm not sure I want to hear that right now," J.R. said. He looked at Dippy. "You've got a way of sapping my strength."

"I'd hate to sap your strength," Dippy said. "But I'm just saying what I saw."

They sat in silence and watched Clarence secure the Green Ugly. The covered trailer had a double zero emblazed on its side.

"Look," Dippy said facing J.R. "I know you don't have capacity to reason correctly, so I don't blame you for being so bull-headed about racing the car. I blame Richard and the rest of these crazy people for putting thoughts in your head. Believe me J.R., I've had the opportunity to interact with the people in this town and other than a few of them, they're all loony. I just watched a greased pig contest back there that should be outlawed and a political debate that ended with two old fat guys trading punches. I think the town would be a great study model for anthropologists studying primitive peoples and National Geographic needs to send a camera crew to get some pictures."

"I don't know what you're talking about," J.R. said, a confused look on his face.

Dippy looked at J.R. with a pitiful look. After a moment, he reached into his backpack and retrieved a compact disc player. "I burned a CD for you," he said.

"Really?" J.R. asked with a big smile.

"Yeah, I recorded some racing music."

"What's racing music?" J.R. asked, taking the CD player

from Dippy.

"It's music you can listen to when you're racing tonight. It'll get your heart pumping. You know... inspirational music for the race car driver."

"Thanks, Dippy."

"Now that you've decided to race, I thought I'd help out in some way," Dippy said. "I still think you'll end up injured or worse, but at least you'll have some good music to listen to."

They sat in silence and looked out the front window as Clarence closed the trailer and Hobbs scampered into the driver's side seat.

"Dippy made me a CD for the race tonight," J.R. said to Hobbs, holding the player. Hobbs started the truck and looked at Dippy suspiciously. "What kind of music?"

"Heart pumping music," Dippy said.

Hobbs frowned. "I don't think J.R. will need heart pumping music. His heart will be beating fast enough as is."

"I think it's great," J.R. said. "Maybe it's just the thing I need to get me by." He stuffed the CD player into a small bag.

"Yeah, Richard," Dippy said. "I'm just trying to help out and be a team player."

Clarence started forward in his truck and Hobbs followed. Horns blared and flags waved from car windows as the caravan started off, carrying the entire town of Anna's Mill to the Macon Speedway.

Chapter 41

The sun cast one last sliver of sunlight over the horizon and for a moment, it painted a canopy of purples and orange in the Georgia sky. At the Bibb County raceway, generators kicked on and stark overhead lights flickered all along the mile-long oval, setting the stage for a hot Friday night of racing action. Spectators searched out prime seats in the stands and formed long lines at the concessions.

Troy Mallard watched the lights flicker and grow bright. He leaned against his black Monte Carlo at the front of pit row and listened to a radio broadcast through headphones. He wore a black flame-retardant racing suit with two white stripes down the sides and looked up at the large press box in the stands where the broadcast originated.

"Welcome to The Central Georgia Amateur Road Stock Car Championship here at Bibb County Raceway," the broadcaster said. "My name is Tommy Durden and my partner, who will be helping me bring the race to you, is legendary stock car driver, Skip Johnson. Skip, welcome back home to Macon."

"It's an honor, Tommy," Johnson said in a heavy southern accent. "As you know, I grew up on this track and got my start nearly thirty years ago trading paint with Jack

Voyals and other fine drivers. I'm glad to be home and to be with you on this special event."

"And special it is," Tommy Durden announced. "Folks, we've taken a break from Friday night football to bring you this historic event. This championship, affectionately known by the locals as the Redneck One Hundred Mile Dash, is the culmination of the amateur season. Race enthusiasts throughout central Georgia have flocked here to the Bibb County Raceway to celebrate amateur racing. This race is the creme de la creme of amateur racing and has attracted the best drivers and mechanics in the region. It'll provide a forum to test their racing prowess in a winner take all skirmish consisting of thirty rough and ready stock cars, traveling at breakneck speeds. Skip, what are your thoughts?"

Johnson cleared his throat. "Tommy, this year's race garnered special attention when news broke from Anna's Mill that Bill Voyals and his family are returning to the track with their famed Green Ugly. Local newspapers and radio stations have raved over the news and it's the reason that I've returned. The Voyals' have been long-time friends and it cheers my heart that they have decided to return to racing."

"What do you think about this new driver, J.R. Rentz?" Tommy Durden asked. "I hear he's from Valdosta."

"I don't know much about the young man. When I talked to Bill Voyals this week, he was closed mouthed. I read in the newspaper that some have called him *The Exterminator*," Johnson said, chuckling. "Whatever name he goes by, if Bill Voyals has given his blessing, then he must be a fine driver."

Troy Mallard removed his headphones in disgust and chucked them into the seat of his car. Everywhere he went these last few days, people talked of the Voyals' and the Green Ugly. If he heard one more word about J.R. Rentz and the Green Ugly he might go off the deep end. He knew that in the next hour before the race, Tommy Durden and Skip Johnson would talk of nothing else. *What about me?* he wanted to yell at the press box. *What about the three-time returning champion?*

Mallard turned his back on the press box and rested his elbows on top of his car. He looked to the track infield and saw three satellite-laden trucks from local television stations. He knew the press swarmed the track looking for news, he'd seen them with their cameras and press passes. *Has anyone bothered to interview the champ?* he thought to himself. *I'm right here, at the front of pit row and nobody cares.* He knew they were waiting on the Voyals' and the Green Ugly. Once the Voyals' and Rentz showed up at the track, they'd be swarmed by the press. *All that's going to change tonight,* he told himself. He had plans for J.R. Rentz and after tonight, they'd have to interview the boy from a hospital bed.

In the distance he heard a police siren and a dull feeling of trepidation settled in the pit of his stomach. The crowd cheered. He closed his eyes and massaged his temples, trying to control his anger and fear. Outwardly he had told friends he looked forward to racing and beating the Green Ugly but inwardly he feared the car and its drivers. Privately he hoped the Voyals' wouldn't show up for the race. But now, at the sound of the siren, his hopes were dashed.

He chastised himself for allowing fears to creep into his thoughts. He blamed the fears on childhood experiences of watching his father get trounced year after year. "I'm better than my father," he said to himself, girding up his courage. "I've already shown that." He concentrated on the low whine of the siren and told himself to face his fears. He opened his eyes and his face fixed into a stone-cold look of determination. "And I'm better than the Voyals'," he said. He turned and watched as the Green Ugly made its entrance.

Along the main road leading to the track, a single police

escort led a long line of cars and trucks decked out in green banners and huge flags emblazed with double zeros. A truck, directly behind the escort, towed a simple white trailer. The fans of Anna's Mill hung from the line of cars and trucks, cheering wildly. The crowd in the stands also cheered as thirty thousand onlookers welcomed back the Green Ugly.

Mallard looked down the length of pit row and saw drivers and support crews strain their necks for a better view. Some clapped and others looked on with a mixture of respect and foreboding. *They look like little baby lambs about to be slaughtered,* he thought to himself. He'd seen the same look from his father every time the Voyals' and the Green Ugly made their grand entrance.

Mallard scowled and he turned back to the procession. The Dodge truck towing the car entered the track through a chain-linked fence. An old red Ford followed behind. The other vehicles headed for the parking lot with horns blaring. Anna's Mill reserved a whole section for its fans along the front stretch and Mallard knew that in about ten minutes that section was going to come alive with a raucous crowd of Green Ugly supporters.

The trucks drove down to the apron of the track and slowly made their way toward pit row. The crowd waved and cheered as the trucks passed. Mallard saw the withered, old arm of Bill Voyals wave from the passenger seat. As the lead truck approached, he saw Clarence Voyals in the driver's seat. He guessed Rentz and his friends drove the old red Ford.

Mallard stepped away from his car and faced the lead truck as it approached. His was the lead car on pit row and the Voyals' would have to pass to get to their position at the end of the line. *Let them know you're not afraid,* he told himself. He scowled defiantly and crossed his arms. *Let them know they've got a race on their hands.*

The truck slowed and inched passed Mallard.

Clarence met Mallard's challenging stare. "You should've stayed in your cabin," Mallard said.

Clarence eased the truck to a stop. "Count your blessings that I ain't racing tonight," he said. "But we'll meet up soon enough."

Mallard smirked and looked at Bill in the passenger seat. "Did you like my little bonfire last night?"

"Move along, Clarence," Bill said with a stern look at Mallard.

"I'll be seeing you," Clarence said as he pulled away. The truck made its way slowly down pit row. Other drivers shook Clarence's hand as he drove slowly.

As the red Ford approached, Mallard looked for the lanky frame of J.R. Rentz. He found him sitting between his friends, looking straight ahead, avoiding eye contact. The truck inched forward, following the slow procession down pit row. "Hey Mr. Exterminator," Mallard yelled into the open window. "Are you ready to race?" He walked next to the truck, attempting to engage J.R.

Rentz avoided eye contact and looked like a scared little child. The burly driver held out a hand and shoved Mallard away from the truck. "Back off," he threatened and stopped the truck. The big man looked ready to get out of the truck.

"Please keep driving, Richard," Rentz said, pathetically.

"Yeah, Richard, keep driving," Mallard said in a mocking voice. "Pretty please..."

The burly man gave Mallard a threatening stare and started down pit row.

"No worries, Rentz," Mallard yelled. "We'll meet up again on the track."

He watched the trucks head to the end of the line of stock cars. He wondered about J.R. Rentz. The lanky driver looked afraid and timid, yet Bill Voyals had given him the nod. *He must have some skills if he's good enough to race the Green Ugly,* he thought. He told himself not to under-estimate the man; his timid nature might be a ploy.

The Voyals' unloaded their car while J.R. Rentz stood to the side, unsure of himself. Mallard studied the lanky driver and decided that at the first opportunity he'd wreck him. The Green Ugly was the fastest car on the track and even a me-diocre driver could win with her. At the first challenge from Rentz and the Green Ugly, he'd take them out of the race.

Chapter 42

Abbey Atwood walked down pit row, ignoring the stares of drivers and pit crews. Her shoulder-length, blond hair waved slightly in the breeze and her blue eyes sparkled with self-assurance. A clean white racing suit fit snuggly to her athletic build and she deftly side-stepped pit crews as they hurried to get their cars ready to race.

"Girls shouldn't be in racing," a bearded man said as she passed.

Abbey smiled at the insult. A few years ago, as a teenager, she may've been offended but after five years on the amateur circuit she had become accustomed to the barbs.

She recognized a middle-aged driver bent over the open hood of a Ford. "Earl McCoy, I thought they set the age limit at seventy-five. What are you doing racing at the championship?"

Earl looked at Abbey and chuckled at her quip. "Why hello, Abbey," he said. He wiped his hands on a grimy rag. "Where are you positioned?" he asked as she walked past. "Second," she said. "I'm right behind the number thirteen car."

"I wouldn't worry too much about Mallard," Earl said. "The real threat is at the end of the line."

"I'm going down right now to see what all the fuss is about," she said.

"Say hi to your daddy," Earl called after her. "And drop a wrench in the engine of that Green Ugly. It'll give us all a chance."

Abbey waved and continued walking toward the end of the line. She looked across the track to the center grand-stands where a couple thousand Green Ugly fans stood, anxiously waiting for the race to start. A large group of fans danced to a version of *Way Downtown* played by their bluegrass band.

In the twenty-ninth stall, just in front of the Green Ugly, Abbey saw a group of teenage boys working on a 1988 Chevrolet Camaro, painted orange to resemble the Dukes of Hazard car. She guessed the boys knew just enough about the workings of an automobile to be dangerous. Nevertheless, they had qualified for the championships and therefore must have some skills. Abbey chuckled and shook her head when one of the boys asked her for jumper cables.

Abbey stopped at the last stall. Except for the car and a tall, lanky man leaning against it, the area was empty. Spare tires and a large tool chest stood on the other side of the cement barricade but unlike the rest of pit row, the stall was quiet.

The man rested his elbows on the top of the green car and looked up into the grandstands. A dull, black racing suit hung like a curtain on his lean body and fell six inches short in the arms and legs. He fingered straps on a faceless white helmet.

"It looks like you've brought the whole town to cheer you on," Abbey said.

The man straightened and turned to face Abbey. He drew a hand through his wind blown hair and smoothed out the wrinkles in his over-sized suit. Abbey watched, amused, as the man tried to look presentable.

"My name is Abbey," she said and offered her hand.

"J.R.," the man stuttered and smiled. "J.R. Rentz." His hand felt rough from hard labor.

He stood a foot taller than Abbey and had long-thick eye lashes. Dimples formed on his cheeks when he smiled.

"J.R., are you gonna race alone without a pit crew?" she asked. "Most people bring a support crew. Or maybe you're gonna race and exchange tires too," she joked.

J.R. glanced at the empty stall. "Everybody is gone. If you want to talk to Bill, I'm sure he'll be back soon."

"Oh, that's okay," Abbey said. "I don't really know Bill. I know of the Voyals', but I mainly race tracks in north Georgia. I just wanted to come down and see the famous Green Ugly. See what all the fuss is about."

"Oh," J.R. said. He moved out of her view of the car.

She looked at him curiously, standing several yards away and trying to blend in with the shadows. Most men in the pits were loud and braggadocios, all too willing to impress her with their wit and bravado.

"You're painfully shy," she said. "That's unusual on a race track."

He looked at Abbey and she noticed his eyes were green and pleasant.

"I'm sorry but I didn't expect to see a girl racer," he said. "I'm useless around pretty girls. Dippy says it's a curse I have."

Abbey chuckled at his honesty and her face flushed. She turned and looked at the car. "Tell Dippy it ain't a curse. Some girls like the tall and quiet type." She smiled at her bold remark. *Let him chew on that thought for a while,* she thought to herself. A little flirting with the competition always worked to her advantage.

Abbey appraised the car and wondered if it was as good as everyone insisted. *How much of the talk was fanciful?*

She asked herself. She knew Troy Mallard and a few other drivers in the top five were serious competitors. But this man, J.R., didn't seem to have the feisty spirit of a race car driver.

"Say, J.R.," she said, turning in his direction. J.R. stood closer than before, smiling at her, dimples and all. She looked into his eyes, momentarily struck by his good looks and calm demeanor.

She smiled back at him. "You said you're useless around pretty girls," she said with a mischievous smile. "I wonder if that rule extends to the race track. Are you going to freeze up when a pretty girl passes you on the track?"

"I don't know; I ain't ever raced before."

She looked at him with a surprised look. "Never?" She wondered what genius decided to put a novice in the Green Ugly.

"I mean against a girl," he said, quickly correcting himself. "I ain't ever raced against a girl." He looked away uncomfortably as if hiding a secret. He avoided eye contact and stared off into the distance and she considered his misfit race suit and worn tennis shoes. He looked and acted like a normal guy off the street, not the menacing Exterminator that everyone fretted over. She suddenly had many questions.

"Why are you here, J.R.?" She knew she shouldn't pry but J.R. seemed so out of place. Several thousand people cheered his name and in minutes, he'd strap into the most revered stockcar in Georgia amateur racing. Everyone with a radio in Central Georgia knew of J.R. Rentz and the Green Ugly, yet here he stood; an ill-equipped novice with no support crew to tend to his needs.

He gave her a confused look as if his presence at the track was obvious.

"Call it a woman's intuition but everything about you says that you don't belong," she said. "I'm sorry to be so blunt but you ain't a stockcar driver."

Initially J.R. didn't respond. He looked at Abbey, dumbfounded. He searched the crowd on pit row as if looking for help. "Richard and Dippy should be back any moment," he said, changing the subject. "I don't know why it's taking them so long to find a few extra engine backup parts for repairs."

Her competitive zeal gave way to concern. A kind and timid man like J.R. didn't belong on a race track. *He'll get eaten alive out there,* she thought. *Especially if he's going to drive a marked car like the Green Ugly.* She knew the drivers in this race and any number of them would consider it the highlight of their career if they could knock out the Green Ugly.

"You've never raced before, have you, J.R.?"

J.R. looked at Abbey with resignation on his face. She got the feeling that J.R. didn't lie very well. *That's a good quality in a man,* she thought.

"They say the Green Ugly is the fastest car on the track," he said. "Who knows, maybe I'll get lucky. Besides, Bill and Clarence want me to race, and see all those people in the stands?" he said, pointing to the rowdy crowd. "They want me to race too."

That's fine, but do you want to race? She wanted to ask. She could tell there was more to the story, but it would do no good to pry further. The distraught look on J.R.'s face told her that she had pried too much already.

"Pass on the outside," she said helpfully.

"Excuse me?" J.R. said.

"If you're determined to race, I might as well give you a few tidbits of advice."

J.R.'s face lightened up. "Yeah, I need all the help I can get."

"Okay, then pass on the outside. Even if you must slow down to let the slower cars move low, you should always pass on the outside. That's the best piece of advice for a new driver."

J.R. nodded his head in appreciation. "Okay, what else?" he asked, eager for more information.

"Well, you're seated in last place. That's good for a rookie driver because you'll not be crowded from behind. Take your time in the back of the pack to feel out the track; find a good line. As the pack thins out, let the slower cars come to you. Most of these boys will hug the inside of the track and so you'll have the outside when you're ready to pass. Your car is fast enough to pass on the outside all night long."

"Okay," J.R. said, staring at Abbey intently. Abbey couldn't believe she was advising the competition, particularly since the competition, in this case, had the fastest car on the track.

"You're driving the Green Ugly, J.R. Most of the drivers will stay clear and let you pass. But there's a few of them that will give you trouble."

Abbey paused, realizing that she was one of the few who intended to give the Green Ugly a run for her money. Breaking that piece of news to J.R. didn't seem right at the moment.

"Troy Mallard is driving the number 13 car." She said. "You should try to be around him as little as possible because he's a dirty driver. And then there's Keith Roth. He's is in the number 52 car and while he's a good driver, he gets ornery toward the end of the race; he'll nudge you if you get too close. Terry Anderson in the number 19 car is usually very safe but he's young and sometimes he takes dangerous risks."

"So, Keith Roth is in the number 52 car?" J.R. asked for clarification.

"Yes," Abbey responded. She looked at the teenage boys in the next stall. "Of course, I'd cast a wary eye at the Dukes of Hazard over there," she said, nodding. The boys finally acquired jumper cables and started the car.

They exchanged high-fives. "People like that are the most dangerous. It's best to just let them crash and take a yellow flag."

"Okay," J.R. said. "I got it."

Abbey watched J.R. as he looked down pit row searching out his main competitors. Somewhere toward the front of the line was her car, the number 24.

"I've got one more piece of useful information for you, J.R."

J.R. looked at her expectantly.

"You should stay clear of cars driven by pretty girls," she said with a playful smile. "I know how you are around pretty girls; we wouldn't want you to freeze up and crash into the wall, would we?"

J.R. laughed and Abbey sensed that the laugh revealed his true and gentle nature. She extended her hand and he took it with both of his. "Good luck, J.R." she said.

"Thank you so much for everything. I'll definitely watch out for pretty girls out there."

She smiled and started off toward her car.

"Abbey," he said to her. She turned. "Maybe I'll see you later after the race?"

"I'd like that, J.R.," she said as two men, one large and one small, walked up and stood next to J.R. They studied her with a quizzical look, as if she was from outer space.

Abbey walked down pit row as the drivers were called to their cars. She wondered if she'd see J.R. during the race and more importantly, she hoped to see him after.

Thoughts of J.R. vanished when she passed Keith Roth. He eyed her and nodded, placing a helmet over his head. A wicked smile crossed his lips.

It's race time, Abbey. She put her game face on and hurried to her pit stall where her father and brothers eagerly waved for her.

Chapter 43

"Who's the pretty girl, Romeo?" Dippy asked. He stood next to J.R. and watched Abbey walk toward the front of pit row.

"Her name is Abbey," J.R. said. "She's pretty ain't she, Richard?"

"Well, yeah. Why was she down here talking to you?"

"I guess she wanted to see the Green Ugly but ended up giving me advice." They watched until Abbey was lost in the crowd. "I think she likes me. She said she likes the tall and quiet type."

Dippy snorted.

"I can't stop thinking about her."

Hobbs gave J.R. a disapproving glance. "You better stop thinking about her. You've got a race to run. Here," he said, handing J.R. his goggles, "put these on."

J.R. placed the goggles over his head as Clarence, Sally, and Bill hurried toward the stall. "It's race time," Bill said excitedly and clapped his hands. The area suddenly swarmed with activity as more people filtered toward the pits. Someone placed a helmet on J.R.'s head. He spied drivers scurry into their cars along the line. Engines fired up and choked out all other sounds.

J.R. felt like a steer prodded toward the slaughter house as hands directed him toward the open window of the Green Ugly. The opening looked like a gapping black hole from which no mortal should venture. Even if he wanted to quit the race, there was no turning back now. He let himself be hoisted through the hole.

Hobbs stuck his head and arms into the car and harnessed J.R. to the seat. "Are you still thinking about that girl?" Hobbs asked.

J.R. shook his head *no* and swallowed hard, looking down the long line of mean looking cars. His body felt glued to the seat. A trickle of sweat ran down his brow and cheek.

Hobbs switched the ignition and the Green Ugly came to life. J.R. grasped the steering wheel of the 3,500-pound beast and felt the vibrations of its powerful engine. He saw that the sleeves of his ill-fitted suit barely passed his elbow. *What am I doing,* he thought to himself *Abbey's right, I don't belong.* He had barely survived the drag through Anna's Mill, how could he think he'd survive one hundred miles of frantic racing?

Gaseous vapors emanated from the hood of his car, casting a distorted view of the orange car in front. Skid marks scarred the dirty-brown surface of the track and retainer wall. A long smear of red paint marked the spot where a car had crashed into the wall.

J.R. wondered if he'd contribute a splash of green to the wall tonight.

Drivers to the front revved their engines to the delight of the crowd. J.R. saw the Anna's Mill section come alive with a flurry of waving green flags and pom-poms. *God, help me,* he thought. *Help me out of this trap.* He struggled against the restraints, hyperventilating. Hobbs placed a steady hand on his chest.

"Be calm," Hobbs said. He returned J.R.'s terror-stricken gaze with steady composure. "Breathe slowly."

"I'm scared, Richard. I don't know if I can do it."

Hobbs smiled. "That ain't you talking, J.R. It's fear. And if you quit now, you'll kick yourself for the rest of your life."

J.R. looked deep into his friend's eyes, searching them for the strength he needed.

"It's almost time, Richard," Clarence said behind Hobbs.

"You've faced down worse than this," Hobbs said and J.R. thought of his troubled childhood. Richard had helped him through his fears then and J.R. believed in him now.

J.R. returned his gaze to the line of cars to his front. The pit crews retreated behind the retainer wall and the cars waited to move out.

"Water," he said.

Hobbs squirted a mouthful of water into his mouth and J.R. swallowed. Hobbs hugged J.R.'s neck. "Be safe," he whispered into his ear and then he was gone.

Clarence attached the window mesh and pounded the top of the car for luck.

J.R. looked to the Anna's Mill section of the stands. The entire town focused their attention to the back of the line where their prized car waited. The cars to the front had gone idle, as they waited to head off onto the track. J.R. engaged the clutch and powered down on the gas. The engine roared like a lion and thirty thousand people stood and cheered wildly. The sound of their car threw the Anna's Mill section into a pitched frenzy. J.R. smiled and waved as pit crews looked to the rear of the line with looks of concern.

A flag dropped and the long line of cars began to make their way down pit row and onto the track. J.R. placed the Green Ugly into gear and looked one last time to Hobbs. With a reassuring nod from his friend, J.R. released the clutch and eased her down pit row toward the track.

Chapter 44

Abbey eased her 2001 Camaro beside the number 13 Monte Carlo as two lines formed for the warm up laps. Mallard wore a mirror tinted face mask and when he turned in her direction, Abbey saw a reflection of her car; white with orange lettering. She imagined a smirk behind the mask and smiled when Mallard took his hand off the steering wheel and lifted his middle finger at her.

Loads of class, Troy, she thought.

Mallard forced Abbey's car high in turn two. *Easy, Troy, it's just warm ups.* She watched the wall close in and slowed to prevent from nicking it. Keith Roth crowded her back bumper, pushing her to stay with Mallard. The race hadn't even started yet and the boys were already sending her none too subtle messages. *You're with the big boys now, little girl,* they were saying, *and you don't belong.*

"We'll just see about that," she said to herself. She moved alongside Mallard again and wagged a finger. She rounded another turn and headed onto the front stretch for another warm up lap. *Two more laps and all hell will break loose.*

When they passed the Anna's Mill section of the stands, Mallard raised his middle finger and was greeted with a chorus of derision.

Abbey reminded herself not to back down from Mallard when the race heated up. The last time she faced him, on a dirt track up in Dalton, she backed down from his aggressive antics and ended up lost in the pack. Troy was a gritty competitor and if he could bang and block other drivers in full view of the officials without being penalized, then he had a method and skill that Abbey had to respect. The key, in her mind, was to stand up to him and hand him some of his own medicine.

She kept her left front panel steady with the Monte Carlo's right rear panel, just far enough back to stay in Mallard's blind spot. Keith Roth nudged her from behind, but Abbey intended to stay right where she was; at least until the green flag dropped.

Her muscles tensed as she and Mallard led parallel lines of cars around the final turn and approached the starting line. *Okay girl, it's race time.* Abbey sensed, but did not hear, the roar of the crowd. She accelerated with Mallard and the roar of thirty engines increased into an incessant whine.

Forty, fifty, sixty miles per hour, the cars screamed in unison in a well-scripted rush to the green flag. In quick, steady motions, Abbey shifted gears, commanding the car to surge forward. She adjusted her speed to that of the pole sitter and then waited, her senses placed on high alert for any untoward movements of the black car that traveled mere inches from her left side panel. The green flag fell, and Mallard veered hard into her space. Abbey anticipated the move and drove high on the track and adroitly tucked herself behind Troy while at the same time fending off other cars that bit savagely at her heels like a pack of wild dogs. *Second place is good,* she thought, *for now.*

She sensed the race shaping up to be a wild and crazy affair and in case Troy thought that she would back down at the slightest intimidation, she floored her car into his back bumper. Troy momentarily lost control but recovered expertly and continued in his front position. Abbey was keeping score and now Troy knew it.

The lights of the track glared down on the Green Ugly as it slowly traversed the paved oval. J.R. looked past the lights and caught glimpses of twinkling stars. He smelled fried hamburgers and barbeque and was surprised that he didn't smell motor oil and gasoline. The Green Ugly behaved well, responding to J.R.'s directions; moving right and left, slowing and accelerating. *So far, so good,* he thought to himself with relief.

He carefully worked around another turn and saw the two lines of cars enter the turn on the opposite end of the track. He knew he should've kept pace but navigating the one-mile oval, even at slow speeds, seemed challenging enough. *Pick up speed,* he told himself and he lightly applied the gas.

He passed the Anna's Mill section of the stands and heard the crowd yelling for him to catch up. If he couldn't even keep pace during the warm-up laps, he wondered how he was going to keep up when the race started.

He entered the final lap of warms up and noticed Dippy's CD player on the floor next to his seat. Wires from the player extended up his chest and under his helmet. He realized that Dippy must've placed the plugs into his ears during the confusion before the race. *I could use some inspirational music just about now,* he thought. Perhaps a fast beat might give him the nerve to push the Green Ugly faster. Some high-tempo bluegrass Banjo picking from the likes of Earl Scruggs might do just the trick.

The constant beat of the car engine grated on his nerves. He reached for the player, fumbled with it for a moment, and pushed the play button. He listened to the silent lag at the beginning of the CD and entered turn one, accelerating.

Of course, Dippy hadn't said that Earl Scruggs' banjo would be picking in his compilation of "inspirational" music. The Soggy Bottom Boys would be okay too even though they sometimes sang songs that made J.R. sad. Any foot-stomping tune would do, he figured.

As J.R. maneuvered the Green Ugly onto the back-stretch, he heard the distant echo of an electric guitar and frowned. He hated electric guitars and the head-banging bands that played them. If played loud enough, rock music made his brain vibrate, clearly a sensation to be avoided. The brief notes of the guitar diminished and then came back stronger than before. *This ain't even Country music,* he realized. He sensed an ominous and dark mood in the sound of the guitar. Like an approaching, slow-moving thunderstorm, the intermittent and increasing wail of the echoing guitar clouded J.R.'s thoughts. He envisioned a dark presence approaching, slowly working its way from the CD player into his mind. He reached for the player, meaning to turn the volume dial to zero. He found the dial with his thumb and turned it to its limit. The volume increased fully and a fiendish human howl filled his ears. J.R. gritted his teeth at the assault, dropped the CD player, and involuntarily mashed the accelerator to the floor. The car drove high into the third turn, glanced off the fourth, and screamed toward the starting line at a blistering pace.

The two drivers at the end of the pace line looked into their rear-view mirrors with horror as the legendary Green Ugly descended upon them like a wild banshee. They glanced at their speedometers and realized that sixty miles per hour would do them no good against a car traveling well over one hundred. With little room for three-wide racing, they braced for impact.

Chapter 45

"Lord Jesus, save us all!" Aunt Mae exclaimed as she stood on the front row of the stands and watched J.R. and the Green Ugly tear down the front stretch toward the starting line.

"What's J.R. doing?" she asked Martha Baker who stood nearby.

"Well Mae, I guess he plans on passing the whole pack before he gets to turn one. If he keeps up that pace, he'll lap them other boys ten times," Martha said as the Green Ugly flew by and threw dust into her hair. "I wonder if there is a mercy rule in racing."

Aunt Mae had never seen anything like it and the crowd stood in awe-struck silence as the Green Ugly rear-ended the Dukes of Hazard in a terrific collision that caused even the most hardened and blood thirstiest of fans to shiver. The rear tires of the orange car lifted two feet into the air. The car shuddered and made a beeline for the infield wall.

The Green Ugly lurched forward, it's front-end mangled. The car looked as if it might roll to a stop on the track apron. But it suddenly accelerated, leaving fresh tire marks on the pavement.

"Now we know why they call that boy The Exterminator,"

Martha Baker said to Aunt Mae. "I guess he plans on taking them out one by one."

After regaining consciousness, J.R. vaguely remembered a flash of orange and the sound of impact. He'd seen the underside of the orange car and the muffler coming unhitched and slapping the frame like loose shutters in a storm. The images came to him like fragmented and unrelated scenes of a movie.

Like a bad after-taste, the lingering stars slowly faded and J.R. turned to see an orange, twisted mass resting in a cloud of dust next to the inside wall. A trickle of blood ran from a nostril and he tasted it in his mouth; wondering why the surface of the track looked deep blue and wavy, like the ocean. *Where's my hearing,* he thought. Colorful images on the outside wall attracted his attention and he studied them with unfocused eyes. Beyond the wall he noticed movement and slowly the faces of onlookers came into focus. *Why are they staring at me? Where am I?*

He felt pain and looked down at his hands. They rested on his lap and one knuckle looked misplaced. He lifted his right hand, studying the odd protrusion and recognized the steering wheel. *A car,* he thought, *I'm in a car.* He grasped the wheel and looked out the front window, *not an ocean,* he realized, *but a race track.*

He mashed the accelerator and his head slammed against the seat rest. The black path veered to the left and he navigated a turn. On the backstretch, he saw cars in the distance. *I'm in a race,* he realized. The front end of his car looked turned up and slightly twisted to the right. *Double zeros on a green hood; the colors of the Anna's Mill car, the Green Ugly.* "My God, I'm racing the Green Ugly." The fog in his mind cleared and he pushed the car high into a turn, realizing that he was still deaf. He remembered the collision and hoped the teenager in the orange car was not hurt badly.

As J.R. pulled onto the front stretch and passed the wrecked Dukes of Hazard car, he became aware of a rhythmic, low-pitched beat on the fringe of his senses. *Thank God, my hearing's coming back. Strange though,* he thought, *that the car engine sounds kind of like the beat of drums and the high-pitched howl of guitars. The collision must have messed up the suspension.* His hearing hadn't returned fully and so it was difficult to assess the real problem. If it got much worse, he'd have Richard check out the damage.

Even with the messed up front end and strange noise, the car seemed to behave well. He pulled the car onto the backstretch and noticed he'd closed distance on the pack.

He drove high into the turn and passed a yellow car. The noise still nagged him, it was getting louder. He frowned. The noise flitted in his ears like a pesky mosquito but with increased intensity, like the approach of a powerful locomotive. In horror, he remembered the CD player and felt the wires pressed into his ears. He frantically looked to the floor, searching for the player. He saw it protruding from under the seat and reached for it. As he fumbled with the box, his hearing returned, and the wailing guitar slammed into his brain like a jack hammer. Now, a high-pitched vocalist screamed into his ears and J.R. gritted his teeth. He dropped the box. The muscles in his body twitched and tensed into a conglomeration of knots. His foot found the floor once more and the Green Ugly shot forward like a bat out of hell.

"*Welcome to the jungle We've got fun 'n' games,*" the song screeched into his ears.

A baby-blue car swerved high to escape the oncoming green car. J.R. ignored the empty space below the car and quickly found a left rear bumper, sending the car into the wall in a shower of sparks that reminded J.R. of a multicolored fireworks display.

"If you got the money, honey. We got your disease," the singer yelled again.

J.R. pushed the Green Ugly in a random line, traveling low on the apron and then shooting wide to send up sparks along the wall. Competitors, sensing danger, avoided the erratic car; they went high, they drove low, and some slowed. Only the truly terrified drivers attempted to out run her. The yellow caution flag fluttered vigorously from the official's stand.

J.R. shouted at a red and white Dodge Charger to get out of the way. He saw the terrified look of the driver's eyes in the rearview mirror just before executing a bump and run maneuver that left the Charger spinning down the center of the track in a cloud of black smoke.

Yet still, the song played on, grating on his nerves and causing his teeth to grind. *"Watch it bring you to your Knees, knees,"* it exclaimed.

J.R. marveled at the stupidity of other drivers that attempted to out run the Green Ugly. *Don't they know I've no control of the car?* He bounced off a wall and careened into the side of a Ford Taurus, vaguely aware that the impact forced the Taurus into stacks of tires at the entrance to the pits. Tires scattered into the pits and onto the track. Pit crews ran away from the carnage.

"I wanna watch you bleed," the singer yelled into his ears.

God help me, he prayed. The incessant beat of drums and evil crooning consumed every fiber in J.R.'s being. His brain shook and rattled and a pathetic, whining sound emanated from his throat as another competitor was forced from the track. Still the music played on.

Chapter 46

"This is your fault, Richard," Dippy screamed while Hobbs watched the Green Ugly speed past the pit area, tires bouncing in its wake. "You should never have allowed that dim wit to drive on this track or any other track. He's going to end up killing himself and we'll be lucky if he doesn't take a couple people with him."

Dippy hid behind the cement retainer wall and yelled at Hobbs from a distance.

When the Green Ugly drove past the pit area, support crews stepped back in case J.R. should decide to veer their way.

"What possessed you to think that you and J.R. could fix up that car to race?" Dippy yelled. "Are you crazy? Did you think that J.R. could somehow win this race? Oh yeah, that's a great idea," he said sarcastically. "Let's put J.R. behind the wheel of a racecar, even though he's never driven before, and then watch him win some money so that we can buy tickets to the Atlanta infield. What a joke."

Hobbs ignored Dippy and watched the Green Ugly careen around the track. He wondered what was going inside J.R.'s mind. *Surely, he's frightened beyond comprehension,* Hobbs thought to himself. He hoped the track officials would stop gawking at the ugly scene and call an end to it by pulling the Green Ugly from the race.

As Dippy continued his tirade, Hobbs thought of Bill and Clarence Voyals and Anna's Mill. The town folk seemed bewildered as they watched from the stands. Some shook their heads in disgrace and others shook angry fists. Bill Voyals had shown kindness to Hobbs and J.R. *and now look how we've repaid that kindness,* he thought bitterly. In just five short minutes, J.R. had managed to tear down a racing dynasty that had taken three decades to build.

Clarence and Bill looked somber and refused to look in Hobbs' direction; *no doubt, too polite to show their disgust.* In the end, no matter how awful it got, Hobbs knew that Bill would put a positive spin on the disaster; he'd likely pat J.R. on the shoulder and say, "good try."

"You screwed up, man," Dippy yelled again from behind the wall as cars roared by. "You and J.R. screwed up big time. And after all Bill's done for us, it's a crime what you've done."

Hobbs turned to see the head official, Levi Cassel, approach with a black flag in his hand. "I'm gonna have to black flag your driver, Bill," Levi said. "I was willing to overlook the first couple of times that he knocked off other drivers but now I see a definite pattern. He'll have to be penalized a lap."

"Only a lap?" Bill Voyals responded. "I wish you'd disqualify him so that he doesn't cause any more damage."

Levi shook his head. "The fans have been waiting a long time to see the Green Ugly race," he said. "Let's get your boy in here and calm him down. If he don't shape up after a rest period, I'll pull him."

Levi climb over the pit wall and walk bravely onto the track apron, traffic screaming passed. When the Green Ugly rounded the fourth turn and headed down the straightaway, Levi pointed at J.R. and waved the black flag vigorously.

The Green Ugly clipped the wall and shot into the pits causing panicked crews to dive for cover.

J.R. skidded sideways and halted next to Hobbs.

"Make the noise stop," J.R. pleaded through the netted window. Hobbs released the net and looked into J.R.'s terrified face. Dried blood smeared from his noise and lip to his left cheek, windblown in large, crusty droplets. His eyes pleaded for help.

"You tried to kill me!" someone yelled close to Hobbs. The intruder pushed Hobbs to the side and grabbed J.R. by the neck. Hobbs gripped the man's ear and forced his face to the tarmac. He recognized the intruder as the teenaged driver of the Dukes of Hazard car. The boy howled in pain as Hobbs applied a vise grip and twisted, feeling cartilage crackle and pop. Hobbs lifted the boy by the ear and held him under his arm like a sack of grain. He turned and saw an angry mob of injured drivers and pit crews, gathered like vultures to pick at whatever remained of J.R. He dropped the boy to his knees and kicked his rear end until the boy scampered into the mob.

Hobbs marched to the mob, picking up a large wrench. *They'll lay their grimy hands on J.R over my dead body,* he thought. "Move out," Hobbs bellowed. The mob dispersed over the retainer wall and cursed J.R. from a distance.

Hobbs dropped the wrench and hurried back to the car. Clarence bent over J.R. and when Hobbs approached, he turned from the car window clutching wires and a CD box.

"He got spooked by music coming from this player," Clarence said. Hobbs placed the ear phone close to his ear and winced. *No wonder he was out of control,* he thought.

He grabbed the box from Clarence and turned to Dippy. The CD player shattered into pieces at Dippy's feet. "I guess that's yours, Dippy," Hobbs said and ran to the car.

"It was the music," J.R. said to Hobbs. "It made me crazy. I hope I haven't caused too much trouble."

Hobbs squirted water into J.R.'s mouth and washed off the caked blood on his face. "You *have* caused trouble," Hobbs said, trying to control his temper. He wanted to pull his friend from the car and make a run for it before the angry mob regrouped. "You've been black-flagged, and the race is over for you." Hobbs started to unbuckle the safety harness.

J.R. wrestled his hands away. "I'm still in the race," J.R. shouted. "I got black-flagged. That's a one lap penalty."

"Get out of the car," Hobbs demanded angrily, stepping back from the car.

J.R. grasped the steering wheel with his good hand and looked to the official blocking his way onto the track. He revved the engine and the official waved his hands. "Not yet," the man yelled.

Bill stood next to Hobbs. "It's probably best that you get out of the car," he said to J.R.

A tear ran down J.R.'s cheek as he grasped the wheel with his injured and swollen hand. Hobbs had not seen the injury before. The knuckle on his pinky finger looked like it had been pushed to the side of his hand.

Clarence pushed between Hobbs and Bill and attached the net to the window. "That boy's mind is made up," Clarence said to Hobbs, "and there ain't nothing to do but let him see this through."

Bill and Clarence retreated as J.R. revved the car once more. Hobbs bent low to peer through the net at his friend. A sick, helpless feeling came over Hobbs as he watched tears stream down J.R.'s face. Despite the tears, J.R. looked determined.

The official waved J.R. through and the Green Ugly sprinted to the track in cloud of burnt tire rubber.

Dippy approached Hobbs. "I was only trying to help," he said pitifully. Hobbs ignored the attempted apology and watched, stone-faced, as J.R. picked up speed into the first turn. On the backstretch, J.R. held a straight line and drove low into the far turn. He braked for traffic to clear and accelerated passed two cars on the front stretch. As the Green Ugly flew by the pit area, Hobbs thought he saw J.R. shoot a thumbs up in his direction. *Keep that up, J.R.,* Hobbs thought with a thin smile.

He walked to the retainer wall and stood next to Clarence and Bill. "He's a brave man," Clarence said as he watched the Green Ugly pass another car on the high end of the track.

"I've never realized as much until just now," Hobbs said.

"He shouldn't drive with that hand," Bill said. "It ain't good for a driver to race in so much pain."

The Green Ugly made another pass in front of the pits, faster than before. The car eased low into the turn and coasted as traffic cleared. J.R. accelerated and passed four cars in a bunch.

"There's nothing to be done, Bill," Hobbs said. "Pain or no pain, J.R. is determined to finish the race."

The Anna's Mill section cheered wildly as J.R. passed. The Green Ugly was back on track and perhaps the town could salvage some level of respect before the night ended.

Chapter 47

From her second-place position, Abbey studied every line of the black Monte Carlo. From her vantage, Mallard guarded the inside line like a jealous lover, even in the turns, he forced his car low and to the inside.

Abbey followed Mallard early in the race, figuring he knew the fastest line. But as the race progressed, and she and Mallard pulled away from the field, Abbey began to experiment. She learned, for instance, that turns three and four banked sharply and allowed a fast-outside line. So fast, in fact, that Abbey found herself coasting to keep from passing Mallard.

She could take the lead at any time, but Abbey saw no need to hurry. She liked having the Monte Carlo in her sights. Occasionally she bumped Mallard for good measure. *In five more laps, I'm going to take you, Troy,* she thought to herself as she coasted once again on the far turn. She allowed Mallard to pull ahead and placed her Camaro on his bumper. *In five more laps, I'm not coasting off the turn, and it'll be adios amigo and see you at the Winners Circle.*

She passed the Anna's Mill section of the stands and her thoughts drifted to J.R. She worried for his safety, especially since he'd been involved in so many wrecks. The black flag he'd received was warranted and Abbey breathed a sigh of relief when she saw the Green Ugly in the pits. She hoped J.R. was safe and secure off the track but didn't know for certain since the Green Ugly had left the pits on her second go around. Possibly, the car had been taken into the infield for repairs.

Dropping a lap in a one-hundred-mile race was a death sentence and she suspected that not even the famed Green Ugly could recover from such a deficit. She wished J.R. no ill will but there's no charity on a race track; not even for a good guy. She liked to think he watched the race from the infield, cheering her on. *That's a safe enough place for him.*

A small piece of debris hit her windshield, startling her. *Get your mind back on the race,* she chastised herself. *I can't believe I'm thinking about a boy in the middle of a race.*

She followed Mallard low into a turn and passed two slower cars on the front stretch. A loud roar came from the Anna's Mill section of the stands, causing Abbey to check her mirror. *Was it a wreck?* She saw slow traffic in her mirror and several other cars ahead but nothing out of sorts. The roar from the crowd intensified as she passed the main stands, drowning out the sound of her engine. Fans stomped to bluegrass and large green flags pumped back and forth in the air. *Something got them fired up and it ain't a wreck because the officials ain't signaling.*

She took another turn and glanced back toward the far side, searching but finding nothing. When she passed the pit area, Abbey sought out her father and brothers hoping they might give a signal. But they ignored her and strained their necks, looking back at the far turn. *Thanks a lot, guys,* she thought bitterly.

Other pit crews also watched the far turn. *Something*

is going on back there, she thought, checking her mirror. She hated not knowing and sensed a threat. Her heart rate increased.

Get your mind on the race, she told herself again. *There's nothing you can do about it anyway.* Her preoccupation cost her two car lengths on the Monto Carlo. She accelerated but found it difficult to catch up; Mallard had picked up speed. She pushed her car faster, flooring the accelerator. With the crowd noise and increased speed, Abbey suddenly found herself in a frenzied race.

Her car struggled but slowly closed the distance. She realized that Mallard had been playing possum. He'd purposefully held his car back but now went full out, pushing his car to its limit. For over sixty miles he'd let Abbey bump and nudge him from behind and then suddenly he begins to sprint when he hears the crowd noise. It made no sense to Abbey. *He's running from something,* she thought, *but what? Not me, I've been here all along.*

She followed Mallard to the outside and he nearly clipped the backstretch wall. *He's taking more risks now,* she thought. *He's running faster and to the outside.* In a desperate and dangerous move, the Monte Carlo cut off a slower car and squeezed inside another. Abbey gritted her teeth and followed, taking the turn low and hard. She swung high on the front stretch and found herself bumper to bumper with Mallard.

Abbey sensed the race retreating from her grasp. Moments ago, it felt like a cake-walk and suddenly all hell broke loose. Mallard had come to race after all and if she didn't act now, it might be too late. *It's time to pass and get this race back under control,* she thought. Whatever Mallard was running from could wait; she had a sticky piece of driving ahead.

Like a lioness hunting prey, Abbey's heart pounded with anticipation. She gritted her teeth and pushed on the accelerator until she felt the petal might break through the floor board. Her bumper pushed on the Monte Carlo and she prepared to pass. The frenzied crowd noise increased. *This feels like the last lap of the race,* she thought, *and there's still thirty-five more to go.* She held her breath. The car deviated from the cautious line and swung high into the turn. She risked losing control and slamming into the wall. Colorful logos rushed passed. She leaned hard against the turn, concentrating on the center of the track, and praying that her tires held firm. *Too fast,* she thought. The Camaro's right panel nicked the wall and the car shot down onto the front stretch.

The Monte Carlo met her left panel and Abbey prepared for a rough ride. The two cars tore down the stretch, racing side by side and trading paint. For Abbey, the turns ahead loomed large. With a dangerous driver like Mallard, she had no intention of racing side by side into the turn. She veered and pushed the Monte Carlo toward the track apron, hoping to draw a response. Mallard recovered and came after Abbey, veering toward her. Abbey acted quickly, touching the brakes and driving low and behind the black car.

Mallard gave up the inside and Abbey took it, placing her front end at Mallard's left rear panel. She took the turn low and Mallard found Abbey's rear bumper on the straightaway. The pass was well made, and Abbey breathed a sigh of relief. *Now you have to pass me on the outside,* she thought, looking in the mirror as Mallard banged his steering wheel in frustration.

The black car nudged her twice more and then fell back a few car lengths. The race seemed under control once more. Abbey knew it would heat up again toward the end but for now she intended to take a breather and keep a wary eye on Mallard. The two cars were equally matched, and she knew another pass would be difficult.

Movement in the mirror caught her attention. The Monte Carlo veered from her sight in a sudden and awkward move toward the outside. *Are you trying to pass me already, Troy?* She thought. *You'll have to try better than that, you've got no speed.* The car veered back into her mirror again. Surprisingly, it had dropped further behind. *That's strange,* she thought. She wondered if he'd popped a tire. *No, that didn't make sense; he would've pulled off the track.* Again, the black car veered hard to the outside. To Abbey it looked like Mallard was up to his dirty tricks again, trying to block another driver and racing hard. When she looked again, Abbey caught the movement of another car, barely perceivable as it glanced briefly in the rearview mirror.

It must be Roth, she thought with surprise. Somehow, he'd crawled back into the race and now she had two cars to deal with. The crowd noise had not let up and Abbey realized they had been cheering for Roth as he made his run. *Unbelievable, if it's not one thing, it's another.* She mashed her accelerator and smiled, remembering why she loved this sport so much. *Here we go again, so much for my breather.*

She took a turn and accelerated toward the Anna's Mill section of the stands. It was pure bedlam as fans jumped up and down. All along the track people screamed and Abbey wondered when Keith Roth had become such a crowd favorite. She glanced at the pit and saw her crew waving wildly, urging her faster. *I'm going as fast as I can,* she wanted to scream.

She saw Mallard's black car in her mirror, several car lengths behind. Apparently, Mallard had failed in blocking Roth's progress and now Abbey felt the other car just off her right rear panel and traveling fast; unbelievably fast. She turned, expecting to see Roth's red car in her rear window. Instead, she saw a flash of green.

"*Green?*" She turned her head to the track and drove

low into the turn. The driver of the green car matched her speed and entered the backstretch even with Abbey. When she turned again, she saw the wide-eyed smile of J.R. Rentz, saluting her from inside the Green Ugly.

"J.R.?" she asked with confusion.

J.R. pumped his fist as if pulling a train whistle and then zoomed by. Abbey sat dumbfounded as she watched the Green Ugly grow smaller as it sped away.

Lord have mercy, that's a fast car, she thought.

She read the back panel of the car as it drove off; *Pride of Anna's Mill.* "I guess so."

The crowd cheered and Abbey chuckled to herself, thinking of the goofy look on J.R.'s face when he passed.

Chapter 48

"Look at him go!" Bill exclaimed, slapping Hobbs on the back. "Yee Haw, Go J.R., go!" Hobbs smiled, pride for J.R. welling up. He watched the Green Ugly scream around the far turn and onto the front stretch.

"Is J.R. winning?" Dippy asked Hobbs loudly. Traffic zoomed passed the pits and Hobbs could feel the hot breeze rush by.

"No," Hobbs responded. "He was a lap down. Now he's made up the penalty lap and he's on the same lap as the leaders. If he can catch up and pass them in the next thirty-five miles, then he's the winner."

"It'll be a close call," Clarence said over the noise. He clicked a stopwatch in his hand as J.R. sped by. He checked the time and wrote briefly in a notebook, comparing the speeds of the front runners with J.R.'s speed. "At the pace he's setting, he's got a slim chance."

"Look at the fans, Clarence," Bill shouted. The old man pointed to the stands, his eyes sparkling. "They've gone hog-wild. It's just like the old times when your Daddy raced."

Hobbs wished J.R. could see the celebration in the stands. The town folks celebrated with wild abandonment and Hobbs suspected their ruckus could be heard for miles.

Young and old, they pounded and shook the grand-stands, taking to the aisles for a wild dance.

"No, it's better than that," Clarence said to Bill loudly as more cars rushed by. "The Green Ugly's been gone too long. They're just making up for lost time."

Hobbs looked at Clarence and remembered the grumpy recluse who only a few days ago made every effort to keep the Green Ugly from racing. *J.R. did that,* he thought to himself.

The Green Ugly flew by again and Hobbs watched the lanky frame of his friend working her controls. He mar-veled at J.R. Rentz, his friend, and a man who could bare-ly solve a sixth-grade crossword puzzle; yet here he was, driving for the lead, and in the process, bringing joy to a down-and-out small town and smoothing over the deep emotional wounds of a divided family.

He followed J.R.'s path down the back straightaway and thought of the pain he must be enduring. He didn't doubt J.R.'s hand had swollen to twice its size, yet his friend con-tinued to race. The hopes of an entire town rested on J.R.'s boney shoulders, yet he continued to push the car hard, ignoring the pain.

You're a winner no matter what, Hobbs thought as he watched J.R. come off a turn.

J.R.'s misfit helmet sat slightly askew and his head bounced as the car traveled over a slight bump. Hobbs chuckled at the sight.

Another bug splattered and its yellow guts flowed up the windshield in a thick, gooey streak. Debris from the track and bug juice covered his windshield and J.R. fig-ured it'd be completely covered in another fifty miles or so.

He looked past the bug juice and concentrated on the turn ahead, driving high and passing a brown Impala.

He passed the pits and saw Clarence holding up a marker board signaling fifteen laps to go and 27 seconds behind the leader. *Thank God,* he thought. His hand throbbed and the heat coming from under the seat was almost unbearable. He looked forward to pulling into the pits for a tall glass of cool water and an ice pack. *They might as well splash some water on my backend to put the fire out back there,* he thought.

The time differential between him and the leaders had dropped considerably. However, J.R. could not be certain where he stood on the track. Occasionally he caught sight of Abbey's white car but there were several white cars in the race, and he couldn't be certain which one led.

He decelerated into a turn and realized that his driving had become routine. Cars moved out of his way and other than the tricky piece of business to pass Mallard's Monte Carlo, he rarely deviated from his line of travel. He marked the oval by the Coca-Cola sign in turn one and the blue paint marks on the backstretch wall. Like the passage of time and the rising of the sun; he counted on the landmarks at each go around.

He liked seeing the surprised look on Abbey's face when he passed her and was glad to see her in first place, in front of Mallard. If J.R. couldn't win, he hoped Abbey did. She'd been kind and helpful and by the tattered look of her car, she battled fiercely with Mallard. Of course, Mallard's car looked just as bad and J.R. suspected Abbey gave as good as she got. *Keep it up, Abbey,* he thought, searching the other side of the track, *only fifteen laps to go.*

He passed the main stands and heard the Anna's Mill contingent chanting his name. When he passed the pit area, Richard held a marker board that read *Good Pace! Keep it Up*. J.R. liked the written messages of his pit crew. They gave him encouragement.

Earlier in the race Dippy held a sign that simply said, *sorry,* in big black letters. He meant to give his small, grumpy friend a big hug at the end of the race.

J.R. took a turn and headed onto the backstretch. The fans all along the track picked up the Anna's Mill chant and he heard his name shouted by thirty thousand people. Like a comforting hand on his shoulder, the fans urged him forward toward the finish line. He pushed his helmet on straight and hunkered down for the next ten or so miles.

The Green Ugly still felt powerful. To J.R., it seemed like the car desired to be at the front of the pack. She wanted to catch the front runners. J.R. pushed further on the accelerator and the Green Ugly responded, soaring passed two cars and heading for the lead. The front runners came into sight in the distance and then took the far turn. *Go! Go! Go,* the marker board read. J.R. took a turn and now the Monte Carlo and Camaro were closer than before. He had them in his sight.

Chapter 49

Abbey felt fatigued by miles of relentless jostling with Mallard. Like a pesky horse fly, he buzzed in and out, taking small pieces of flesh at each pass. He latched onto her back bumper and pushed, punched, and bullied her to give up her front position. Abbey responded by using every trick in the book to block his progress; moving left and right to match his efforts while at the same time pushing her car to gain some distance. She weaved through traffic, looking for the fastest line, yet she could not shake him.

Jolted once again by rear end contact, Abbey grimaced, and her arm muscles ached with every shaking move. With frayed nerves, she passed the pits with three laps remaining. Abbey knew her car had reached its limit. She felt the erratic vibration of the steering wheel and saw small wisps of smoke drifting from the hood; the needle on the temperature gauge pointed firmly in the red zone. She had never pushed a car so hard and over the last several miles, as Mallard picked up speed, she came to realize her car was primed for the picking. Unless she blocked his advance, the Monte Carlo would surely pass. She reminded herself to remain professional when the pass came. She'd do what she could to block it, but if it was meant to be, she had no intention of causing a bush-league wreck.

With two laps remaining, Abbey passed a slower car and saw an open track ahead. *Not good.* The passing lanes were open. Abbey checked her rearview mirror and as Mallard veered to the right, Abbey matched the move. *I can't block him for two whole laps,* she thought to herself. She braced for rear end impact, but Mallard feinted to the inside and when Abbey moved low to block, the Monte Carlo accelerated to her outside panel. *Well, that's it,* she thought, *he's going for the pass.*

Mallard pulled even with her into the turn and the two cars banked high. When they came to the backstretch, Abbey turned to see Mallard's head turn in her direction. His mirrored face shield revealed a battered white car, blackened and dented by numerous collisions with the Monte Carlo; black fluid from the hood flowed over the door panel in small streams.

Make the pass, why don't you? Abbey thought. *You've beaten me half to pieces.*

Instead, Mallard stayed even, looking at her and no doubt gloating, Abbey thought. Sparks streamed from the Monte Carlo's rear and she saw a small piece of metal from the undercarriage dragging on the pavement. On further inspection, Mallard's car looked as battered as Abbey's. The back end looked slightly turned up and white paint steaks covered his door. She'd not realized the punishment she'd dished out and she found comfort in the fact that he was likely as worn-out as she.

He can't pass me, she realized as they drove into a turn side-by-side and then lumbered down the front stretch. *His car's just as bad off as mine.* Hope for victory welled up as the white flag dropped, signaling one lap to go. The crowd stood, cheering as the two cars entered the first turn. Abbey pushed hard on the accelerator, summoning the last burst of speed from her car. Mallard responded and the two cars fought neck and neck onto the backstretch. The path ahead remained clear and the cars howled and surged forward like two battle-hardened warriors, giving everything to gain a few inches of the lead.

Abbey caught movement in her mirror and looked up to see the Green Ugly in the distance but approaching at a fast clip. The car traversed several car lengths in a matter of seconds and for a moment Abbey had the frightening thought that the car might open its mangled front end and gobble her whole. Its movement under the sparse lighting looked sporadic like the strobe lights of a horror movie and Abbey could feel the vibrations of its growling engine. The Green Ugly approached to within centimeters of her back bumper, exhaling hot embers of fumes.

The goofy smile on J.R.'s face was gone, replaced by a serious and determined glare. J.R. looked to her car and then shifted his gaze to Mallard. *He's looking for a way to pass,* Abbey thought. J.R. ran up behind Mallard and bumped his rear end, causing more sparks. Mallard looked in his mirror, intently studying J.R.'s movement. The Green Ugly moved back and forth like a caged animal and finally it reappeared in her rear-view mirror. J.R. looked frustrated, almost resigned. The far turn approached and the Green Ugly's way to the lead was blocked.

Sorry J.R., Abbey thought as she started into turn three, *there ain't no room.*

Abbey ignored the menacing presence to her rear, and with the crowd cheering wildly, she concentrated on the last half mile. On the final turn, the Monte Carlo surged forward as Mallard made his move toward victory. The Camaro sputtered when Abbey attempted to match Mallard's speed and she sat helpless as he pulled away on the turn. *He's used me to block the Green Ugly and has saved his speed for a final push,* Abbey thought. She pounded her steering wheel in frustration. "Go car, go," she yelled.

Surprisingly, Abbey felt a jolt of speed and her car

accelerated onto the final stretch. She passed Mallard and ran into the lead. Confused at the sudden burst of speed, she looked at her controls. Finding nothing, she checked her rearview mirror and saw the Green Ugly nestled onto her bumper and pushing hard.

She hooted and hollered with exhilaration. The finish line approached, and with J.R. pushing her into the lead, no one could catch her. *I gonna win,* she thought, *I'm gonna win.* She blew a kiss to J.R. and screamed with delight.

She saw J.R. wave at her in the mirror; and then, Troy Mallard crashed into the left side of the Green Ugly. To Abbey it seemed like a huge black hand had swatted J.R. and his car into the infield grass.

She turned to see the Green Ugly speeding over the grassy infield, throwing thick clouds of dirt into the air and coming dangerously close to the retainer wall. J.R. recovered and charged back onto the track, colliding with the outer wall and bouncing into the center of the track where Mallard was waiting to finish the job. In vivid colors, textures and rapid movements, Mallard accelerated and rammed the Green Ugly. Blows from the Monte Carlo sent sparks of black and green into the air. Shards of green metal from J.R.'s car erupted from contact with the wall. Abbey watched horrified at the violent, rag doll movement of J.R.'s body behind the steering wheel.

The sight in her rear-view mirror sickened Abbey as Mallard battered J.R.'s car mercilessly. Steam erupted from the Green Ugly and hot black smoke billowed from its exhaust. Amazingly J.R. maintained control of the car and aimed it toward the finish line. But still, Mallard waited. He lined up his car to deliver the final blow.

Later, Abbey would remember the final embrace between the two cars as dance-like. As Mallard drove his car at the Green Ugly, J.R. slowed and veered his left forward bumper into Troy's right-rear panel and the cars performed a pirouette. Her view became obscured in a thick cloud of smoke and Abbey caught split second glimpses of the Green Ugly and the black Monte Carlo as they spun out of control. After several violent collisions, the Monte Carlo suddenly erupted from the billowing smoke and tumbled onto the infield grass. The smoke parted and the Green Ugly emerged to the thunderous applause of the fans.

Abbey crossed the finish line and like a wounded warrior, the Green Ugly limped to second place.

Chapter 50

Hobbs watched the Green Ugly coast off the track and onto pit row. He remembered how the car once looked; pristine and shiny, surrounded by trophies and old photographs; impressive but useless, like a museum exhibit. Hobbs preferred the look of her now; dented, gnarled and well used.

The car sputtered to a stop, too exhausted to go one foot further. Like a sad sigh, the engine exhaled and died.

J.R. squeezed the last drop from her, Hobbs thought. He reached into the window and gave J.R. a hearty hug. "You've done good," he exclaimed, extracting J.R.'s helmet. "You've done real good." Hobbs noticed J.R.'s mangled right hand, resting in his lap.

"I didn't win," J.R. said with disappointment.

"First place don't matter," Hobbs said. "You did better than anyone expected."

"Hey, Richard?" J.R. said, pulling the safety harness from his shoulders.

"Yeah?" Hobbs said, watching a large crowd of Green Ugly supporters gather around the car. They chanted J.R.'s name.

"My butts on fire," J.R. said. "I'd sure like to get out of this car and get some fresh air on my britches."

"The Doc has to tend that hand too," Hobbs said and helped his friend from the car. When J.R. landed on his feet, Bill Voyals reached up and placed his hands on J.R.'s cheeks, pulling him close to speak. The crowd noise drowned out Bill's words and Hobbs figured it was probably right that only J.R. could hear what was said. Bill's moistened eyes and quivering lips revealed a deeply appreciative old man. After a while, Bill hugged J.R.'s neck and then reached into his pocket for a handkerchief.

"You made us proud," Clarence said, patting J.R. on the shoulder. He raised J.R.'s left arm into the air and turned to the crowd.

J.R. smiled modestly as spectators applauded and cheered. Some attempted to raise him on their shoulders but Hobbs thwarted the attempt, claiming J.R.'s hand was too badly damaged. Hobbs called for the doctor.

As the doctor weaved through the crowd toward them, J.R. searched the crowd. Finding Dippy Jordan crammed between two large men, J.R. pushed forward, his broken hand held high. Hobbs followed, attempting to make a path.

"We've got to get that hand tended," Hobbs yelled as fans prodded at J.R., patting him on the shoulders and offering their congratulations. J.R. reached into the crowd, extracting Dippy by the collar. "You can't hide from me," J.R. said to Dippy in a reproachful tone.

"I was only trying to help," Dippy protested. "I didn't mean no harm."

J.R. looked at Dippy with a stem face that gradually softened. "There's no harm done and so there's no need to hide either," he said with a smile. "Come here." J.R. pulled Dippy into a bear hug. "And you said I couldn't race," he said with an arm around Dippy's shoulder and a broad smile across his face.

"Well, you didn't win, did you?" Dippy responded quickly.

Always the pessimist, Hobbs thought to himself

"You got beat by a girl," Dippy added.

"Ain't nothing wrong with that," J.R. said. "Especially when she's as nice as Abbey, ain't that right Richard?"

The doctor arrived and cared for J.R.'s hand. He wrapped it with a cold pack and administered pain medicine. Surgery would be called for, the doctor said. He provided directions to a hospital with a strict warning to J.R. that he should get to it as soon as possible.

Clarence approached and whispered into J.R.'s ear. It was time pick up the prize money.

Chapter 51

Hobbs, Dippy and Clarence escorted J.R. to the awards ceremony at the administrative trailer. J.R. walked on shaky legs and occasionally leaned on Hobbs for support.

"Twenty-five hundred dollars should do the trick," Dippy said.

"That amount ought to get you into the Atlanta race," Clarence agreed. "It'll leave you with some spending money to boot."

J.R. had almost forgotten about the professional race in Atlanta. *Had it only been five days since they first arrived in Anna's Mill?* It seemed much longer; so much had happened. He felt emotionally and physically drained and a weekend at the races would go a long way toward recuperation.

They walked down an infield service road toward several double-wide trailers. J.R. liked being away from the crowd in the pits. It gave him the opportunity to stretch his weary bones and to breathe in the cool October night air.

As they approached, J.R. noticed a large contingent of drivers and support crew gathered under a generator-powered overhead light, next to the trailer. He heard angry shouts from the crowd and Hobbs stopped the group short and listened.

"I reckon those drivers up there won't be too happy to see J.R." Hobbs said. "He caused a lot of them to wreck and it's likely they're protesting J.R.'s second place finish."

"Well, we've got pick up our money," Dippy said. "You'll have to fight 'em off, Richard."

"I know a back way," Clarence said. The small group walked through a maintenance yard and came upon the trailer from the rear. Clarence tried the back door and knocked when he found it locked. A baldheaded official answered and greeted Clarence. The official allowed J.R. to enter but the others were told to walk around the trailer and join the crowd out front.

"I'll be on the front row, J.R. Don't worry about a thing," J.R. heard Hobbs say as he was escorted into the trailer. The official closed the door and locked it. "I ain't ever seen a mob that's as angry as the one waiting for you out front," the official said.

The poorly lit trailer contained several paper-strewn desks and racing posters decorated its walls. J.R. followed the official to the front door. Loud and angry voices came from the other side and J.R. felt like he was about to be thrown to the lions.

"If I were you," the official said, holding the door knob, "I'd get the money and skedaddle. I'd not look back either. Don't get me wrong, you raced well towards the end of the race. But at the beginning, you made enough enemies to last a lifetime."

J.R. thought of the adorning fans at the pits. He wished some of them would've showed up for the awards. *I've walked several hundred yards and have gone from hero to villain in the process,* he thought to himself.

When the official opened the door, the angry crowd fell quiet. J.R. saw their angry faces and felt like running out the back door. Then Abbey stepped into his view. She smiled and took his hand, leading him out onto a metal landing. Four steps, running parallel to the trailer, led from the landing to the ground and Abbey directed J.R. to the step below the platform. The third-place driver stood on a lower step; the man nodded as J.R. took his second-place position on the platform.

Someone cursed J.R. from the crowd. He looked at his feet, praying that someone would hand over the money, and quick.

"Thanks for that extra push at the end, J.R.," Abbey said. He turned and looked at Abbey's smiling face. Even though she stood on the top landing, J.R. stood slightly taller. He heard more curses and now angry shouts from the crowd made him grimace. "Don't worry about them," Abbey said. She leaned into his shoulder and kissed his cheek.

"They're just jealous."

Levi Cassel, the head official, stood between the crowd and the stairs. In one hand he carried a sawed-off broom stick, twirling it like a cop on the beat. "I make up the rules here," Levi exclaimed defiantly.. "Mind your manners, all of you. I won't stand for no driver revolt at my track."

The teenaged driver of the Dukes of Hazard car emerged from the crowd and addressed Levi. A large wad of blood-stained gauze covered his right ear. "I've got a complaint against your second-place finisher," the boy said loudly for all to hear. He pointed an accusing finger at J.R.

Levi lowered the blow horn and J.R. could see angry, pulsing veins emerge on his forehead. The official held the broomstick firmly, as if ready to strike. "I don't take complaints, boy," he said, trying to control his anger. "I ain't even got a complaint box so back off before you force me to commit child abuse."

"He back-ended me," the boy complained in a squealing voice. He looked at J.R. with hatred in his eyes. "I didn't even get to the starting line and you back-ended me. I ain't gonna let you get away with it neither." The boy rushed at

J.R. but a large hand grabbed his collar and threw him, rag doll-like, back into the crowd.

Hobbs released the boy's collar and engaged the mob with a critical eye. *No one could calm a crowd like Richard,* J.R. thought.

The boy stood up holding his neck. He looked at Hobbs with a hurt look and slithered away into the mass of people.

"Take that as a lesson," Levi spoke to the crowd through his blow horn. "Even if you're able to get passed this burly fellow up front, you'll have to contend with me, so it ain't even worth a try." He paused to stare down several cantankerous drivers.

"First place goes to Abbey Atwood," Levi called out. A smattering of applause came from the assembled as Levi stood on the ground and extended a money order to Abbey.

"That was a beautiful piece of driving, Abbey," Levi said with a smile. "You can race here anytime you want."

Abbey stuffed the five-thousand-dollar money order into a pocket and waved to her father in the back of the crowd.

"Second place goes to... "

"Levi, it ain't fair," one of the drivers in the front called out. "The Green Ugly should have been disqualified after the first lap. You're just playing favorites. If it had been any other car, you'd have kick them off the track."

"I make up the rules here," Levi exclaimed defiantly.

"You're just interested in the money, that's all you're interested in," said a grease stained mechanic. "The Green Ugly brings in a crowd and that's why you're playing favorites. It ain't fair."

"If I want to sell hotdogs, that's my business," Levi retorted.

Several angry men objected to Levi's reasoning and shouted objections. J.R. imagined a posse stringing him up to the nearest tree. He eyed the prize money in Levi's hand and wished the man would drop the formalities and just hand over the cash. He wanted to high-tail it.

As if reading J.R.'s thoughts, Levi extended the money to J.R. "You ought to get going," he said. "I can't hold 'em off for long."

J.R. grabbed the money order and stuffed it into his pocket. Abbey took his good hand and pulled him into the trailer. They ran, hand in hand, through the back door and into the shadows of the maintenance yard; Abbey laughing and J.R. looking over his shoulder. He heard the thunder of Levi's voice over the plaintive clamor of the mob. J.R. hoped Levi held off the posse long enough for him to have a few minutes with Abbey. After that, he wanted to escape to Atlanta with his buddies.

Chapter 52

J.R. and Abbey rounded an abandoned trailer and ran through a dark field to a cluster of garages. They skirted a stack of old tires and found a darkened corner in which to hide. A Coca-Cola vending machine hummed close by and gave off a red glow. In the distance, J.R. heard sounds of automobiles and the distant clamor of voices.

Slumping into sitting positions, their backs against the cement wall of a deserted garage, they huffed and puffed and shook their heads at the absurdity of it all. Abbey retrieved her hand from J.R.'s and hugged her knees. *She looks beautiful,* J.R. thought to himself. Even with the dirt and grime of the track covering her face, she still looks beautiful. Tears of joy and laughter revealed streaks of white skin under the dirt and she looked at him with raccoon eyes where her goggles had stamped their impression. The skin around her eyes looked puffy as if she'd just awaken and although her eyes were slightly **blood** shot, J.R. had never seen blue eyes so striking. They seemed to shoot right through him.

A lock of blond hair covered her mouth and she regarded J.R. for a moment. With a puff of breath, she blew the lock of hair and it fell upon her neck. "Why did you do it?"

she asked with a smile.

"Do what?" J.R. replied with a curious look. He breathed heavily and his heart pounded like a jack hammer. He knew the thump and rhythm of his heart had nothing to do with the moderately strenuous sprint through the infield.

"You know what I'm talking about," Abbey said. She shifted positions and rested her shoulder against the wall, her body and full attention directed at J.R. "You helped me win the race. Why?"

J.R. looked away modestly. He felt a stuttering spell coming on. She looked so pretty, so awesome and so... *interested in me!* He could tell she liked him by the way she searched his eyes; could feel it even as she studied his profile. *Hold it together,* J.R. commanded himself. He started to respond and then swallowed the words, his heart pumping. *It's no use,* he thought, *I'm just no good around a girl like Abbey.* He wished his friends would come to his rescue. *And how pathetic is that?*

"You're not going to stutter now, J.R.," Abbey commanded. "You can't. Not after what you've done for me and not after what we've just been through."

J.R. looked toward Abbey. He found something in her face that gave him courage. "Like I said before the race," he said, looking away. "I'm no use around pretty girls."

"You can't use the same line twice to pick up a girl," Abbey said with a playful smile.

"I didn't even know that was a pick-up line," J.R. said. He turned to her and smiled. "Did it work?"

"Sure, it did. But you can't to use it twice," she said with mocked sternness. "That line is reserved for me."

J.R. chuckled. "Okay, I promise not to use it again." Abbey made him feel relaxed. She was so easy to talk to.

"You know J.R., you had me fooled," Abbey said. "All along I was thinking you were a timid guy. Kind of like a victim, helpless and all. But then on the track, when you drove up on me with the Green Ugly, I saw stone-cold determination on your face."

J.R. fidgeted and looked away, uncomfortable at the complement. After a few moments, he looked back at her.

"You come off shy and timid but under that modest exterior you've got strength," she said, her eyes penetrating his like laser beams.

"My friend Richard is strong," J.R. said. "I don't guess I'm very strong compared to Richard."

"There's more to strength and bravery than pure muscle, J.R."

J.R. wondered where this conversation was going. He'd never met a girl like Abbey; someone full of compliments and unafraid to speak her mind.

"After the race, my father told me what you did for the Voyals' and how you helped Clarence to get back on his feet. It's a wonderful thing you did. You had no experience in racing, yet you crawled into that car and put your safety at risk to help a desperate man. I'd call that a strong and brave thing to do. I bet that even your friend Richard wouldn't have had the guts."

J.R. remembered the fright he was under during the race. He hadn't thought he'd been particularly brave. *Naive, sure, but brave?*

"I guess I wasn't strong enough because I got bested tonight," J.R. said, smiling at Abbey.

"Well of course you were bested, you were racing against me, weren't you?" Abbey said with a cock-sure tone. She smiled and took his wounded hand in hers. "Does it hurt badly?" she asked, applying tender strokes.

"The doctor gave me pain medicine and it's taken the edge off."

She held his hand for a moment and then placed it back into his lap. "I want to thank you for helping me tonight," she said.

"Well, you were kind to me earlier," J.R. said. "Besides, you would've won without my help."

"We both know that ain't true," she said.

"Troy Mallard had nothing left," J.R. said. "You would've taken him on the last stretch."

"Maybe you're right about that and during the race I thought his car was faster," she said. "But his car wasn't the fastest car on the final stretch." She looked at him with an intense gaze. "I've been reviewing the final stretch in my mind," she said, "and it's occurred to me that when you pushed me forward, you created a space. You could've passed, but you didn't."

J.R. couldn't peel his gaze from her hypnotic eyes.

"You didn't pass because you wanted me to win," she said. "When you hung back, you exposed yourself to Mallard. I get the feeling you go through life without a thought for yourself. I'm afraid with that attitude you'll never become a great race car driver."

J.R. chuckled. "Well, I guess I'll just have to live with that deficiency and leave the racing to the pros."

They sat in silence for several moments; him, looking into the dark night and she, looking at his profile. "You're a breath of fresh air," she said finally. "You're brave and modest. And your friends must think you're the best guy in the whole world."

J.R. turned and held her gaze, unafraid to look away. He needed someone like this; someone to build his confidence and someone with compassion. He wanted this new friendship. He wanted to nurture it and grow it and see what it might become.

J.R heard someone walking rapidly toward them. "Stand up, Rentz," a harsh voice in the darkness commanded.

Abbey responded to the intruder's voice without hesitation. She bolted to her feet and stepped bravely into the darkness, toward the oncoming footsteps.

Chapter 53

Troy Mallard pushed Abbey aside with his shoulder and grabbed J.R. by the collar, pinning him against the wall. Blotches of dried blood caked his lip and chin. His recently broken nose stood at an odd angle with ugly purple bruises and his black jacket opened to reveal a bony chest, sparsely populated with long, sweaty hair. Blood-shot eyes peered out from puffy black circles and his breath reeked of recently consumed alcohol.

"You wrecked me," Troy growled at J.R. "You totaled my car and broke my nose." A disgusting crackling sound accompanied every word as the loose cartilage and bone in his nose grated against each other. He spoke with a nasal tone.

"Leave him alone, Troy," Abbey yelled. "I'm the one that beat you. If you want a fight, pick on me." She struggled against one of Mallard's friends who held her by the arms.

"Oh, I'll get to you Abbey," Troy said, looking back at her with hate-filled eyes. "I promise you'll receive my undivided attention after I deal with Mr. Exterminator here." He handed a bottle of whiskey off to his friend and placed his forearm across J.R.'s neck. He leaned his weight into the cement wall, cutting off J.R.'s windpipe.

J.R. struggled against the hold, clawing at Mallard's forearm and catching quick gasps of oxygen.

"How's that feel?" Troy sneered.

J.R. hoped that his last moments on earth were not spent looking at the distorted and hatred-filled face of Troy Mallard. Shades of yellow and brown began to appear at the periphery of his fading vision and pinpoint sized stars danced around like pixies in a midnight dream.

"Stop," Abbey yelled. She broke free and attacked Mallard's hold on J.R.

With one hand, Mallard grabbed a fistful of hair and threw Abbey backward. She tripped and hit the pavement like a one hundred and twenty-pound bag of flour.

Seeing Abbey thrown to the ground like a rag doll brought the fight out of J.R. He punched Mallard in the ribs with his good hand and forced the thumb of his damaged hand into his left eye. Mallard grunted in pain and grabbed J.R.'s bandaged hand, slamming it against the cement wall. Waves of pain washed through J.R. and his knees buckled.

Mallard grabbed J.R.'s neck and formed a fist, ready to strike.

Suddenly, Richard Hobbs appeared, and grabbed Mallard's wrist. He pulled him from J.R. and Mallard swung at Hobbs with his free fist. A beefy hand quickly engulfed his fist and Troy Mallard found himself face to face with Hobbs.

"Hi, Troy," Hobbs said. He held Mallard's wrists like a parent restraining an irate child. Mallard's face grew pale and he struggled to break free of the hold. He watched his companion slither away into the darkness. "Let me go," he yelled.

"Unfortunately, you've been making some poor decisions recently," Hobbs said. "First you run over Bill with your car, then you burned all of Bill's old cars and now you're trying to beat up my buddy; poor choices, Troy." Hobbs took Troy's fist and thumped it against his nose. To J.R., the blow looked comical except that Troy's broken nose had already been splintered into a crooked mass.

Mallard cried out in pain, tears streaming down his face. He kicked Hobbs in the knee. "Let go of me," he yelled and cursed.

"That nose looks like a red radish," Dippy Jordan said, standing on the tips of his toes to get a better look. "Lord have mercy, it's pulsating." He recoiled with a look of revulsion.

Mallard spat blood from his mouth and regarded Dippy. No doubt, he felt like a pinned frog in a high school dissection pan. He cursed again with a raspy voice, his face red with anger. Every time Mallard's mouth moved, J.R. heard crackling noises, not unlike the snap, crackle, pop of his breakfast cereal.

"Save your breath," Dippy said with a painful look on his face. "Don't talk, it hurts just watching."

J.R. knelt next to Abbey and helped her to her feet, cradling his mangled hand next to his chest. Abbey brushed off her pant legs, found Mallard and marched toward him with fists clenched.

"Now hold on, Abbey," Mallard said, showing fear for the first time. He attempted to step back but Hobbs held him in place.

"I wasn't gonna hurt you," Mallard said.

Abbey bounded forward and in one swift motion, delivered a straight legged kick to his groin, lifting Mallard and inch off the ground. The blow made Hobbs and Dippy wince.

"Damn, Abbey," Mallard croaked. His eyes rolled in his head and his body went slack.

Hobbs broke Mallard's fall and eased him to the ground gently.

Hobbs looked up to Abbey, an astonished look on his face. She stared down at Troy's motionless body. "He was hurting J.R. and he threw me on the ground," she said defensively. "Nobody treats me like that."

"I guess not," Hobbs managed to say.

"Should we call an ambulance?" Dippy asked. Mallard lay face down; his rear-end sticking up in the air. He blew small puffs of dust from the ground at each exhale. Dippy leaned down and checked Mallard's pulse. "His heart is still ticking," he said.

"He's breathing too," Hobbs said, standing and regarding Mallard with pity. "I guess he'll recover. Come on, let's get out of here."

Troy Mallard felt cool gravel against his cheek, vaguely aware of the tingling pain in his midsection. He felt no great desire to move. In fact, he had an overwhelming desire to remain exactly where he was, with his face in the gravel and his rear sticking up in the air. The last thing he saw before blacking out again was Hobbs' truck as it sped away. He hoped that he would never again be unfortunate enough to meet up with Hobbs and his gang. Most importantly, he vowed never to race on the same track as Abbey Atwood; she was tougher than nails and didn't fight fair.

Chapter 54

The overhead lights of the track went dark as Hobbs drove along an infield service road toward the lighted pit area. On the far end of the pits, Hobbs saw a small gathering of fans around the Green Ugly while several track employees and a few straggling drivers busied themselves with stowing equipment and cleaning up trash. The dark and deserted grand stands gave the race track an eerie, lonely feel.

Abbey's father and brothers waited patiently for Abbey next to their van and car trailer. When Hobbs pulled to a stop, Abbey's father opened the passenger side door. "I was worried," he said to Abbey. Abbey sat between Hobbs and J.R. while Dippy tried to stay comfortable in the back of the truck with the camping supplies.

"I'm fine, Daddy," Abbey said. She and J.R. got out of the truck. "I want a few minutes with J.R.," she said to her father.

While Abbey and J.R. walked a short distance away for privacy, Dippy jumped into the passenger seat. "There's no comfortable ride to be found back there," he said to Hobbs. "It's getting cold and it's awfully late. If we don't get up to Atlanta soon, we'll have to pull off and sleep in a rest stop."

"We've got to get J.R. to the hospital first," Hobbs said.

"After that we'll head up to the track. We'll strike camp by midnight or soon after." He watched Abbey and J.R. talking. She handed him a piece of paper and J.R. stuffed it into his pocket. He'd seen J.R. stammer and freeze up around girls and it occurred to Hobbs that Abbey must make him feel comfortable and at ease. They laughed and Abbey leaned against him and placed a goodbye kiss on his cheek. Even in the darkness, he saw J.R. blush.

J.R. turned and walked back to the truck with a big, goofy smile of his face. Hobbs wondered how J.R. would respond to a love interest. With a girl like Abbey, Hobbs knew that J.R. couldn't go too wrong.

"Get in Romeo," Dippy said, holding the door for J.R.

J.R. crawled into the truck and Hobbs drove slowly toward the small gathering of friends at the far end of the pits, next to the Green Ugly.

"So, did you get her phone number?" Dippy asked.

"She gave me her address too," J.R. said. He pulled out a piece of paper and handed it to Dippy. "We plan on meeting next weekend for a date," he said to Hobbs. "She's says there's a race on her local track and she wants me to help out in the pits."

"Well, since the last pro race of the season is tomorrow, I guess you'll be free," Hobbs said.

"You're invited too," J.R. said to Hobbs.

"That's a good thing since you ain't got a ride," he responded. "What about Dippy?"

"Count me out," Dippy said. "After tomorrow, I'm gonna take a break from racing."

The comment did not surprise Hobbs. For two years, they had traversed the country several times with Dippy and had made life long memories. Dippy tolerated the hard living because professional racing provided a challenge for his analytical mind. Hobbs would sorely miss his grumpy friend.

"What's next for you, Dippy?" Hobbs asked.

"I don't have plans past tomorrow," he said.

"Well, perhaps we'll partner up again next year when the race season starts up again," Hobbs said.

Dippy remained silent. "Maybe," he said eventually.

Hobbs pulled to a stop next to the retainer wall, opposite the Green Ugly. Voyals family members and close friends waited close by.

"First thing, first," Hobbs said, turning the truck off. "Let's say our goodbyes and then we'll head off to the hospital."

Hobbs pulled himself from the truck. He straddled the retainer wall and walked with Dippy and J.R. toward the small group. The entire Voyals clan walked toward them with warm, welcoming faces. Bill and Aunt Mae led the pack, followed closely by Clarence, Sally and Maggie, holding hands. Bobby Lee Reynolds approached with his wife; Reeves Carter brought up the rear. Hobbs recognized several other close friends; *all good people,* he thought.

The family looked complete; they looked happy and fulfilled and for a brief instant, Hobbs thought of Clarence's father, Jack. He wondered if Jack Voyals still lived. *If he did live,* Hobbs thought, *he was missing out on a good thing.*

"We need to head off," Hobbs said to Bill. "We've got to stop by the hospital before we drive to the race track in Atlanta."

Bill passed up the hand shake Hobbs offered and hugged the big man with frail arms. Hobbs welcomed the gesture and gently patted Bill's shoulder. The old man felt fragile in Hobbs' burly arms.

"Thank you," Bill said. "Thank you for all you've done."

Hobbs held the embrace for a moment and then turned to Aunt Mae and squeezed her tight. "You take care of J.R.," she said. To Hobbs, it felt like a demand.

"Yes ma'am," he responded.

Sally Voyals embraced J.R. while her husband, Clarence, patted him on the shoulder; *a perfect image of a grateful*

---

man. Reeves exchanged contact information with Dippy and for several minutes, Hobbs and his friends exchanged goodbye's to dear friends who, only a few days earlier, were complete strangers.

"We ought to be leaving," Hobbs said finally. Aunt Mae came forward with a picnic basket full of food that looked like it could feed an elephant. "For the ride up to Atlanta," she said.

"Did you include an apple pie?" Dippy said, practically salivating over the basket.

"Of course," Aunt Mae said. "And there's a sampling of biscuits and gravy too. But mind you, it's only a sampling. You'll have to come back to Anna's Mill for more. We've got an endless supply and you're always welcome."

"Thank you, Aunt Mae," Dippy said as he rummaged through the basket, cataloging its contents.

"That reminds me," Clarence said. He held his sleepy-eyed daughter in his arms. "If you're still interested in jobs, you'll be interested to know that I'm looking for a few good mechanics. We plan on an increase in business now that the Green Ugly is racing again."

J.R. turned to Hobbs and raised an eyebrow as if to say, *let's do it.*

"You're welcomed to live in Clarence's old cabin," Sally offered "It's quiet and peaceful out in the woods and thanks to you boys, Clarence won't be needing it anymore."

Bill and Aunt Mae faced Hobbs with expectant looks and he had the feeling that a significant amount of strategizing had gone into the offer.

"We'll be neighbors," Clarence said.

"More than that," Bill said. "You'll be like family."

Family, Hobbs thought. It was a wonderful thought for a man who had grown up in foster homes. He loved J.R. like a brother and had never imagined, nor expected, that there could be more.

"Thank you for the offer," Hobbs said with a look of gratefulness. "J.R. and I will have to discuss it."

"Dippy too," Bill said.

"Actually Bill," Dippy said. "I appreciate that, but I've got other plans. As much as I'd love to wake up to Aunt Mae's biscuits every morning, I'm afraid Anna's Mill is a bit slow-paced for me."

"The offer stands if you ever change your mind," Bill said.

After a few moments of awkward silence, Hobbs said, "Well, we ought to be going." Hobbs and his friends filed into the truck and with a final wave, started slowly down pit row toward the exit.

Hobbs noticed debris on the track and a long green splash of green paint on the racetrack wall where J.R. and the Green Ugly had left their mark. *Battle scars*, he thought to himself. *A reminder that sometimes the risks we take in life tend to work themselves out in the end.*

Hobbs turned and noticed a lone figure approaching, slowly making his way toward the Voyals family. The man walked tentatively with his head down and occasionally glanced up at the family.

"Slow down, Richard," J.R. said and sat up to study the approaching man.

Hobbs stopped the truck and allowed the headlights to provide more detail. The man wore baggy blue jeans with a dirty brown sweatshirt. With trembling hands, he fingered a green baseball cap. The resemblance of the man to Clarence was unmistakable and the appearance of Jack Voyals staggered Hobbs. His strong chin and broad shoulders mirrored those of his son, but three years of unrelenting guilt had battered the man. With no one to turn to, he'd become a shadow of the strong and brave man he had once been.

The stories told by friends conveyed a gregarious and

compassionate nature; an expressive and sensitive man who sometimes cried and always sought out opportunities to laugh and enjoy life. Bill liked to say Jack Voyals lived on the sunny side of life. But from the look of the man walking down pit row, sunny days for Jack Voyals had been few and far between.

As Jack Voyals approached the passenger side window of the truck he stopped and gave them a weak smile.

J.R. reached over Dippy and rolled down the window.

"Do you think they'll have me?" he said weakly. His stubbly chin quivered slightly, and Hobbs noticed tears glistening in his weary eyes.

"Yes, sir," J.R. said.

Jack nodded and looked toward his family again. "Thank you," he said and continued his walk.

Hobbs and his friends turned in their seats to take in the scene. Aunt Mae was the first to respond. She covered her mouth and took a few steps toward the approaching man, as if to get a better view. "Oh Jack..." she exclaimed. Even from a distance, Hobbs could see her dismay at the disheveled condition of her brother-in-law.

Now others in the family turned. Each unsure that the approaching stranger could possibly be the Jack Voyals that Hobbs had seen in news clippings and family photographs. A man, once full of vigor and gusto and now a common beggar who probably lived on the street and in shelters. Once, a loving father, brother and grandfather, Jack Voyals stood before them beaten, wrecked and ashamed.

"I am so sorry," Jack said as a tear ran down his cheek.

Still the family looked on, dumbfounded.

Jack turned to leave.

"No..." Clarence shouted and ran toward his father. He caught Jack in a loving embrace and both men sobbed onto each other's shoulders. Bill, Aunt Mae and Sally joined the embrace as the others gathered around and wiped tears from their eyes.

Hobbs turned in his seat and looked up at the green paint that decorated the racetrack wall and then glanced into his rearview mirror as the family continued their long embrace.

Battle scars, he thought to himself with a smile. He placed the truck into drive and eased off the track and through the exit.

CPSIA information can be obtained
at www.ICGtesting.com
Printed in the USA
LVHW041013010820
662075LV00002B/152